CALDER COUNTRY

The Calder Series by Janet Dailey

THIS CALDER RANGE

STANDS A CALDER MAN

THIS CALDER SKY

CALDER BORN, CALDER BRED

CALDER PRIDE

GREEN CALDER GRASS

SHIFTING CALDER WIND

CALDER PROMISE

LONE CALDER STAR

CALDER STORM

SANTA IN MONTANA

The Calder Brand Series
CALDER BRAND

CALDER GRIT

A CALDER AT HEART

JANET DAILEY

CALDER COUNTRY

KENSINGTON
PUBLISHING CORP.

www.kensingtonbooks.com

KENSINGTON BOOKS are published by

Kensington Publishing Corp.
900 Third Avenue
New York, NY 10022

After the passing of Janet Dailey, the Dailey family worked with a close associate of Janet's to continue her literary legacy, using her notes, ideas, and favorite themes to complete her novels and create new ones, inspired by the American men and women she loved to portray.

Library of Congress Card Catalogue Number: 2024934898

ISBN: 978-1-4967-4474-6

First Kensington Hardcover Edition: August 2024

ISBN: 978-1-4967-4478-4 (ebook)

10 9 8 7 6 5 4 3 2 1

Printed in the United States of America

CALDER COUNTRY

CHAPTER ONE

Miles City, Montana
July 1924

AT TWENTY-SEVEN MINUTES PAST MIDNIGHT, THE CHICAGO, MIL-
waukee, St. Paul, and Pacific passenger train pulled into the Miles
City depot. Running late, it paused just long enough to let a solitary figure descend from the second-class coach. After a last-
minute call of "All aboard" and a blast from its whistle, it picked
up speed and raced off into the night, bound for the Dakotas and
points east.

Mason Dollarhide gazed up and down the empty platform. A
solitary light burning in the closed station house was the only sign
of life. He'd wired his arrival time to his mother, but he should
have known that she wouldn't have sent anybody to meet him.
Amelia Hollister Dollarhide had probably grown forgetful in the
five years since he'd seen her. Or more likely, she hadn't forgiven
him for getting arrested and sent to prison, leaving her to live
with his disgrace and run their ranch alone.

Miles City had grown in Mason's absence. But some things
didn't change. At this late hour, lights along Main Street told him
that, despite the government edict, the brothels were still thriv-
ing. He hadn't been with a woman in more than five years, and
the urge was there, like a hot coal smoldering in his belly. But that
indulgence would have to wait.

On his release from the old State Prison at Deer Lodge, he'd been given fifty dollars cash, a shoddy, ill-fitting suit, and a pair of cheap shoes that pinched his feet. He'd spent a good part of the money on the train ticket; prices had gone up since he'd last traveled. What remained would be barely enough to buy him a few fingers of illegal moonshine and a private room with clean sheets on the bed.

Tomorrow morning, when the bank opened, all that would change.

Shouldering his duffel, which held little more than his work boots, a change of underwear, and a few toiletries, he ambled down the platform, taking time to stretch his cramped legs. He'd gone no more than a few steps when he realized he was being followed.

A furtive glance told him there were two men behind him—unkempt, ill-dressed thugs, husky but obviously none too bright. Otherwise they wouldn't be sneaking up on a man who had *ex-convict* written all over him.

He slowed his pace, letting them get close before he turned around. "Gentlemen," he asked politely, "is there something I can do for you?"

The pair looked startled, maybe because their quarry had shown no fear. Recovering, the bigger man flashed a knife. Glancing at the smaller man, Mason glimpsed a baseball bat. "We'll take that bag off your hands, mister, along with anything that's in your pockets. Play nice now, or we'll gut you like a pig."

Mason's pockets were empty except for the few dollars that remained after buying his train ticket and a cheese sandwich at one of the stops. The contents of the duffel were worthless. He could hand it over without regret. But after five years behind bars, where a man could barely take a piss without supervision, a little action might be just what he needed.

He straightened to his full height of six-foot-two. "I've got a better idea," he said, holding up the duffel. "If you want this bag, you can take it away from me."

The two thugs glanced at each other. For an instant, Mason

thought they might turn tail, which would have been a disappointment, since he was itching for a fight. But then the knife blade flashed in the moonlight as the big man came at him.

Mason swung the duffel hard. The blow knocked the man off balance, leaving him open to a crushing belly blow from Mason's fist. The breath whooshed out of him. He staggered backward, still gripping the knife.

Mason dropped the duffel at his feet and flexed his fingers. The impact with the man's gut had hurt his hand, but the pain felt good. In his prison time, he'd missed the thrill of an all-out fight with no guards wading in to break it up.

Now the smaller man charged in with a baseball bat. In a lightning move, he cracked the bat across Mason's wrist. Pain shot up Mason's arm. He lunged for the little man and aimed a hammer punch at his jaw. His doubled fist found its target with a satisfying crunch.

The man with the knife came at him again. Mason felt the blade slice into his cheek as he ducked. Adrenaline surged. He swung a solid kick to the man's groin, a move he'd learned in prison, where there was no such thing as a fair fight. The man grunted and doubled over, dropping the knife.

Scooping up the weapon, Mason flung it past the far side of the tracks. Blood from the knife cut drizzled down his cheek. He would tend to it later.

The smaller man had retreated to the edge of the platform. He crouched there, whimpering and cradling his jaw, the fight gone out of him. As Mason swung toward the big man, emotions held back for five long years burst in him like floodwater through a broken dam. The chain gangs, the bullies, the long nights, the isolation, the vermin, the constant humiliation—memories crashed in on him, driving him to an uncontrolled rage. His first punch knocked the big man off his feet. Then Mason was on top of him, his fists pummeling the man's face, his head, his body, pouring fury into every blow.

"Please stop, mister." The voice filtered through his awareness. It was the smaller man, standing somewhere behind him, pleading. "Please, mister, don't kill him. He's my brother. He can't hurt you no more."

Don't kill him . . . he's my brother. Somehow the words got through. Mason forced himself back onto his heels. His enemy lay on the platform, his face purpled with bruises, his eyes swollen, his nose and lip bloodied. With effort, Mason pushed to his feet. The big man was stirring, trying to get up. His brother moved to his side, tugging at his arms and supporting him as he struggled to his feet.

Mason stepped back. "Take him and get out of here." His voice was a growl. "Don't ever come near me again." Picking up the duffel, he watched the pair stumble away, the big man leaning on his brother.

He had a brother of his own, Mason reminded himself—a half-brother by the same father. But if he were to find Blake Dollarhide lying beaten and helpless somewhere, Mason would just walk away and leave him to bleed. And Blake would no doubt do the same to him.

Mason had a son, too—a son Blake had raised as his own. Joseph would be nineteen now, on the cusp of manhood. A bright, handsome boy to make any man proud. But after Mason's arrest, Joseph had disavowed all kinship between them. Any hope for a reconciliation would be asking too much.

The cut on Mason's cheek stung, but it didn't feel deep. Rummaging in the duffel, he found a clean sock and pressed it to the wound. The blood was already beginning to clot. With a bit of cleaning, it would heal fine. And one more scar wasn't going to make much difference in his looks.

Finding a pump outside the station house, he wet the sock and did the best he could to sponge away the blood. Then he left the platform and headed down Main Street. He'd meant to find a bar and pay under the table for a few fingers of moonshine before turning in. But he soon gave up on that idea. The few bars surviving as speakeasys had gone underground with Prohibition and wouldn't be easy to find. Besides, he looked like hell. If word got around that Mason Dollarhide had turned up in town, dressed like a bum, bleeding from a knife wound, and searching for a drink of illegal booze, it was bound to be bad for future business. He'd be smart to lie low until he could show up in style.

Keeping his face in shadow, he checked into an older back-street hotel where nobody was likely to recognize him. He'd hoped for a room with a private bath, but the only accommodation he could afford had a shared bath down the hall. Everything had gone up in price since his arrest ended the life he'd known—a life he was determined to get back, starting tomorrow.

The bathroom was empty, but there was no tub, and the hour was too late to ask for one. Mason splashed himself as clean as he could, returned to his room, and sank into the bliss of clean sheets, a warm blanket, and a padded mattress. No clanging of iron doors or moaned curses of prisoners. No snores from his cellmate. No squealing, scampering rats. No midnight inspections or communal showers. For the first time in five years, he was free.

Mason had expected to fall asleep at once. But his mind was churning with plans. His prison time hadn't been entirely wasted. He'd met other men there—men who, like him, had been sentenced for trafficking in illegal liquor, home-brewed or smuggled from Canada.

Mason had listened and learned, especially from the more recent arrivals. His former operation, trucking in crates of bottled Canadian whiskey and selling them out of his barn, was small-time now. And hiring local help, as he had done, carried a high risk of getting caught. If bootlegging had been big business back then, it was even bigger now. But even in a backwater like Eastern Montana, a man who was serious about getting rich these days needed access to a big-city network. An up-front cut paid to the right connections would enable him to tap into the market, find buyers, and arrange for delivery. Once trust was established, much of the business could be handled by wire or a simple telephone call.

Mason had emerged from prison with an education; but the lessons hadn't been free. He'd paid for information with favors—

everything from delivering cigarettes and messages to serving as protection for his mentor, Julius Taviani, who was doing ten years for violating the Eighteenth Amendment, which prohibited the production, importation, transportation, and sale of alcoholic beverages.

Taviani's sentence was double Mason's because he'd controlled a much bigger market, including a private source with a secret route from the Canadian border—for which he'd gone to jail rather than divulge. A diminutive, graying man who looked more like a bank clerk than a bootleg king, he was in frequent touch with his team of lawyers who, he insisted, would soon have him cleared of all charges.

Meanwhile, Mason had served as the man's unofficial bodyguard in exchange for a master course on how to set up and run a successful bootlegging operation. All that he'd learned, including contact information, he had committed to memory. The startup would take time, which he had, and cash, which, for now, would have to come from the ranch income. Once the bootlegging operation was bringing in good money, the cattle would serve as a front for the real business.

His strong-willed mother might be an impediment, especially since she was the legal owner of the ranch. Maybe he could persuade her to retire and move to someplace like Helena, where she could live in a stylish town house and enjoy social activities such as shopping, restaurants, and the theater. At the very least he needed to get power of attorney, something she'd never been trusting enough to give him.

Toward dawn, he drifted off. He was awakened by the mutter of voices and the sound of footsteps outside his door. For an instant he struggled to remember where he was. But then it all came back to him. He was in Miles City. And he was free to start his new life.

The morning light pouring through the cheap calico curtains told him he'd overslept and would likely have to wait for the bathroom. He sat up and swung his legs to the floor. His heel kicked the metal chamber pot, partly hidden under the bed. He pulled it into view and made do with it.

The bank wouldn't open until nine o'clock. Until then, his prison-issued suit would have to suffice. But once he withdrew enough cash to spend on a bath, a good barbering, and a quality suit of clothes, he would begin to feel like himself again. He'd noticed a couple of taxicabs parked along the street last night. He would take one home to the ranch, on the far side of Blue Moon. The ride was long and wouldn't be cheap. But once he accessed the ranch funds, he could afford to arrive in comfort and style.

Downstairs, he spent his last dollar on a simple breakfast of coffee, toast, and fried eggs. By the time he'd finished eating, it was almost nine o'clock.

He cut through an alley to the bank, which had just opened. Jason Coppersmith, the balding, middle-aged assistant to the bank president, recognized him at once.

"Mr. Dollarhide." There was no mention of how Mason looked or where he'd been. The man was nothing if not discreet. "How good of you to stop by. What can I do for you?"

"I'd like to withdraw some cash from the Hollister Ranch account," Mason said. "Five hundred dollars should be enough for now."

Coppersmith's expression did not change. "Would you kindly step into my office, Mr. Dollarhide? There's something you need to see."

Nerves prickling, Mason followed the man to his office behind the row of teller windows. As in the past, he'd expected to be handed the cash without question. Was something wrong?

The office was small and impersonal, the walls bare except for a calendar, a modest-sized desk, a metal file cabinet, and three chairs. Most of the desktop was taken up by a tray of papers and a large, leatherbound book which Mason recognized as an account ledger.

Coppersmith stepped behind the desk, opened the ledger, and leafed through the pages. The account names were listed alphabetically. It didn't take him long to find the page he was looking for. He turned the ledger around so that Mason could see it from his side of the desk. "Here you are, Mr. Dollarhide. Take a look. I'll be happy to answer any questions you might have."

Mason stared down at the page, scanning the lines and columns— the dates, the deposits from cattle sales, the withdrawals, mostly for ranch expenses, he surmised. Then, abruptly, the entries ended with a large withdrawal and a stamp that said *ACCOUNT CLOSED*.

Mason felt his stomach drop as if he'd swallowed a twenty-pound lead weight. This couldn't be happening.

"Two years ago, your mother came in here, cashed out the account, and closed it," Coppersmith said. "We suspected something might be wrong, and we tried to change her mind. But it was her money and her right to take it. There was nothing we could do." He shook his head. "I take it she didn't let you know what she'd done."

Mason forced himself to speak calmly. "I only got a few letters from her, and none of them mentioned this. She's managed the ranch for decades, ever since her father died. She's always done fine. I just assumed she was angry. You know my mother. She's not one to let go of a grudge."

"I understand," Coppersmith said. "But I suggest you go home and get to the bottom of this. Your mother isn't getting any younger. She could be ill or under the influence of someone who's out to take advantage of her."

"Of course." Mason's plan to enjoy a clandestine drink of Canadian whiskey, groomed and dressed like a gentleman, was swiftly evaporating. "I'll be heading right home. But first, I'm going to need your help with a small matter."

Twenty minutes later, with the help of a one-hundred-dollar short-term loan from the bank, Mason was on the road back to Blue Moon and the ranch, which lay a few miles beyond the town. The taxi, a rusting Model T, had clearly seen better days, as had the driver, whose ravaged face bore the physical and emotional scars of war.

The taxi rattled along the unpaved road, leaving a trail of dust to settle in its wake. Mason sat in the back seat, hunched low as the cab neared the small town of Blue Moon. He cursed the prison staff for neglecting to give him a hat. The vehicle was missing its canvas top, which left Mason's prison-pale skin bare to the brutal sun and exposed his downtrodden condition for all to see. There was more traffic on the road than he remembered, mostly autos and trucks these days, with an occasional horse-drawn buggy or farm wagon. Sooner or later, he was bound to pass someone who recognized him. Then, in the way of small towns, the word would spread that Mason Dollarhide had come back, sneaking into town like a whipped dog.

But that was the least of his worries. What had his mother done with the money from the bank? There'd been more than fifty thousand dollars in the account, including the income from his whiskey sales, which he'd mixed with the ranch funds to hide it from the authorities.

Had the money been stolen? he wondered. Had Amelia squirreled it away out of spite or distrust? And then there was the most pressing question of all—if the money was gone, what would happen to his plans to start a new business?

Mason hunched lower in the seat as the taxi passed the turnoff to the Calder Ranch. He had little doubt that Webb Calder would still be in charge, or that he would be wealthier than ever, damn his greedy, grasping hide. Aside from sharing the same father, Mason and Blake had one other thing in common—their hatred of the Calders and all they stood for.

Webb's father, Benteen Calder, had been among the first to settle this part of Montana. He had consolidated the land grants so he and his men could claim the biggest plot of ranchland in the territory. Webb had continued the Calder practice of land grabbing, taking advantage of bad luck and hardship to expand the family kingdom. His teenage son, Chase, would no doubt grow up to do the same.

The taxi was coming into Blue Moon, a town that had known days of boom and bust before settling into quiet obscurity. The place didn't appear to have changed much in the five years

Mason had been gone. The grocery store, which also functioned as a gas station and a post office, was as he remembered it. Next door was a café, and, next to that, a roadhouse called Jake's Place, with a private gaming room in the rear and rooms upstairs where Jake's so-called nieces plied their trade. There was also a hardware and dry-goods store, an abandoned grain elevator, and a schoolhouse for the children who lived in town and on the surrounding farms and ranches. Nearby was the sheriff's office and the adjoining jail, where Mason had spent time before being bound over for trial in Miles City.

Three boys on bicycles were coming up the road toward him. Torn by an unaccustomed longing, Mason couldn't tear his gaze away from them. But as they drew closer, he could tell that none of them was old enough to be his son. Joseph would be tall now, his body filling out to become a man's.

The boys appeared to be excited about something. They were pumping their bikes hard, glancing up at the sky as they rode. Only as the overhead drone of an engine reached his ears did he understand why. Looking back over his shoulder, Mason could see the biplane—a Curtiss JN-4, the model known as a "Jenny"—coming from the direction of Miles City to swoop in low over the town.

As the plane passed overhead, paper leaflets came fluttering down to scatter like a flock of white pigeons. The boys had stopped their bikes and were scrambling to catch as many leaflets as they could grab with their eager hands.

Mason understood what was going on. Barnstormers were nothing new, even to this small town. They flew around the country, putting on airshows and offering plane rides to the locals for a few precious dollars. Among the leaflets there might be one marked with a special stamp, entitling the finder to a free ride. That was the reason the boys were clambering after the leaflets.

As the taxi pulled around them and drove on, Mason happened to glance down at his feet. One of the leaflets had landed on the floor of the vehicle, the edge just touching his shoe. Reaching down, he picked it up and read the printed message:

Art Murchison's Flight Show. 1:00 today.
See death-defying stunts.
Admission: 25 cents for adults, 15 cents for children
Plane rides: $4.00

Below the message was the print of a rubber stamp framed and lettered in red ink.

Present this ticket for a free 15-minute plane ride.

Mason stared at the stamp. Evidently he had found the lucky ticket for a free plane ride—or rather, it had found him. Somewhere, the Fates must be laughing.

Today, of all days, with so much going wrong, the last thing he needed was a free plane ride. He thought about ordering the driver back to where the boys were and offering them the ticket. But there were three boys and only one ticket. They'd probably fight over it. Why cause trouble?

He tapped the driver's shoulder. "Could you use this ticket for a free plane ride today?" he asked.

The driver shook his head. "Not me. You couldn't get me up in one of those contraptions for a million dollars. I saw too many of 'em go down over France."

As the taxi moved beyond the town and neared the ranch, Mason folded the leaflet and slipped it into his vest pocket. He had no plans to use the free ticket.

His gaze swept the familiar hayfields and barbed wire fences, the grazing red-and-white Hereford cattle, and the towering Lombardy poplars planted in long rows along the property lines to serve as windbreaks.

Minutes from now, he'd be arriving at the Hollister Ranch to face his mother.

Anything could happen.

As the biplane swooped low over the sprawling ranch complex, Ruby Weaver scattered the last packet of leaflets advertising the afternoon show. As the papers fluttered to the ground she gazed past the edge of the cockpit, struck by the immense spread of buildings, corrals, pastures, and vast herds of cattle below. Everyone in Montana had heard of the Calders and their Triple C Ranch—the biggest in the state. But Ruby was seeing it for the first time. From the air, the place looked more like a town—or even a kingdom—than the property of a single, powerful family. How could anyone be rich enough to own all that land, that grand house, and all those horses and cattle?

But that question shouldn't concern her. All that mattered was flying the plane, putting on a show, and moving on to the next town.

The sound of the engine was too loud for conversation. As the plane began to climb, Ruby signaled to her father, who was piloting the aircraft from the tandem cockpit behind her, that she had no more leaflets to drop. It was time to land, eat the lunch they'd packed, refuel the plane, top off the radiator, and fill the tires before the show.

Ruby checked her seat belt for the descent and landing. The biplane was a training model, built to carry an instructor and a student, one behind the other. In her cockpit, the stick and foot pedal bar moved in ghostly sync with the ones her father was using to control the aircraft.

As the climb leveled off, he reached forward and touched her shoulder. Ruby knew what he expected. It would be up to her to take the controls and pilot the plane to a safe landing.

Her pulse skittered as she grasped the stick and placed her feet on the pedals. She could feel the quiver of resistance as her father released contact and turned the flight over to her. As she banked the plane for the turn, tilting the wings at a steep angle, her heart drummed like a trapped bird against the walls of her chest. Only after she'd leveled the plane out and headed back the way they'd come did she allow herself a deep breath.

Ruby's father, Art, who'd served as a flight instructor during the war, was an excellent teacher. But Ruby had only been flying for a few months. Every time he gave her the controls, she battled the fear of making a critical mistake that would send them both plunging to their deaths. Now he was placing his life in her hands, trusting her to keep them both safe. But Ruby knew he had another, deeper motive. Art had brought her into the sky to save her.

CHAPTER TWO

*T*HE TAXI DRIVER LET MASON OFF AT THE FRONT GATE. MASON HAD paid in advance for the ride, but he gave the man a fair tip, as a gentleman would do.

The stately brick house, its broad porch sheltered by the over-hanging roof, appeared unchanged. But the front yard was weedy and overgrown. Mason's mother had always taken pride in her home's outward appearance. For as long as he could remember, she'd paid a gardener to keep the place mowed, weeded, and trimmed.

Apprehension growing, he opened the gate and started up the walk. The place was quiet except for the piping of a quail and the whisper of leaves in the wind.

As Mason mounted the porch, a savage barking from inside the front door reached his ears. His mother's two huge mastiffs had been her constant companions. The dogs would be old now if they'd even survived this long. What Mason was hearing sounded more like one animal than two. But he knew better than to open the door and walk in.

Raising his hand, he rapped the brass knocker.

"Who's there?" His mother's voice came from the direction of the parlor. At least she sounded the way he remembered.

"It's me, Mother. It's Mason. I've come home." He shouted the words over the barking.

At a sharp, spoken command, the barking ceased. "Come in," his mother's voice said.

Mason opened the door and stepped into the entry. The house looked clean enough, but there was a shabbiness about the place. The rugs, the furniture, even the wallpaper looked worn, dusty, and faded. Or maybe he was just looking with fresh eyes.

His mother was seated in the high-backed, brocade-covered chair that Mason had always thought of as her throne. The massive hound that crouched protectively at her side was one of the pair he remembered—the other beast must've passed on. This one was showing the white of age around its muzzle and cataract-blurred eyes, but when it growled, pulling back its lips, its yellowed canines appeared as sharp as ever.

Amelia Hollister Dollarhide was thinner than he remembered. The red hair of her younger days had turned silver. Aside from that, she had changed surprisingly little. Dressed in an outdated green voile gown that matched the shade of her striking eyes, she looked fit and healthy. She wasn't that old, barely over sixty, Mason reminded himself. But something wasn't right. What had possessed her to close the bank account?

"So you're back." There was no hint of welcome in her voice.

"Yes." Mason paused in the middle of the room, still wary of the dog. "Didn't you get my telegram?"

She shrugged. "I might have. But I figured that if you really wanted to come home, you'd find a way to get here on your own."

"You don't sound happy to see me." He said it teasingly, hoping to get a rise out of her. But her expression didn't change.

"Why should I be happy to see you?" she snapped. "I raised you to grow up and help me run the ranch. But then you got that wretched girl pregnant and had to leave. When you finally came home, and the girl was safely married to your brother, I had hopes you might stay. But no, you had to fool around with the law and get yourself arrested. Having you as a son never did me a lick of good. I'm tempted to sic my dog on you and run you off the ranch."

Not a good beginning, Mason reflected. Winning her over could take time—time he didn't have.

"I went to the bank in Miles City this morning, Mother," he

said. "They told me you'd cashed out the ranch account and closed it."

"I did. The money's safer with me. You can't trust anybody these days, especially bankers. As far as I'm concerned, they're all a bunch of crooks."

"Where's the money?" Mason asked, keeping his voice gentle. "What did you do with it?"

Her laugh was humorless. "You think I'd tell you—a man who just got out of prison? I don't trust you any more than I trust those bankers. You'd help yourself to the money and burn through it like a hot knife through butter."

"I'm your son. Your own flesh and blood." He took a step toward her. The dog growled and edged forward. Mason halted. "I'm your heir, your only family. If you can't trust me, who can you trust?"

His mother silenced the dog with a touch. "So far, Mason, you've been worse than no family at all. For as long as I've been your mother, I've never known you to think of anything but yourself—your own pleasure, your own convenience, your own gain. When you went to prison, I was tempted to change my will and send you packing when you came home. But in the hope that you've learned your lesson, I'm willing to give you one last chance."

"What do I have to do?" Mason was grinding his teeth with impatience, but he knew better than to show it.

"You're not stupid. You can figure it out for yourself." She took in his appearance, her upper lip curling with distaste. "The first thing you can do is change out of that godawful suit. Your old clothes are still in your room. They'll do you for now. You're lucky I didn't burn them or give them to the first bum that came to the kitchen door."

Picking up a small silver bell from a side table, she gave it an extra loud shake. The man who shuffled in from the kitchen was dressed in a black suit. His thin, white hair hung in strings to his shoulders. His body was stooped and gnarled like the trunk of an ancient tree that had survived more seasons than a man could count.

"Madam?" His sonorous voice was the same. Mason had assumed that his mother's aging butler would've long since gone to meet his maker—not that he'd given much thought to the old man.

"Sidney, bring me a glass of claret."

"Yes, madam." He vanished into the kitchen. Wine was illegal, as was any other alcoholic drink, but Mason was aware that his mother kept a store of her favorites in the cellar. He knew better than to think she might invite him to share.

She glared at her son. "Get out of my sight. I don't want to see you again until you've changed your clothes. And don't expect me to tell you what to do. You're a man. Use your eyes and ears—and your head if you've acquired any common sense in the past five years."

"And the money?" Mason couldn't resist asking. "When will you give me access?"

She shook her head. "Not until I can trust you to act responsibly."

"And how long will that be?"

She shrugged her bony shoulders. "Days. Weeks. Maybe never. Meanwhile, the money is safe. I'll pay you a salary for managing the ranch, but only if you do your job."

I'm not your employee, Mother. I'm your son! When you're gone, this ranch will be mine!

He wanted to shout the words at her, but that would only steel her resolve to control him. For now, he would pretend to go along with her plan. But he couldn't get back into the bootlegging business without seed money up front.

His bedroom was much as he'd left it, his clothes and boots in the closet, his socks and underthings in the bureau drawers. Mason liked dressing well. In his first sojourn away from the ranch, he'd spent money on expensive clothes—shirts of linen and silk, leather jackets and vests, trousers of fine wool gabardine, and custom-made boots—the kind of things that didn't go out of style. Even his work clothes were of exceptional quality. Dressed, he could pass for a wealthy rancher—even if, for now, his mother controlled his every dollar. That would soon change, he vowed. It would have to.

After enjoying his first real bath in five years, he shaved, dressed, and combed his hair. Groomed and dressed in his own clothes, he'd expected to look much as he had before his arrest. But as he stood before the full-length mirror, it was a stranger he saw looking back at him—his hair showing strands of early gray, his intense green eyes framed by leathery creases. There was a hardness about his mouth—a mouth that had all but forgotten how to smile—and a determined set to his jaw. His nose, broken in a prison brawl and never properly set, gave him the look of a street tough. His clothes hung on his lean, sinewy body in a way he'd never noticed before.

His discarded clothes and shoes, courtesy of the Montana Corrections System, lay in a heap on the floor. The smell that rose from them recalled the five-year nightmare of prison—the kitchen slop that passed as food, the steaming bleach scent of the laundry, the toilets, the stench of sweating bodies. Mason shuddered. He would roll everything into a tight bundle, take it downstairs, stuff it into the trash bin, and forget it. He wanted nothing to remind him of that time. The scars on his body would be enough.

As he lifted the vest, a folded sheet of paper fluttered to the floor. It was the leaflet that had been dropped from the airplane. Mason unfolded it and reread the announcement about the air show.

Maybe he should go.

The more he thought about the idea, the more it made sense. Sooner or later, he would have to face his old acquaintances in Blue Moon. Putting it off would only make things harder. He'd been seen driving through town. Word would already be spreading that Mason Dollarhide was back.

So, why not show up dressed like a gentleman and standing tall? True, he'd been in prison, but not for harming anyone in Blue Moon. His crime had been a violation of federal law—a law that many people hated and believed to be unfair. Now that he had paid the price with five years of his freedom, with a few months' probation for good behavior, he owed no one an apology.

Refolding the paper, he slipped it into the hip pocket of his trousers. It was early yet. He'd have time to look over the ranch before leaving for town. Among other things, he needed to know how many cattle and horses were on the place, what condition they were in, and who was taking care of them. The sooner he stepped into running the ranch and took a firm hand, the better his chances of accessing the money he needed.

An hour later, he was on his way back to town. His old car, a high-end Model T, had been kept in running condition, probably to transport his mother on her errands. Mason had seen newer and nicer autos in Miles City today, and not just Fords. There were Chryslers, Oldsmobiles, and Buicks; and he'd seen ads for luxury Cadillacs and Packards that would be a dream to own. But getting a fancy car would have to wait until he could afford it. Meanwhile, he had his work cut out for him.

What he'd seen of the ranch had dismayed and worried him. Most of the cattle had been sold off last year. With no stock to breed, there'd be nothing to ship to market this fall. Even the horses, the best ones, were mostly gone. What had his mother been thinking? Surely she couldn't have been that desperate for money. Mason could only conclude that she was ill, not in her body but in her mind.

For now, he would put his gloomy thoughts aside and try to enjoy the air show. In a town like Blue Moon, where exciting events were rare, the chance to see a plane close up and maybe even ride in one would draw a crowd. Would Blake's family be there? Would Joseph be with them?

In prison, after Joseph had rejected him, Mason had told himself that he didn't care about his son. But now, the prospect of seeing the boy triggered a surge of hope. Maybe Joseph's youthful anger had mellowed. Maybe they could talk and become friends. He might even offer Joseph the ticket for a free plane ride.

Blake wouldn't like that. Neither would Blake's wife, Hannah.

The innocent girl Mason had impregnated twenty years ago—the girl Blake had married after Mason skipped town—had matured into a lovely, confident woman. And for his unselfish act, Blake was reaping the rewards of a beautiful family—a rich dynasty for any man.

Neither Blake nor his wife had any use for Mason. If they happened to be at the air show today, and if he were to approach them, they would probably turn their backs.

But others would welcome him. His half-sister, Kristin, a doctor, would never turn her back on him. And his boyhood chums, the ones who'd stayed in Blue Moon, would greet him with open arms. With luck, he might even meet a woman—preferably a widow, who knew the score and wouldn't mind his company on a lonely night. She wouldn't even have to be pretty as long as she was willing. Otherwise, his only recourse would be to visit one of the "nieces" at Jake's Place. His need of a woman was becoming an itch that demanded to be scratched.

The printed announcement hadn't specified where the air show would be staged. But the open field east of town, once used to park heavy grain wagons and stable the giant draft horses that pulled them, was the logical choice. Now used for ball games, horse races, community picnics, and other functions, the field was spacious enough for a small plane to land and take off, with no nearby trees, fences, or grazing animals to worry about.

In Blue Moon, people were moving toward the field, some walking, some in autos and buggies, and others, mostly boys, on bicycles. It was early yet. Mason took his time driving down Main Street. His eyes scanned the passing crowd for people he might remember. There were surprisingly few. A man in overalls gave him a grin and a wave. He looked vaguely familiar, but Mason couldn't recall his name.

As he parked the Model T with other vehicles along the near side of the field, he could see the plane sitting in the open. The Curtiss Jenny models had been mass-produced for use in the Great War, mostly for pilot training. After the fighting ended in late 1918, the surplus planes had been sold at bargain prices to the public. The sturdy, lightweight Jennies, as they were called, were bought by the hundreds, many of them by pilots who'd returned from the war, who used them to make a living, flying from town to town, putting on shows and selling rides. The practice was known as barnstorming.

Glancing down the row of parked vehicles, Mason spotted a shiny, new dark green Buick, a car that had big money written all over it. Only one member of the community would drive a car like that—Webb Calder, who ruled the Triple C Ranch like a feudal lord.

Webb, who towered over most of his neighbors, was easy to spot among the gathering crowd. Now in early middle age, he still moved with a cowboy's easy grace, his body built for the saddle. His taciturn presence commanded respect. Webb Calder was the man that other men wanted to be. But, as Mason reminded himself, Webb had done nothing to earn his wealth and power. His most telling accomplishment was having been born a Calder.

But it wasn't Webb that Mason had come to see.

The crowd, kept at a distance from the plane by a staked rope, was growing. Mason scanned the newcomers, hoping to spot a familiar, boyish face. But there was no sign of Blake's family. With a ranch and a sawmill to manage, Mason's half-brother probably wouldn't spare the time for an outing. Blake had kept his nose to the grindstone all his life. He was probably raising Joseph the same way. Pity. Young manhood should be a time for fun and adventure.

Another man, even taller than Webb, moved past Mason, balancing a small, golden-haired girl on his shoulder. Mason turned aside to avoid being recognized. Sheriff Jake Calhoun had been the one to arrest and jail him five years ago. The man had treated him decently, but the memory of that time evoked nothing but humiliation.

The glint of a silver star on his vest confirmed that Jake Calhoun was still sheriff. But the tiny girl on his shoulder, dressed in a rumpled pinafore, with her hair in a lopsided braid—that had to be an interesting story.

"Mason?"

Startled by the soft but firm voice behind him, Mason turned to face Britta Anderson, the town's longtime schoolteacher. A plain, big-boned spinster with wheaten hair and cornflower eyes, she was also the sister of Blake's wife—and a woman whose family history gave her every justifiable reason to detest him.

"Hello, Britta. It's nice to see you." He spoke in a mocking tone, knowing he was probably the last person she wanted to see today. Mason had abandoned her pregnant older sister and then, unwittingly, contributed to the ruin and death of the younger one. A related incident had led to her father dropping dead on his doorstep.

"When did you get back?" she asked.

"Just today. I'll be helping my mother run the ranch. I was hoping to see Blake's family. Do you know if they'll be here?"

"I doubt that they'll take the time. But I'll let them know you're back in town."

"Not that I'm expecting any dinner invitations. How are they—the family?"

"They're fine. Hannah has a new baby girl. Our mother passed away a few months after you left. It's safe to say that she died of a broken heart."

Her meaning wasn't lost on Mason. Inga Anderson had suffered the loss of her two sons, her husband, and her youngest daughter. But none of those deaths had been Mason's fault. He couldn't help it if pretty Gerda had gotten pregnant by her boyfriend and tried to hang the blame on him. Or that the girl's father had assumed the worst, come after him with a shotgun, and died of a stroke brought on by his own rage.

Mason chose not to argue the point. "What about Joseph?" he asked. "How is he?"

"Joseph is growing up. He's got big dreams, but Blake is grooming him to run the ranch and the sawmill." She paused, her stern blue eyes gazing directly into his. "Leave Joseph alone, Mason. The last time you were here, you almost ruined his life. He doesn't need your meddling. Do you understand?"

"I understand," Mason said. "But if Joseph wants to talk to me, I won't turn him away."

"Don't hold your breath." Britta gave him an angry look before walking off to greet someone else. Mason didn't blame her for resenting him. But he couldn't change the past. He could only seize the future and make it his. If his plan worked, he would have all the wealth and respect he'd ever wanted.

He scanned the crowd one more time, but failed to see his family or anyone who might welcome him. That shouldn't be surprising. He hadn't exactly left a lot of friends behind when he'd gone to prison. And as he reminded himself, for the past five years, life had moved on without him.

The two people who'd arrived in the plane were working their way through the crowd, collecting money and rubber stamping the hands of those who paid. For the price, the pair couldn't be making much of a profit. By the time they paid for fuel and other expenses, there wouldn't be much left over.

A man was moving toward him with a tin box for collecting payments. He had a wiry build, dressed in khakis, with a white, fringed scarf flung rakishly around his neck. He appeared to be nearing sixty, his face long jawed and narrow, with a neat moustache. His graying hair was plastered to his head, as if by a helmet he might have worn earlier.

Occasionally he stopped to make change, but most people had the required coins. They clinked into the box like donations in a church collection plate.

A smaller figure, in a loose-fitting khaki jumpsuit cinched at the waist with a webbed belt, followed at his elbow with a rubber stamp and an inkpad, stamping the image of a miniature biplane in blue on the back of each payer's hand. A floppy newsboy cap shadowed the features below. A lad, Mason assumed. Maybe the man's son or grandson.

The pair approached Webb Calder. The owner of the Triple C dropped his quarter in the box and had his hand stamped. Moments later, the man with the tin box approached Mason. With a smile, Mason took a dollar bill out of his wallet and laid it in the box. "Keep the change," he said loudly enough for Webb and those around him to hear. The gesture was a small one, purely for show. But Mason liked the way it made him feel.

"Your hand, sir." The feminine voice startled him. Mason found himself looking down at a stunning face below the cap's raised brim. Coffee-colored eyes crowned by dark, unplucked brows gazed up at him. Even at first look Mason sensed a secret sorrow in their depths. Her features were balanced by full lips, chapped by the wind to a deep rose. A curl of auburn hair had escaped the cap to tumble down her cheek. For a moment he was mesmerized. Good Lord, how could he have believed this beauty was a boy?

"I need your hand for the stamp, sir." She spoke with a note of impatience. Mason complied, palm down. She used her left hand to apply the blue stamp. His heart sank as he noticed the thin gold band on her ring finger. Married. That older man collecting the money must be her husband. As she walked away, Mason muttered a curse. Life wasn't fair—that beauty was wed to an old man. A woman like that should be dressed in silks and lace. And she deserved to be thrilled in bed—as Mason could imagine thrilling her.

He remembered how, years before, Webb Calder had fallen for a young immigrant woman, married to a man who was old enough to be her father. Ignoring all common sense, Webb had pursued the woman and ended up getting shot by the jealous husband—a wound that had nearly killed him. Eventually the husband had died. Webb had married the widow, who gave birth to a son before dying herself in a shooting gone wrong. Webb had never remarried.

Lesson learned. This woman was off-limits, Mason admonished himself. But a little harmless flirting would not be crossing the line. Those luscious lips might not be his for kissing, but he wouldn't mind coaxing them into a smile.

The air show was about to start. The woman, her cap replaced by a leather helmet and goggles, stood at the front of the plane. The man climbed into the rear cockpit.

"Switch off!" the woman called.

"Switch off!" he shouted.

The woman gave the wooden propeller a couple of turns, then braced her feet. "Contact!"

"Contact."

Showing a strength that surprised Mason, she swung the propeller hard. There was a sputter from the engine, a puff of acrid smoke, then a churning sound as the engine caught and the prop became a blur of motion. The woman scrambled onto the wing and into the front cockpit. Head lowered, she took an instant to fasten her seat belt before the plane taxied out to the end of the field, a safe distance from the crowd.

Mason had come to the air show with the idea of seeing who else might be there. He hadn't expected to be interested in the airplane—he'd seen others over the years, some of them flying low over the prison. But as the little Jenny's engine revved for takeoff and headed down the makeshift runway, he felt his heart creeping into his throat. The craft was so fragile looking, like a child's toy made of paper and matchsticks. A sudden wind gust could send it crashing to the ground.

He almost forgot to breathe as the plane droned down the field. At the last possible second, the wings caught the air. The craft lifted off the ground, carrying the woman with the haunting face into the sky.

Mason watched the plane do loops and barrel rolls. These were standard fare for most air shows, but he had to admire the skill and courage involved in the stunts. It took a special kind of bravery—or perhaps madness—to put on such a display. The pilot could have flown in the war, although he looked too old to have been in combat.

And too old to be married to that stunning woman. She was no young filly, but she couldn't be much over thirty. Maybe she was his daughter—but the ring on her finger didn't lie. The beauty was taken.

The plane circled and raised its nose, climbing until it was little more than a dot against the blue. Mason could guess what was coming next—a parachute jump. Was that why the woman had gone up in the plane? Was she going to be the jumper?

What was the old man thinking? Mason muttered a curse. So help him, if the Fates were to give him a woman like that one, he would never risk her anywhere near a plane. He would keep her in a mansion, dress her like a queen, and make love to her every night.

He savored the fantasy for a moment, letting it dissolve slowly, like the sweet taste of brandy on his tongue. Someday he would have the mansion, the wealth, and a woman made for treasuring—not the woman he'd just met, but one equally beautiful and meant only for him.

He would have it all—any way he could get it.

CHAPTER THREE

*R*UBY HAD TAKEN OVER THE CONTROLS. WITH THE STICK AND FOOT pedals, she kept the plane stable while her father, wearing parachute gear, climbed out of the cockpit and onto the lower wing. This was the most dangerous part of the stunt, when the wrong move on her part could throw him off before he was in position. She gripped the stick, balancing the pedal bar and holding steady.

Grasping a strut for support, he dropped to a crouch and hurled himself into space. When she knew he was clear, she banked the plane, turning it around for the long descent to the field. A downward glance confirmed that her father's war surplus parachute had opened. It floated below like a billowing white blossom, growing smaller with distance. Now it would be up to her to land the plane.

Ruby flew with more confidence when her father wasn't with her. The awareness that he was watching her every move and that his survival, along with her own, was in her hands, tended to make her nervous. Flying alone, with the wind sweeping past her face and the engine throbbing in her ears, she felt a rare sense of freedom, as if nothing mattered except the moment, not even her life.

She had married her childhood sweetheart, Brandon Weaver, trusting that their love would give them a lifetime of happiness together. Then the war had come. That great and noble cause had taken her beloved husband and returned a stranger, scarred and blistered by mustard gas, which had done as much damage to the inside of his body as to the outside. After many months in an army hospital, he'd been released to come home to her in Missoula. Ruby had done everything in her power to make him feel loved and valued. But she had fought a losing battle. Depression had eaten away his will to live. She'd come home from running errands one day to find his body hanging from a rafter in their barn.

Days later, Ruby had lost the baby she was carrying. For months afterward, she hadn't cared whether she lived or died.

It had taken her widowed father to rouse her from her fog of pain, guilt, sleeping powders, and laudanum. He had nursed her back to health and brought her with him into the sky. Flying had probably saved her life. But the darkness was still there, deep inside, where she kept it hidden.

Maybe that was why she hadn't said no last night when he'd told her about his latest "business opportunity." A few days earlier, a prosperous-looking friend from his past had approached him after one of the air shows and taken him aside for a private talk. Only last night had Ruby learned what the man had in mind. He and a group of associates were looking for pilots to deliver their product by air. Ruby didn't need to ask what that product would be.

"Think about it, Ruby." Her father's eyes had shone with an excitement Ruby hadn't seen in years. "The pay for one delivery would be more than we're making in a month of air shows. We could have a real home somewhere. No more living on the road. If the arrangement works out, they'll even buy me a bigger plane to carry more weight."

"But what about the revenuers? What if we get caught?" Ruby had demanded. "We could end up going to prison."

"I'm aware of the risk. That's why there'll be no 'we' in this venture. I'll be making the runs alone. I'm not getting any younger, girl. If anything happens to me, I don't want to leave you with nothing."

Ruby had stood firm. "You know I won't go along with that, Dad. If you decide to get into this business, I'll be right there with you. That's the only arrangement I'll accept. Think about that before you say yes to your friends."

Ruby had hoped her stand would dissuade him. But something told her that Art Murchison had already made up his mind. It was time to prepare for whatever was to happen next.

Now, as the plane descended, she could see the field below. Her father had landed safely and was keeping the crowd back to clear the way for her landing.

Calm and in control, she aligned the plane's path with the improvised landing strip and glided earthward. She felt the bump as the wheels touched down and rumbled over the uneven ground. Her thundering pulse eased as she taxied the plane across the field to where her father stood, with the crowd waiting behind him.

After switching off the engine, she climbed out of the cockpit, lifted away her goggles, and pulled off her helmet. Her sweat-dampened hair tumbled loose in the light breeze. She had finished piloting the plane for the day. Her father would fly the paid rides while she packed the parachute and kept an eye on the thinning crowd.

Most of the people who'd come for the show but lacked the desire or the cash for a plane ride were leaving. Only a handful stayed to watch the four brave souls—three younger men and a tall, plain-looking, blond woman—queue up for their fifteen-minute flight.

The man at the front of the line was talking to Ruby's father. They seemed to be arguing about something. As Ruby left the plane and walked closer, she recognized him—tall and handsome with chestnut hair, mocking green eyes, and a broken nose that gave him a rakish look. She'd had to ask him twice to hold out his hand for the stamp. When their eyes had met, she'd felt a subtle tension, an unvoiced challenge.

Seeing him with her father, she felt it again. Something in the man's looks and manner whispered *trouble*.

"Ruby, this gentleman has a special request," her father said. "He has a coupon for a free plane ride. But he's offering to pay double the regular price if you'll be his pilot. I told him that would be up to you."

Ruby hesitated. She'd never taken a passenger up before, and there was something unsettling about the man. "What if I say no?" she asked her father.

"Then I'll accept his coupon and give him his free ride if he still wants it," Art said.

Ruby sighed. Eight dollars was enough to pay for their meals and rooms in Miles City, where they'd be spending the night. Still, she hesitated.

"Why would you pay extra for me?" she demanded, speaking to the stranger for the first time. "My father's a much more experienced pilot. I don't have my license yet. It probably isn't even legal for me to fly with a passenger."

His smile was slightly lopsided and absolutely charming. "I'm willing to take a chance," he said. "Maybe I just like the idea of taking a ride with a beautiful woman."

"Mark my words, mister," she said. "If I agree to do this, a plane ride is all you're going to get."

"I understand. And I promise to behave. Thank you."

Had Ruby just consented to this madness? The stranger seemed to think she had.

"Dad—" She gave her father a pleading look. But she knew him well. He was already counting the extra dollars in his mind. She loved him dearly, but he did have an avaricious streak. That was why he'd jumped at the offer to deliver bootleg liquor for his so-called friend.

She took the spare helmet and goggles from her father and handed them to the stranger. "Put these on," she said. "Then follow me. You'll see a set of controls in your cockpit. Whatever happens, don't touch them."

Wearing the leather helmet and goggles, Mason strode behind the woman to the plane. He'd learned from talking with the pilot that she was his widowed daughter, not his wife. That intrigued him—but Mason knew better than to think he could talk her into bed. He'd learned the hard way that when it came to their women-folk, fathers tended to be even more protective than husbands. And Ruby—the name he'd heard from her father—was no ordinary woman. The fact that she had the skill and courage to pilot a plane demanded his respect.

But something about her rankled him. She was *uppity*, damn it, treating him like some fool kid on a carnival ride. She barely looked at him when she motioned him into the front cockpit. He might have said something, but conversation would be difficult with both of them wearing leather helmets that covered their ears. And it would be impossible once the plane's noisy engine started.

She gestured toward her waist, indicating that he should fasten his seat belt. When she stood on the lower wing, leaning close to make sure his belt was pulled tight and securely fastened, Mason inhaled her womanly aroma beneath the oil-stained jumpsuit. He fought the urge to reach out and touch her cheek, to turn her face and make her look at him with those mesmerizing eyes. But this woman was about to take him on a dangerous ride. Annoying her wouldn't be smart.

A nervous chill passed through his body as she climbed into the cockpit behind him. Mason had always thought of himself as an adventurous man. But he'd never been in an airplane before, let alone with a beautiful woman who'd confessed to being a fledgling pilot. What if something were to go wrong? Maybe this flight wasn't such a good idea.

Standing in front of the plane, her father gave the propeller a hard spin. The engine sputtered and stopped. It wasn't too late, Mason told himself. He could unbuckle his seat belt, wave his arms, and tell her he'd changed his mind.

But then the engine coughed and roared to life. The plane shuddered and began its taxi to the far end of the field. Mason could see the stick and pedal bar moving in the cockpit, as if being worked by some ghostly hand. He remembered Ruby's admonition not to touch them. But when he watched them, it was fascinating to see how she controlled the plane.

Mason's pulse hammered as the craft, which seemed no more substantial than a dragonfly, turned into the light wind and began moving forward. The wheels rumbled over the bumpy ground. Then the air caught the wings. The rumbling stopped, and the plane began to climb.

Mason's stomach dropped as he looked over the side of the cockpit and saw the Montana landscape slipping away beneath him, everything below growing smaller. Even the distant Calder spread appeared miniature—unimportant in the vast scheme of things. Mason began to laugh. "I'll be damned," he muttered out loud. He was beginning to enjoy himself. This was better than being drunk.

With the wind battering his goggles, he put up a hand and made an okay sign with his fingers. Since Ruby was directly behind him, piloting the plane, he had no way of knowing whether she'd understood. But he liked to think she had.

He would have enjoyed inviting her to dinner at Jake's after the other flights—probably with her father along. But his small windfall of cash from the bank loan had dwindled to pocket change. With time and funds running out, he needed to learn what his mother had done with the money from the bank. That would be his first priority when he got home. But for now, he was soaring in the azure sky with a goddess. He'd be a fool not to savor every moment.

Ruby glanced at her wristwatch. Fifteen minutes. That was how much of her time the stranger had bought with his money. She could hardly wait until the ride was over and she had him safely back on the ground.

The man struck her as arrogant—as if he thought his wealth could buy anything, or anyone, including her. Art should have refused his offer to pay extra for her services. But she'd lacked the spine to say no, and now here she was.

What did she know about him, this hard-edged stranger with

scars on his face and hands? He was obviously wealthy. But she sensed dark secrets lurking behind those striking green eyes. And the way he'd looked at her, as if he were reining back forbidden urges . . .

Collecting her thoughts, she checked her watch again. *Thank goodness.* It was time to turn the plane around and descend to a safe landing.

She banked the plane, tilting the wings to an angle that was guaranteed to get her passenger's pulse racing. Coming out of the turn, she leveled off and began the gradual descent to the field where her father waited.

That was when it happened—the sputter of the engine, followed by the most terrifying sound a flyer could hear—dead silence.

She checked the fuel gauge. No problem there, but something had killed the engine. This had happened once when she was flying with Art. He'd managed to start the plane again, opening the throttle and manipulating the switch until the engine caught and the propeller began to whir. But Ruby had yet to master the trick. She tried once, then again. Nothing happened.

She was running out of time. She would have to glide down, trusting the air to carry the wings as she used the rudder to steer the plane to a safe landing spot.

Willing herself not to panic, she moved the stick back, raising the nose of the plane slightly. Aiming downward, in the direction she wanted to go, could trigger a deadly dive. The only sound was the whisper of air rushing beneath the wings. Using the controls, she eased the plane into a long, shallow glide.

In the front cockpit, her passenger didn't appear to be moving. Was he paralyzed with fear or had he simply passed out? She couldn't worry about him now—not when the slightest error on her part, or even a stray gust of wind, could send them both plunging to their deaths.

Time froze. Ruby forced herself to breathe, as if her life force alone could keep the craft in the air. Ahead and below, she could see the field. The people along the side looked as small as insects, the cars like toys. Was she coming in too low? Or maybe too high? Her knuckles whitened on the stick. If the glide was too high, she would overshoot the landing and rip the plane apart in the tall scrub at the end. If it was too steep, she would crash-land, destroy the plane, and possibly kill her passenger and herself.

Her teeth bit into her lower lip, drawing blood as she came in for the landing. *Easy . . . easy . . . like lowering a baby into its cradle . . . Stick, ailerons . . .*

She felt a jarring crunch as the wheels touched the bumpy ground, then an upward bounce, followed by another crunch. The wheels rumbled over rocks and badger holes, coming to a halt a few yards short of the junipers and sage clumps that would have slashed the plane's fuselage to ribbons.

When the forward motion stopped, Ruby unfastened her seat belt and climbed out onto the wing. Her passenger was stirring. He appeared unhurt, but first things first. After jumping to the ground, she found a hefty rock to block one wheel and keep the plane from rolling. Then, pulling off her helmet and goggles, she turned and waved her arms to signal that she was all right. Her father had already started across the field with his tool kit.

Ruby's passenger had climbed out of the plane and vanished into the brush, probably to relieve himself. Standing by the plane, she weighed the idea of climbing onto the wing to raise the cowling doors and peer into the engine. She was a fair hand with a spanner. Maybe with a bit of tinkering, she could find the problem that had caused the engine to quit.

But no, minutes from now, her father would be here. Art Murchison was a master mechanic. Unless the trouble was major, like a broken part, he would tighten a few nuts, check the belts, make some adjustments, and have the engine working in no time.

"That was quite a performance, lady!"

Startled, Ruby wheeled to face her passenger. He was standing a few steps behind her, the helmet and goggles in his hands. His mocking grin showed a slightly chipped front tooth.

"I hope you got your money's worth," she said. "I was afraid you might be terrified."

"Terrified?" He chuckled. "I can't remember when I've had so much fun. If you were trying to scare me, it didn't work."

"Trying to scare you?" She gaped at him, scarcely believing her ears. "*Trying to scare you?*"

"Like when you shut down the engine and coasted to the field. I've been on some wild carnival rides in my time, but that tops them all."

"*When I shut down the engine?*" Did the insufferable man think she'd done it on purpose? Fury welled in her, like a pot boiling over on a hot stove. She barely stopped herself from slapping his insolent face. "Listen, you fool! I didn't lose engine power to entertain you! The danger was real. We could have died if I hadn't—"

Ruby broke off as she noticed the deepening dimple in his cheek. He was struggling not to laugh at her. That was when she realized she'd just been played.

Her hand balled into a fist. "Why, you insufferable—"

She might have punched him or at least finished her sentence, but just then her father arrived on the scene.

"Are you all right?" He directed the question at the man, but it was Ruby who answered.

"He's fine, Dad. But if you ask me to do that again, I'll tell you no. I said I wasn't ready, and I was right."

"You brought the plane down to a safe landing." Her father climbed onto the wing to reach the cowling doors. "You're closer to being ready than you think you are. Just a few more hours in the air, and you'll be ready for your license."

"How can you say that? It was sheer luck that I made it. I could just as easily have crashed the plane and killed two people."

The stranger looked as if he might have something to say, but Ruby turned to him before he had a chance to speak.

"Your ride is over, mister. I trust you got your eight-dollar thrill. And since you won't be getting a lift back to the other side of the field, you might as well start walking."

"Understood." The stranger thrust the helmet and goggles into her hands. "Is there anything I should tell the folks who are waiting for their rides?"

"Tell them the rides are done for the day," Ruby said. "The ones who've already paid will get their money back."

"Not so fast!" Art had the cowling doors open and was peering into the engine. "I don't see anything broken. Could be just a blocked fuel line, or a spark plug gone bad. Tell those folks I'm working on the engine and hope to have it fixed soon."

"I'll pass on what you said. Thank you again for a most memorable ride, Miss Ruby."

The sardonic note in his voice was not lost on Ruby. She bit back a sharp retort as he gave a farewell nod and strode away, headed across the field.

"Pass me that box of spark plugs, Ruby," her father said. "And while I tinker with this engine, maybe you can explain why you were so rude to a paying customer."

"I didn't realize I was being rude." She found what he needed and passed it up to him.

"Did he make a pass at you? I could tell he wanted to."

"Heavens, no! If anything, the man was condescending, as if he thought he was better than the likes of me." She gave a raw laugh. "Me—a woman who lives like a nomad and smells like a garage."

"A woman who's as smart and courageous as she is beautiful. You're wrong, my dear. I saw the way he looked at you. A man like that, wealthy and experienced in the ways of the world, could be worth cultivating."

"Experienced in the ways of the world? You mean, on the shady side of the law?"

"That's not at all what I meant, Ruby. I meant cultured. The kind of man who knows the right kind of wine to order in a restaurant. A man who's done some traveling, maybe some reading."

"Dad, you could be describing a typical con artist."

"Or maybe just someone who knows what he wants and how to get it. I'd just like to see you happy again, with a man who appreciates your worth. Maybe you should have been friendlier with the fellow, gotten to know him better."

"I found him annoying. That was as much as I wanted to know."

"Well, since he didn't measure up to your standards, I met a man who would. While you were in the air, I was talking with Webb Calder, who owns that big ranch. He's as rich as King Midas, and he's a widower. Hand me that small flashlight, will you?"

Ruby found the flashlight in the tool bag. "Stop trying to match me up, Dad. I'm quite happy as I am. And Webb Calder could probably have any lady who caught his fancy. Why should he be interested in someone like me—a woman pushing thirty with no fine manners and grease under her fingernails?"

She reached up and passed him the light. "What did the two of you talk about?" she asked, shifting the subject.

"We had an interesting conversation." Art focused the thin beam of light into the engine. "Calder agreed with me that aviation is the way of the future. He's already looking into building an airstrip and a hangar on his ranch. He asked me what he'd need to get set up, and I told him. But I advised him to wait on the planes. The Jennies are easy to buy and operate, but the new models coming out of Europe are sturdier, faster, and more efficient—like that fleet of De Havillands the post office bought from Britain to carry the mail."

"I take it he didn't offer you a job," Ruby said.

"His plans weren't that far along, or he might have. Anyway, I've already got a job. We'll be meeting with some key people tonight in Miles City. This could be a big turning point in our lives, girl." He probed deeper into the engine. "I think I've found the problem. Dollars to doughnuts, it's a speck of dirt in the fuel line. Once I get it cleared out, she'll be running like new."

Ruby stood back and watched him work. Art was the eternal optimist, always cheerful, always counting on the luckiest outcome. But life had taught Ruby that nothing was guaranteed, and that heartbreak was just as likely as the rainbow around the bend.

Looking back over the field, she saw that her passenger's long legs had carried him all the way across to the far side. He must have been moving fast, as if he had somewhere urgent to go.

Up there in the sky, they had faced death together. Afterward, he'd made a joke of the experience, as if that sort of thing happened to him every day. Ruby had never learned the intriguing

stranger's name. But that didn't matter. He was already gone
from her life.

The four people who'd lined up for rides were still waiting at
the edge of the field. Mason had agreed to pass on the message
that the engine would soon be repaired. But additional flights
could still be risky. Any passenger who climbed into that cockpit
would be taking their life in their hands. He owed them the truth.

The first two in line were cowboys that Mason didn't recognize.
Next to them stood Britta—what a surprise. Mason would never
have guessed the woman had an adventurous streak. He was
about to speak to her when she silenced him with a sharp look.

Standing a few paces behind her, his gaze fixed on the plane,
was Joseph.

Mason would have known his son anywhere. Joseph had been a
boy of fourteen when they'd last met. He was inches taller now,
still filling out through the chest and shoulders. With his rangy
frame and dark hair, he resembled his late grandfather, Joe Dollarhide, Mason's father, who'd founded the family dynasty and
built the rambling log home on the bluff overlooking the valley.

In his younger years, Mason had spent time with his father's
second family, sharing good memories with Joe, his wife, Sarah,
and their children, Blake and Kristin. But over the years, alien-
ation had taken root and grown bitter. Now, for Mason, seeing
Joseph was like seeing a younger version of Joe Dollarhide—the
man he remembered from his childhood.

He felt a firm hand on his arm as Britta guided him out of
hearing, behind a row of parked autos. The blue eyes that leveled
with his own were like tempered steel. "I told you to leave Joseph
alone, Mason," she said. "He doesn't need you in his life."

"I understand, Britta. I already said I'd respect the family's
wishes. But I didn't expect to see him today. What's he doing
here?"

"If you must know, Joseph is crazy to fly. He's never been up in
a plane, but all he talks about is wanting to become a pilot. No
one could have stopped him from coming here today."

"I can imagine how Blake must feel about that. But what about you? Are you planning to switch careers?"

"Hardly." She lowered her gaze a moment, looking almost like a wistful young girl. "Don't laugh. I've spent most of my life looking after others—my family, my students. I've never had a real adventure. I thought maybe it was time."

"So you brought Joseph along?"

"No. I came by myself. He just showed up, and I couldn't make him leave. All I could do was make him promise that he'd let me go first, to make sure the plane was safe. If I decide the ride is too dangerous, then I won't allow the pilot to take him."

"Then you need to hear what I came to say. That plane is a death trap. The engine quit while we were in the air. The woman who was at the controls couldn't start it again, so she had to glide to a landing. It was scary as hell. We could have crashed. You need to tell Joseph and those two cowboys."

Britta turned away, shaded her eyes, and looked out across the field. Following the line of her gaze, he saw the plane, its propeller a spinning blur, taxiing over the ground. The two cowboys were nowhere in sight. Joseph stood alone, waiting at the field's edge.

CHAPTER FOUR

*T*HE PLANE TAXIED TO A STOP, ITS ENGINE STILL CHURNING. STAND-
ing with Britta behind the row of vehicles, Mason watched his tall
son race onto the field to meet it.

"Joseph, stop!" Britta shouted. "Wait for me!" But her voice failed
to carry over the sound of the engine. Whatever she'd meant to
do, Joseph clearly had a different plan in mind.

Mason sensed Britta's dilemma. Joseph was well ahead of her,
determined to get his plane ride before his aunt could go first
and decide to stop him. Now he was holding up his hands, pointing to the double stamp as evidence that he'd already paid. Ruby
was climbing down from the front cockpit to give him her place.
At least, this time, her father would be at the controls, although
there was still no guarantee that the plane was safe.

But there was more to Britta's situation. If she were to interfere
now, and insist on taking the first flight, Joseph would be left on
the ground with his estranged father—a man she had every reason to distrust.

"The boy will be all right, Britta," Mason said. "The man's a
good pilot. I took a chance, flying with his daughter, but her father's had plenty of experience."

Britta's posture was rigid, her jaw set. Her determined look reminded Mason of her father, the late Big Lars Anderson, who'd
had every reason to hate him.

"I can't stop Joseph from getting his plane ride," she said. "But you've done our family enough harm. You're not to be here when he comes back. I mean what I said—if you care about that boy, you'll leave him alone."

"I understand," Mason said, and he did. "All I really wanted was to see my son. Now that I have, I'll be content to mind my own business."

"You have no right to call him your son," Britta said. "Now get into your automobile and leave."

"As soon as I know he's safe," Mason said.

Joseph had donned the goggles and helmet and climbed into the plane's forward cockpit. Ruby checked his seat belt, jumped down from the wing, and made a hand sign to her father. Moments later, the biplane was headed back to the foot of the landing strip. On the near side of the field, Ruby had spread the parachute over the dry grass and begun preparing it to be packed.

Feeling the tension in his own body, Mason watched the biplane as it turned into the light wind. Droning like an angry wasp, it headed over the ground, gaining speed until the wheels left the earth. As it gained height, mounting the sky, Mason took a deep breath of relief.

He had promised to leave. But he would watch from his auto until the plane was safely on the ground again. Only then would he turn for home to resolve the issue of his mother and the missing money.

As the plane banked and leveled off, Joseph filled his gaze with the infinite blue above him and the land below—the toylike town and the patchwork of fields and pastures, rising to the scrub-dotted foothills and the forested peaks beyond. He'd expected to be nervous, even scared. But all he felt was a joyous bursting sensation in his chest. This was like magic—better than magic because it was real. He was flying.

The flight was a short one. As the plane banked again to head back to the landing strip, it passed over the Dollarhide family ranch and sawmill. Joseph could see the sprawling house on the bluff, the yellowed pastures spreading below, where red-and-white Herefords grazed on the dry stubble and drank from the cattle tanks that had to be filled almost daily from the dwindling creek that flowed out of the canyon. Blake, who was Joseph's father in every way but one, had voiced fears that the cattle might have to be sold off early. But as long as the animals continued to put on weight—which would determine their sale price—they would likely remain until fall, when they'd be rounded up, sold, and shipped off to feed lots in places like Chicago.

At the foot of the bluff, the sawmill complex spread like a yellow fungus. Clouds of sawdust drifted above the open sheds where the big rotating blades shrieked as they cut the logs into slabs and boards. Heavy wagons, carrying logs and orders of cut boards, rumbled along the roads. Since the closure of the lumber mill in Miles City, the Dollarhides had cornered the local market on wood for the postwar building boom. The mill, which employed more than half the men of Blue Moon, had made Blake Dollarhide a modest fortune.

Joseph hated the sawmill. He hated the dust, the noise, and the demands it had always made on his father's time. Most of all, he hated the idea that one day it would be his to manage. The prospect that awaited him was like a looming prison sentence.

And it wasn't as if he could wait for Blake to pass on or retire. His father was already involving him in the work, teaching him every step of the process that turned rough logs to smooth, straight boards for building—the ordering, hauling, and stacking; the different types and grades of wood, and the sawyer's craft that would ensure the measurement of every cut.

Once—and only once—had Joseph dared to suggest that running the sawmill might not be the life he would choose. Blake had put him down angrily. "This isn't about you, Joseph. This is about your responsibility to take care of our family. It's about building on the legacy that your grandfather began. Now, no more of this foolish talk. Get to work."

Joseph hadn't told Blake about the air show, and especially not about the plane ride. There was always the chance that Aunt Britta would give him away. But as the plane descended, the earth below growing closer and larger, Joseph knew that whatever punishment he might have earned, he would never regret what he'd done. He had found his soul—and nothing was going to keep him from returning to the sky.

There was something else Joseph had decided not to mention. He had recognized the man he'd glimpsed talking with his aunt. His father, Mason Dollarhide, was out of prison and back in Blue Moon.

Not that it should matter. Five years ago, Mason had hired Joseph and his friends to help with his illegal booze deliveries, guiding the trucks and unloading crates of Canadian liquor. The danger and the pocket money had provided a heady lure for three fourteen-year-old boys. But for Joseph, getting to know the glamorous father he'd never met had been an even more compelling draw. The adventure had ended when federal agents showed up. The boys had narrowly escaped arrest; and their friend, Chase Calder, who'd come to warn them away, had been shot and barely survived.

Joseph had concluded that a man who'd risk his own son, as well as the safety of the other boys, was no father of his. He'd visited Mason for the last time in jail and told the man he wanted nothing more to do with him—ever.

Now Mason was back—like a swashbuckling pirate from a Hollywood movie. Joseph had barely glimpsed the man, but his instincts told him that prison hadn't changed his father. Not that it mattered. He was through with Mason—for good.

Britta was waiting when Joseph climbed out of the cockpit. Dropping to the ground, he stripped off the helmet and goggles. One look at the radiant grin on his face told her everything she needed to know. This was trouble—the kind of trouble that would need to be handled with kid gloves.

"You promised to wait for me, Joseph," she said.

The glow faded a little as he handed off the helmet and goggles and walked toward her. "Forgive me, Aunt Britta. You'd stepped out of sight. I saw my chance, and I was afraid of losing it. I could say that I'm sorry, but that would be a lie. It was wonderful."

"I understand. But I almost wish I didn't."

"Are you going to tell Dad?" he asked.

"No, *you* are. As soon as you get home. Better he hear it from you than from me."

"He'll take a strip out of my hide—and he's bound to keep me at home for the next month."

"Yes, he will. But you pay for your thrills. It's time you learned that." Britta wondered whether Joseph had seen and recognized Mason. Maybe not, since the boy hadn't mentioned it.

"Excuse me, ma'am." The woman who'd flown with Mason caught Britta's attention. "I remember that you paid for your ride. Do you still want to go? If not, you can have your money back."

Her dark eyes narrowed. "Don't worry. If you take your flight, my father will be the one at the controls. He's an excellent pilot."

Britta hesitated. What had she been thinking when she'd paid for the ride?

Most of the people who'd come to see the show had gone, but some of them had stayed to watch the plane take off and land. Britta could imagine what they'd be saying.

Look at her! The old maid schoolmarm going up in an airplane. And her a model of behavior for our young girls! What next? Will she be bobbing her hair and shortening her skirts like one of those flappers?

If she had any sense, she would take her money and leave, Britta told herself. But somewhere deep in her compliant spirit there burned a flame of defiance. While her pretty sisters had broken rules and flung away their virtue, she had remained the good daughter, the sensible, dutiful daughter—the one who was never likely to marry or leave Blue Moon.

Climbing into that plane would constitute a small act of rebellion, one she desperately needed.

Did she dare?

"Go for it, Aunt Britta." Joseph stood just behind her, urging her on. "Who knows when you'll get another chance?"

She took a deep breath. "All right, I'll do it," she said.

The pretty woman in the oil-stained jumpsuit handed her the

helmet and goggles. "Come on. I'll help you into the plane," she said, taking Britta's arm. "Mind your skirt and petticoat."

With help, and despite her narrow, ankle-length skirt, Britta made it onto the wing and into the front cockpit. She was tucking her hair—a long, pale blond braid that wrapped around her head like a crown—into the helmet when she happened to glance back at the small group of people who'd gathered to watch. Standing next to Joseph was the last man she would choose to see her make a fool of herself—Sheriff Jake Calhoun.

Five years ago, there'd been a flicker of attraction between them. He'd whirled her around the floor at a dance, leaving her as flushed and giddy as a teenager. But in the weeks that followed that magical evening, she'd lost both her father and her younger sister, followed a few months later by her mother. Grief and family duties had kept her from responding to Jake's show of interest. As time passed, Jake had married pretty Cora Rushland and fathered a baby girl.

Today he was carrying his four-year-old daughter on his shoulder. Perched like a little doll, the golden-haired child kept a tight grip on the big hand that kept her securely balanced.

The sight tugged at Britta's heart. Cora, a porcelain-skinned beauty, had always been fragile. After the little girl's birth, Cora's health had slowly declined. She'd passed away sixteen months ago, leaving Jake to raise their daughter with the help of Cora's aging grandmother.

A number of attractive younger women had tried to capture the handsome sheriff's attention. Britta, at twenty-nine, wasn't one of them. She'd had her brief chance. The timing had been wrong. Love had passed her by.

Still, she had her pride. She'd avoided Jake, not wanting him to think that she was pursuing him. If he was interested, he could let her know. He hadn't.

And now, by chance, here he was. Just when she was about to do something crazy.

Joseph gave her a wave of encouragement. Britta waved back as the plane made a right-angle turn and taxied back across the field. Britta's heart crept into her throat. She was really doing this. What would people say? What were they thinking, especially Jake Calhoun?

But what did it matter? She was doing this for herself—to prove that she had the courage to push her limits. At least she'd have a story to tell her students when they came back to school in the fall.

Britta willed herself to take deep breaths as the plane picked up speed. She felt the impact as the wheels bounced over the bumpy ground. Then the way became smooth. She felt the lift as the air rushed beneath the wings. She was flying.

But the fear was there, like a cold, quivering lump in the pit of her stomach. As her gaze traveled the distance from the sky to the ground, far below, she couldn't help imagining how it would feel if the plane were to stop in midair and plummet straight down out of the sky. What would her last thoughts be in the seconds before the craft shattered against the ground? Would she be hoping to see her family—her parents, her two brothers, and her sister, who'd passed on before? Would she regret the life she'd chosen? Would she regret not having given Jake more of a chance?

Maybe she was an even bigger coward than she'd led herself to believe.

If she made it back to the earth safely, Britta resolved, she would walk up to him and say hello. She would speak to his little girl and allow him to ask about the flight. What did she have to lose? Maybe they could at least be friends.

It came as a relief when the short flight ended. Britta released a sigh as the wheels touched down and the plane headed back across the field. She could see a few people who'd stayed to watch. Joseph was waiting to congratulate his aunt; and the pilot's daughter stood by to help her out of the plane. But there was no sign of a very tall man with a child on his shoulder.

Jake had gone.

Mason had stayed, watching from his car, until the plane carrying Joseph had landed safely. Only then did he crank the engine to a sputtering start and head back to the ranch. He was proud of his son. Joseph had shown daring and determination when it came to getting what he wanted. Mason possessed those same qualities. He liked to think that he might've passed them on to the boy, along with his striking green eyes.

What if things had been different? What if, instead of skipping town at his mother's urging, he'd remained in Blue Moon, married sweet Hannah, and stayed to raise a family?

But that choice would have been a mistake. He would have ended up feeling trapped and frustrated; and he would have passed his discontent on to his wife and children. He'd done Hannah a favor, leaving her to be rescued by dull, reliable, duty-bound Blake. And he'd done Joseph a favor, too, giving him a secure childhood in the heart of the Dollarhide family.

Still, he couldn't help wondering how things might have been. And he couldn't deny a subtle yearning for what he would never have. But the past was gone and couldn't be changed. All that mattered now was the future. And that future was in his hands.

The ranch house was quiet except for a line of laundry flapping behind the house in the afternoon breeze. He'd noticed a newfangled electric washing machine on the screen porch off the kitchen. But who was doing the laundry remained a question. Except for his mother, Mason had yet to see a woman about the place. Was Sidney, the elderly butler, also doing the wash?

It would be worth his time to learn more about the household routine and the person or persons doing the work around the place. If he planned to be moving crates of bootleg liquor, he would need absolute secrecy. But he would also need to maintain the appearance of a normal, working ranch.

Maybe what he needed was a secret place, away from the house and outbuildings, to carry on his business. He recalled finding the entrance to a cave near the south boundary. He'd discovered it as a boy, but after hearing animal sounds from inside, he'd run away and never returned to the spot.

The place was worth checking again. But until he got control of the money from the ranch account, his hands would be tied.

As he parked in the shed and climbed out of the Model T, his mother's big mastiff came around the house. Its old age was evident in its gait and its white-haired muzzle, but Mason knew that it still had teeth. Seeing him, it stopped a stone's toss away and growled a warning. Then, as if in pure contempt, it lifted its leg on the front tire of the car before trotting away.

Mason cursed. Damned dog. He didn't even know its name or the name of its departed brother, but his mother had loved those two ugly mutts. Probably more than she'd ever loved him.

Reminding himself to have a look at the Model T's engine before driving the auto again, Mason entered the house through the kitchen door. He found Sidney at the counter, cutting crustless egg salad sandwiches into precise triangles.

"Have you eaten, Mr. Dollarhide?" the elderly butler asked. "I'll be glad to make an extra sandwich or two. Your mother likes to lunch late. Tea time, she calls it." The old man was more relaxed and talkative here than in Amelia's presence, where he behaved more like an actor cast in the traditional butler's role.

"Thanks, but I'm fine for now." What Mason really wanted was dinner in town with one of Jake's rare beefsteaks. And maybe a big slab of apple pie for dessert. But his advance from the bank was all but gone.

"We've got some bottled sarsaparilla in the icebox," Sidney said. "Now that you're home, maybe you can talk Mrs. Dollarhide into buying one of those new electric refrigerators. I've seen them in town. They do a dandy job of keeping things cold. I hear that Webb Calder ordered a whole truckload of them for the Triple C."

Webb Calder again—a man rich enough to own anything he wants. Airplanes and even refrigerators.

A man like that was easy to hate.

"Tell me what my mother did with the money from the bank account, and I'll buy you a new refrigerator tomorrow. Hell, I'll replace the whole kitchen."

The old man shook his head. "Even if I knew—and I don't—I would never betray Mrs. Dollarhide's confidence. I'm afraid you're on your own."

Mason stepped aside as the dog padded into the kitchen. Passing Mason, it snarled, showing jagged fangs. It passed through Mason's mind that he could threaten to shoot the dog if his mother didn't give him access to the money. But Amelia was smart enough to recognize a useless threat. As things stood, he had two choices—win his mother's trust, which would take time, or find the money himself.

The surest approach would be to try both.

The dog went to a bowl of table scraps in the corner of the kitchen and chuffed down the food. "We used to feed him on the back porch," Sidney said. "But the coyotes started stealing his food. He was too old and slow to catch them."

"My mother had two dogs when I was here before," Mason said, making conversation. "What happened to the other one?"

Sidney arranged the sandwiches on a china plate. "He just got old. We found him dead on the porch one morning last year. Your mother was fit to be tied. She mourned him like he was her own child. She even buried him in the family cemetery, next to the place she's laid out for herself."

"What about this dog? Weren't they brothers?"

"That's right. I don't suppose old Brutus here will last much longer. Mrs. Dollarhide had both their names carved into the headstone—Brutus and Cassius, like in Shakespeare's play." He picked up the plate, adding a napkin and a glass of cold tea, which he balanced between his large, immaculate hands. "I'm glad you've come back, Mr. Dollarhide. Your mother's a strong woman, but she's getting on, and she needs you to step in and manage the ranch. You can see how it's all gone downhill, most of the cattle sold, the pastures gone to weed, the fences and sheds falling down. You'll have your work cut out for you." He gave Mason a sharp glance. "I do hope you plan to stay around this time."

The old man would know, of course, that Mason had been in prison. What the words implied was the hope that he didn't plan any illegal activities that would land him behind bars again. But what the butler didn't know wouldn't hurt him. And Mason had learned his lesson. This time he would do everything right.

*   *   *

After the air show, Ruby and her father had flown back to the
outskirts of Miles City, where there was a small airport with a runway and a secure enclosure for the plane. They'd taken a taxi
back to the Olive Hotel in town, where they'd left their extra lug-
gage at the desk.

Ruby would've been happy to settle for a light supper in her
room, a warm bath, and an early bedtime. But Art had other
plans. His new "business associates" would be meeting him at dinner. Ruby would need to be there, too.

As she bathed, pinned up her unruly curls, and slipped into
her one good dress—a second-hand pale green crepe with a
dropped waist and pleated hemline—Ruby couldn't shake a deep
sense of foreboding. Her father was excited about the chance to
win them both a better life. But the men they'd be meeting didn't
care about that. All they wanted was to use Art for their own illegal purposes. If things went wrong, they would turn their backs
and leave him to his fate.

She knew better than to try and change Art's mind. All she
could do was be there, support him, and try to keep him safe.
There were times when she felt more like his parent than his
child. This was one of them.

She surveyed her reflection in the cheap mirror that was mounted
on the back of the door. She'd bought the dress from a second-
hand store in Kansas City. Even used, it had been expensive, but
the fit was perfect, the color a nice contrast with her dark eyes
and auburn hair. Her only jewelry was a fine gold necklace with a
tiny airplane pendant. Art had bought it in a pawn shop and
given it to her for her last birthday. Her kidskin slippers were so
old that they fit her feet like gloves. Her only makeup was the
barest touch of lipstick.

A memory of the day flashed through her mind—the tall
stranger gazing down at her, his jade green eyes hard, as he insisted on paying extra to have her take him on his flight. She'd almost killed them both, and afterward he'd treated the whole
adventure as a lark. A man without emotion. She hadn't liked

him. All she wanted was to put the experience behind her, especially the look he'd given her before he'd walked away. But those careless green eyes continued to haunt her.

Ruby forced her thoughts back to the present. Her father wanted her to help him make a good impression tonight. She knew that she'd be putting on an act for his sake. She forced herself to smile at her reflection in the mirror. Her mouth looked convincing enough. But her eyes were like a captive animal's, restless and wary, brimming with distrust.

A rap from the outside of the door blurred her reflection in the mirror. "Are you ready, Ruby? They'll be expecting us downstairs." Her father's voice rang with optimism. Ruby suspected he might've had an illegal drink to bolster his confidence.

"I'm ready," she said, reaching to unfasten the chain lock on the door.

"Then let's be on our way," he said. "This could be the night that changes both our lives forever."

CHAPTER FIVE

WITH THE SUN SINKING IN THE WEST, MASON POCKETED A FLASH-light and a pistol, saddled a horse, and rode south across the pastures to the boundary of the Hollister Ranch. He didn't re-member much about the cave he'd discovered as a boy. But if he could find it again, it might prove useful.

Everything Sidney had said about conditions on the ranch was true—the broken fences, the weedy pastures pocked with clumps of thistle, prairie dog towns and badger holes; the scattered cows, barely enough for breeding stock, their ribs showing through their dusty hides. Everywhere he looked, he saw things that needed attention. But they would have to wait. Right now, he had more urgent matters on his mind.

Pausing the horse on a low rise, Mason surveyed the neglected land. His eyes traced a path along the foothills that bordered the farthest pasture. Beyond the flats, the ranch property was a wilderness of scrubby mesas and shallow box canyons, a hideout for occasional renegades and outlaws, unfit for grazing cattle or any kind of farming.

Shielding his eyes from the setting sun, Mason focused his thoughts on a time in the distant past. He'd been hunting varmints with Blake—back when the two half-brothers were boys and still friends. They'd been tracking a coyote when they lost the trail and came across the cave entrance. They might have gone exploring, but the large bones that littered the entrance had warned them off. Blake had sworn he heard a growl from inside the cave. Mason had taken him at his word. The boys had told no one and never returned to the spot.

Now Mason rode along the edge of the pasture, scanning the foothills for a clue to the cave's location. The overgrown brush and the absence of tracks suggested that no one had been out here in a long time. But where was the entrance? Maybe he'd remembered the location wrong. He kept on looking.

The sun vanished below the horizon, leaving a glow like the last dying coals of a bonfire. Shadows lengthened as twilight crept over the landscape. Even with the help of his flashlight, Mason couldn't see more than a few yards ahead. A bat darted past his face, then another and another. They swarmed into the sky, filling the darkness with their high-pitched cries.

Were they coming from the cave?

Looking toward the source, he saw it, darkly outlined against the risen moon. The craggy outcrop was familiar—he remembered the shape of it now, like the head of a giant wolf. The entrance to the cave would be behind it, concealed in deep shadow.

Senses prickling, he rode closer, dismounted, and tethered his horse to a dead stump. Before moving forward, he drew the pistol, a hefty Colt .45.

Moonlight flooded the ground. Mason breathed easier as he saw that the dry vegetation was untrampled. It appeared that no large animal had been here for some time. But that didn't rule out snakes or even hornets. He'd already seen bats.

Willing himself to stay calm, he rounded the outcrop and stepped into the cave. The entrance was littered with bones, but they were dry and long since picked clean. The odor of bat guano assailed his nostrils. If he used the cave, something would need to be done about that, and the bats as well. That aside, as he directed the flashlight beam at the cave's walls and ceiling, he liked what he saw. There was enough width and height in the entrance to park and unload a good-sized vehicle. From outside, the approach was well beyond the sight of anyone at the ranch house. There was no road to the cave, but the ground could be leveled to drive on. With no easy water source, grazing cattle would be un-likely to wander this far.

The entrance was clear of bats and their droppings, but Mason's nose told him the creatures had come from this cave, maybe from someplace deeper inside. Gripping the flashlight in one hand and the pistol in the other, he followed the narrowing passage for a dozen yards until it opened up into a room the size of a large parlor.

Standing in the entrance, he directed the flashlight beam over the walls and ceiling. This was the bats' roosting place. A few of them were still here, fluttering in the unexpected light. This ap-peared to be a dry cave. There was no sound of dripping water, none of the typical cave formations. All to the good for his pur-pose.

The floor of the cave—that would be the challenge. It was lit-tered with droppings, the bones of dead bats, and heaven knew what else. Snakes? Rats?

Mason had tied his bandanna over his nose and mouth to keep out the worst of the foul odor. The place would need to be fumi-gated with smoke, or more likely burned out. But once it was clear, this room would be deep enough in the hillside to maintain a stable temperature, even in winter. And the space would hold enough crates of liquor to supply a town the size of Miles City for a year.

He could do this. If he could find the money and make his plan work, he'd be rich beyond his wildest dreams. Richer, even, than Webb Calder.

What if the cave went even deeper? Mason used the light to search for another opening. But he found none. This chamber appeared to be the end. For now, it would be enough.

Preparing to leave, he used the flashlight to give the place a final inspection. That was when he noticed something moving through the debris on the floor. A rat—and where there was one, there were bound to be others. Mason hated rats. He'd seen too many of them in prison. Still, he followed the animal with the light as it foraged toward the back of the cave.

That was when he saw something else. His throat jerked as if a noose had been pulled tight around his neck.

Lying against the far wall was the desiccated body of a man.

Mason had seen death before. But the scene that met his eyes now jolted him like an electric shock. Knowing better than to walk into the morass on the cave floor, he stood rooted in the entrance, his hand gripping the flashlight.

It appeared that the man, whoever he was, had been dead for a long time—months or even years—if the cool, dry cave air had helped preserve the body. His rat-eaten face was nothing but bones, crowned by wisps of brown hair, but Mason could see that he'd been tall in life. He was dressed in moldering cowboy clothes—jeans, a plaid flannel shirt, a belt with an ornate brass buckle, and boots with soles that had come loose and curled away from his feet, showing the remnants of worn socks and the bones of his toes.

Did he have a family somewhere—people who'd loved him and might want to reclaim his body? But that didn't matter, Mason reminded himself. He couldn't allow news of this discovery to get out. When he cleansed the cave with fire, every trace of the man, whoever he'd been, would be burned to ashes.

For now, there was nothing more to do here. The next time he came, it would be with enough kerosene and wood to do what needed to be done. Meanwhile, he'd have his hands full finding the money and setting up the connections he needed for moving and selling the liquor.

As Mason turned to leave, a vague awareness stirred in the depths of his memory. A chill crawled up his spine before it passed. *What was it?*

Stopping, he redirected the flashlight beam on the remains of what had once been a man. Once again, he felt it—the gut twinge that told him he was missing a vital clue.

He stared at the dried-out, decaying figure. Something about the dead man touched a familiar chord. It wasn't possible, he told himself; but it was almost as if he'd known the fellow in life. Maybe his imagination was working overtime. But he couldn't shake the feeling. Mason swore under his breath.

"Who are you?" he muttered, speaking to the corpse. *"Who in hell's name are you?"*

The two strangers had taken a table in a quiet corner of the hotel dining room. They rose to their feet as Ruby walked in with her father. Immaculately groomed and dressed in custom tailored suits, they stood out among the locals who frequented the place. Glancing at Art, Ruby could tell he was impressed.

Both men had a European look about them. The tall one, who appeared to be in his thirties, had luxuriant black hair and the kind of well-tended body that a man would take pleasure in showing off. His smoldering eyes roamed over Ruby with an entitled look that made her seethe.

Suppressing the impulse to confront him, she turned toward his younger companion, who was built like a fireplug, with heavy brows, a fleshy face with a scar slash across one cheek, and cold, intelligent eyes.

"Well, Colucci," the shorter man said. "Are you going to stare at the lady all night, or are you going to introduce us?"

The color deepened in Colucci's florid face. Evidently Ruby's father had met him earlier. "Sorry, Boss, this is our pilot, Art Murchison, and he's brought along his daughter, Miss Weaver."

"It's *Mrs.* Weaver," Ruby said. "And I'm a pilot, too."

"An admirable accomplishment, if I may say so. I'm a family man myself." The shorter man raised Ruby's hand to his lips and brushed it with a courtly kiss. "Alphonse Capone at your service, ma'am. We've already ordered dinner. Now let's enjoy it before we get down to business."

The roast beef, served with potatoes and gravy, was as good as could be expected, but Ruby had to force down every bite as she listened to the dinner conversation. She could tell her father was excited, and the more engaged he became, the more she worried. It didn't ease her discomfort any that Colucci, who was seated across from her, was watching her as if he'd already staked his claim. Avoiding eye contact with the big man, Ruby willed herself to focus on the talk at the table and learn as much as she could.

Capone, she gathered from the talk, was on his way to heading up the Chicago bootleg operation. Torrio, the big boss, was in ill health. When he died or retired, Capone would be first in line to succeed him. What kind of talent did it take for a younger man to rise so fast in an organization that was known to be ruthless? Ruby suppressed a shudder at the thought.

"There's a big untapped market for us in Montana," Capone was saying. "But so far, the problem has been with delivery—all that open space and road time, with our trucks and drivers exposed. Airplanes could make all the difference, but we'll need to set it up right. First off, we'll need good, experienced pilots who can land and take off in rough places."

"I'm your man, Mr. Capone," Art said. "I trained pilots all through the war. And Ruby here, she's been taught by the best. A little more practice, and she'll be able to fly for you, too."

"You won't be working for me," Capone said. "I'm just here looking things over before I take the morning train back to Chicago. It's Mr. Colucci here who'll be in charge of the operation—if we can make it work." He turned to his companion. "So what do you think so far, Leo?"

"We won't know for sure until we've taken a few trial runs," Colucci said. "Mr. Murchison, I'm willing to hire you on a probationary basis. You'll be paid a hundred dollars, plus the cost of fuel, at the end of each successful run. Do you understand?"

"And if the run is unsuccessful?" Art was clearly hoping for a better offer.

"You mean if you crash the plane or get caught?" Colucci raised an eyebrow. "If you're as good as you say you are, that shouldn't happen. But if it does, that's your responsibility. Understand?"

The big man's cold gaze met Capone's. It was only for an instant, but what Ruby read in that glance chilled her. For the pilot, getting caught wouldn't be an option.

"Do you understand?" Colucci demanded again.

Art nodded. "Yes, I understand." Ruby's fear deepened. She knew how much her father wanted to buy a better life for her and for himself. But the price was too high. This job was too dangerous.

"Wait." She broke into the conversation, hoping to stall his decision, give him time to change his mind. "I have some questions, Mr. Colucci. What if the buyer doesn't show up, or doesn't pay?"

Colucci shrugged. "The buyer doesn't get the product until he's paid for it in full. And the pilot gets paid after we get paid, Mrs. Weaver. That's how it works. Any more questions?" His manner made it clear that as a woman, she'd spoken out of turn.

"This isn't really a suggestion, Mr. Colucci," Ruby said. "But you need to be aware of something. The Jenny is a small plane—and an old plane. Even stripped down, with no spare fuel and only one person in the cockpit, it can't carry more than a few hundred pounds of cargo. And when you're talking glass bottles in crates, that isn't much. If you want to make money, you're going to need a bigger airplane."

Again, Capone and Colucci exchanged glances, as if the latter needed approval for what he was about to say. "We're aware of that, Mrs. Weaver. But before we invest in an expensive new plane, we'll need to know whether the plan will work. We'll go with your Jenny and pick up another one to use as backup and for your training. Does that meet with your approval, Mr. Murchison?"

"Yes. Yes, I believe it does." Art was nodding, almost smiling. That these men planned on buying a new plane, and that they were willing to train Ruby for future work, appeared to outweigh the risk to their lives.

But then, as she met her father's eyes, the truth struck home. The two of them had already met with these gangsters. They had seen their faces and heard their plans. They couldn't just reject their offer and walk away—not if they wanted to live.

Three nights later, Mason loaded a cart with a stack of firewood and two gallon-sized cans filled with kerosene. With a calm horse hitched to the load, he drove out through the back gate and headed south. Forty minutes later, he reached the entrance to the cave.

Steeling himself for a dirty job, he unloaded the wood and fuel outside the cave. The bats were gone. In the morning, they would have to find a new place to roost.

After moving the horse and empty cart to a safe distance, he soaked the woodpile with kerosene, carried each piece into the cave and tossed it into the dark, hollow space at the rear. He didn't use the flashlight, but he could hear each piece thudding against the wall or clattering onto the floor. Sometimes he heard nothing at all. That was when he imagined the wood striking the soft clothing and crumbling bones of the corpse that had begun to haunt his nightmares. Several rats fled past him as he used the last of the kerosene to pour a trail leading out of the cave. There was just enough to get him past the outside entrance and into the open.

Striking a match on a rock, he touched it to the spilled fuel and stepped back to watch. He held his breath as the flame snaked along the trail of liquid. Anything could happen. The flame could go out. The burst of heat could collapse the cave or set the prairie on fire. The light and smoke could attract unwanted attention from as far away as the ranch or even the town.

The flame vanished into the opening. Seconds crawled past. Drops of sweat trickled down Mason's face.

From the depths of the cave came a roar and an explosion of flame and heat that seemed to suck the air out of his lungs. Tongues of fire leaped out of the cave entrance.

Mason retreated to where he'd left the horse, prepared for a fast escape in case the dry scrub caught fire. But that didn't happen. As the minutes passed and the explosive roar faded to the crackle of burning wood, he realized that, aside from the foul-smelling smoke that rose from the mouth of the cave, everything had gone according to plan.

He waited long enough to make sure the blaze wasn't going to spread, then headed the horse for home. He would give the embers a few days to cool, then return to clean up the mess.

By now it was well after midnight. The sky was clear. The light breeze, blowing from the northwest, would carry the smoke smell away from the ranch. He would put the horse away, sneak up to his room, and go to bed. His mother would be none the wiser.

The house was dark when he pulled through the back gate, unhitched the horse, and left it in its stall with food and water. Stealthily, he tried the kitchen door. It was locked, probably from the inside, and he didn't have a key.

With a muttered curse, he stole around to the front of the house and mounted the porch steps. His mother had always kept a spare key under the doormat. Yes—there it was. He thrust it into the lock. It turned easily. Mason exhaled with relief and reached for the latch.

That was when he heard snuffling and scratching sounds, followed by a low growl from the other side of the door. *Damned miserable dog.*

"Brutus," he whispered, trying to sound friendly. "It's all right, boy. It's just me."

The growling ceased. He could hear the dog's clicking toenails on the hardwood floor, fading toward the parlor. Mason opened the door, half expecting to be attacked. One hand gripped the pistol. He wouldn't shoot the dog except to save his own life, but he couldn't be too careful.

No attack came. As his eyes adjusted to the dark parlor, he could see the dog sitting next to his mother's big chair. Only as she spoke and moved did he realize that his mother was there, too, concealed in the chair's deep shadows.

"Aren't you too old to be sneaking out at night?" Her voice dripped with sarcasm. "You could've at least let me know."

Scrambling for his wits, Mason forced a laugh. "I'm not a teenager anymore, Mother. And since when do I need your permission to visit a lady friend?"

"Does your so-called lady friend entertain her customers in a gas station? Don't lie to me, Mason. I can smell you from here."

He hesitated, knowing he couldn't tell her the truth. "All right. I didn't want to worry you. A couple of saddle tramps were camped out on the range. The fools used some kerosene to start their campfire. I saw it from the house and went out to chase them off. When they heard me coming, they rode away. I had to stamp the fire out. That's what you can smell."

"A likely story!" she snapped. "But even if you told the truth, I wouldn't know whether to believe you. That's why I can't trust you with my money."

"Then how do you expect me to run the ranch? How do you expect me to pay for my own needs?"

"You mean, like your lady friends? I'd say that's your problem. If you need cash for ranch expenses, you can ask me. As for your personal needs, I already mentioned that I'd pay you a small salary in addition to room and board. That should suffice until you've earned my trust, but you'll be expected to earn every cent. And you can start now."

She glanced from Mason to the restless dog. "Brutus needs to go outside and do his business. You can take him and bring him back when he's done. I never let him out alone at night. He's apt to run off and get into trouble."

"What sort of trouble?" Mason couldn't resist some wishful thinking.

"There are skunks out there, even coyotes and bobcats. And if there's a female in season within a mile, he'll smell her and be off like a shot. Not so different from you in that respect—or your father. So keep an eye on him, understand?"

"I understand." Mason knew better than to argue. He switched on the flashlight, opened the door, and whistled for the blasted dog. Brutus trotted out the door ahead of him, crossed the porch, and vanished into the dark.

"Don't just stand there! Go after him!" Amelia snapped.

"What if he won't come when I call him?"

"There's a tin of dog biscuits on the porch. Take one of those."

Mason closed the door behind him, found the tin with the flashlight, and took out a bone-shaped biscuit. By now, the dog was nowhere in sight. He scanned the front yard with the light and caught a flash of tan going around the corner of the house.

"Brutus! Come back here, you miserable mutt!" He called and whistled, holding up the biscuit, but the dog ignored him. He could hear the dry grass rustling as Brutus left the yard and kept going, back toward the small, fenced square of land that served as the Hollister family burial plot.

The wrought-iron fence had a gate that fastened with a simple latch. Brutus waited by the gate, whimpering softly. As he realized what the old dog wanted, Mason's dislike for the animal mellowed to a twinge of sympathy. He unlatched the gate. The dog passed through ahead of him, trotted to a low mound of earth marked with a headstone, and lay down on it, its massive head resting on its paws.

"So you miss your brother, do you, old boy?" Mason shone the light on the marker, a low granite block, a little bigger than a shoebox, with the names of the two dogs, Cassius and Brutus, etched on its surface. The birth dates were the same, the death date filled in for Cassius.

In all likelihood, Mason surmised, the two dogs were the only individuals his mother had loved and trusted. Her parents had separated when she was young. Her socialite mother had passed her off to her father, who'd died so long ago that Mason could barely remember him. Her husband, Joe Dollarhide, had left her to marry his true love, Sarah. As for her son, her only child . . . Mason had to admit that he'd let her down as cruelly as any of them. Even Sidney was only a paid employee. No wonder she'd turned to her dogs for affection and loyalty.

Not that Amelia was an easy person to love.

The dog hadn't moved from the grave. Mason didn't want to risk laying a hand on the creature to move it. It was none too friendly, and those jaws could be deadly. But he was tired, dirty, and impatient to get back to the house.

He still had the biscuit. Stepping back from the grave, he held it out. "Come on, Brutus," he said. "Time to do your business and get back to your mistress."

The dog's nose twitched. It lurched to its feet, lunging for the treat so fast that Mason jumped away and stumbled over a rock. The biscuit flew out of his hand as he pitched forward, catching himself against the headstone.

Pain shot up his arm. For a moment he feared he might have sprained his wrist, but he forgot the injury as he realized that the stone, which he'd assumed was solidly set in cement, had shifted a couple of inches. His pulse raced. Where would his mother most likely hide her treasure, if not with her beloved pet?

While Brutus gnawed on the biscuit, Mason worked his hand under the stone and tilted it onto its side. Without disturbing the actual grave, the ground beneath the stone had been hollowed out. The hole was awkwardly dug, as if Amelia had done the job herself. Fitted into the space was a steel box.

The box was latched, but not locked. Mason held his breath as he raised the lid.

There it was—bundles of cash, most of it in hundred-dollar bills. There had to be thousands of dollars here, money that his mother had withdrawn from the bank and hidden in what she perceived to be a safe place. The woman was clearly not in her right mind. But he would deal with her later. Right now, all that mattered was having the funds to set up his business.

But as he stared down at the cash—more money than he'd ever seen in one place—Mason knew he had to handle this the right way. Siphoning off the money without telling his mother would have consequences when she found out—as she was bound to. So would seizing the funds outright and taking charge by force. The old woman would still have power. She could easily call the law on him or write him out of her will.

The best solution was the simplest—put the money back in the bank with his name on a new account and his mother as beneficiary. The bankers would accept his story that Amelia had grown irrational. There was every reason to believe she could no longer be trusted to handle the ranch's money.

His mother would be furious. But with the bank backing him, there'd be little she could do. Everything would be carried out legally and openly. His action would be seen as that of a dutiful son protecting his family's assets.

Mason hadn't wanted to hurt his mother. But by withdrawing the ranch money from the bank and burying it next to her dead dog, she'd played right into his hands.

He would look after her, of course. He would even keep old Sidney around to make her little sandwiches and serve her tea. But he was the one in charge now—in charge of the money, the ranch and everything.

Mason lifted the box free, replaced the headstone, and whistled for the dog. First thing tomorrow, he would take the cash to Miles City and open a new bank account. Then he would go to the telegraph office and send a coded message to Julius Taviani, who coordinated bootlegging operations from his prison cell. Julius would connect him with the people who could help him set up his business.

He was on his way. Soon, everything he'd dreamed of in that hellhole of a prison would be his.

CHAPTER SIX

Three weeks later

RUBY SWUNG THE BIPLANE INTO THE DAWN WIND AND OPENED THE throttle. The engine roared as the heavily loaded craft lumbered down the runway and caught the air beneath its wings.

As the Jenny began to rise, Ruby allowed herself a deep breath. It was natural to be nervous about this, her first solo delivery, she told herself. She operated the plane from the rear cockpit, packed in front with two hundred pounds of padded cargo and an equal amount behind her, carefully balanced. The flight would be a short one, to a ranch that lay a few miles south of Blue Moon. Piloting a plane that had been stripped of every extra ounce to allow for cargo, she was to land on the rough prairie, collect the money, help unload, and fly the empty plane back to the abandoned farm outside Miles City.

Simple. What can go wrong?

The irony of that thought coaxed a smile from her lips as she banked the plane and headed south, following the map she'd memorized.

Part of the distribution process remained a mystery, as it was probably meant to be. The base of operations was an abandoned farm about twenty miles east of Miles City. The planes, three Jennies now, were kept there in a big barn converted to a hangar.

Crated liquor shipments from Canada—Ruby had no idea how they were transported over the border—were flown out to the clients almost as soon as they arrived.

So far, there were just two pilots, Ruby and her father. Between shipments, they lived at a boardinghouse in Miles City. When a new shipment came in, a car would pick them up and drive them to the old farm, where they would stay and work, swilling coffee and getting little rest, until all the deliveries were made. Early on, Art had made all the flights. Ruby had helped the ground crew and worked on her training. Now that business was picking up, she'd been pressed into service as a pilot.

At this early hour, there was barely enough light to see the contours of the land below—the hills and pastures, the roads and farms. Flying by daylight ran too much risk of being seen and tracked. Art was already making night flights, using the plane's instruments to guide him. But Ruby was still learning. She needed the faint first glow of morning to find her way.

Worries plagued her. So many things could go wrong. The client was new—always an added risk. The landing with the loaded fuselage would be tricky, the added weight changing the dynamics of the plane. Then there was the rough terrain, a sure guarantee of a hard landing.

The worst of it was not knowing what to expect. She carried a small pistol in the pocket of her coveralls, in case she needed to defend herself or her cargo. But in some instances, a weapon would be useless. She could crash or land in the wrong place. Or she could climb out of the cockpit to be surrounded by armed revenuers and carted off to jail.

Stop it! Just remember what you've been taught.

As Ruby flew the plane south over Blue Moon and began a slow descent, she willed herself to focus on her job. Everything would be all right, she told herself. All she had to do was land, collect payment, unload the crates, and take off again. By then there would be enough light to find her way back to the base.

She'd been told that a bonfire would be lit to guide her to the landing. Scanning the ground below, Ruby could see the burning beacon in the shadowy dawn. She was on target. Heart in her throat, she banked the plane, circled, and headed down.

Mason heard the distant drone of the plane before he spotted it in the sky—a dark speck, like a flying insect, above the pale horizon.

He added more dry wood to the smoldering bonfire. Flames leaped, crackling in the morning stillness. The plane banked and turned toward him. Mason's pulse quickened. His first shipment was about to arrive.

The cave was ready, the walls and ceiling cleansed by fire, the ashes on the floor covered with layers of canvas. All that remained of the mysterious dead man was his brass belt buckle, which Mason had dropped into his vest pocket. He had done all the work himself. There was no one he could trust to help him.

The roar of the engine grew louder as the plane swept in for a landing. There was no proper runway out here, and no way to build one without a construction crew. Using a horse and a chain, Mason had ripped out the larger sagebrush clumps, thistles, and cedars; but the long strip of ground was still dotted with low scrub, rocks, and holes. His telephone contact had assured him that the pilot would have the experience to land on the roughest terrain. Mason wasn't sure he believed the man. Now the moment of truth had arrived.

The plane came in low and fast—too fast. After almost skimming the ground, it rose again, banked, and came in for a second try. Mason forgot to breathe as the craft touched down, shot forward, and bounced once, then again, coming down hard before shuddering to a stop.

Mason sprinted toward the plane. The engine had died. The plane's only movement was the lazy turning of the propeller. Coming closer, he could see the pilot struggling in the rear cockpit.

Reaching up, he climbed onto the wing. The pilot seemed dazed, flailing at the controls. Unable to reach the seat belt, Mason lifted off the goggles and yanked off the leather helmet.

He gasped as he saw who it was.

Hand on the stick, feet on the rudder bar, ailerons up . . . the jarring collision with the ground. Where was she now? Was the plane all right? Ruby opened her eyes, but the cracked lenses of her goggles blurred everything.

Then the goggles and helmet came off, as if ripped away by an invisible hand. Her vision cleared, along with her mind. She was still in the cockpit. A face hovered above her—piercing green eyes, oddly familiar, gazed into hers.

"Thank God you're alive, Ruby." The voice seemed to echo in her head. And how did the speaker know her name?

"Is the plane all right?" She muttered the first concern that came to mind.

"It appears to be fine. It's you I'm worried about."

That rough-edged baritone. Where had she heard it? Ruby stared at him, finally remembering. "You," she said. "I never expected to see you again."

He shrugged. "Small world. Right now, we need to get you out of the plane. If you'll unfasten your seat belt, I'll give you a hand."

She unbuckled the strap, ignoring his proffered hand as she climbed out onto the wing and jumped to the ground. "I'll be fine. I just need to collect your payment, unload the cargo, and be on my way."

"You're not going anywhere until we make sure you're all right. Sit down on that log. I'll get you some water."

"I'll be fine." Still standing, she struggled to collect her thoughts. She couldn't remember stopping the plane, only the rough landing. The seat belt would have kept her from being thrown very far, but she could have struck the instrument panel or the windscreen, the impact cracking her goggles.

She needed to get back to the base. Returning late from her first delivery would worry her father and land her in no end of trouble with their employers. She owed Art that much.

"Here, drink this." He handed her an open canteen. Ruby tilted it to her lips. The water was fresh and cool. She took several deep swallows and returned the canteen to him. She did feel a bit shaky, but that would pass, she told herself. Meanwhile, she had a job to do.

"Now sit down," he said.

"Business first. I'll take your payment now."

"Fine." He withdrew a white envelope from the inner pocket of his leather vest. "You can count it if you want. The money for this shipment is all there, along with a down payment on the next one. But we're not unloading those crates until you've had some rest and we've made sure you're all right to fly."

Ruby took the envelope and tucked it inside her flight jacket. All she wanted was to leave. Surely, even without goggles, she'd be fine for the short return flight. But she couldn't take off without unloading the heavy crates, and she couldn't lift them out of the plane by herself.

With a sigh of impatience, she sank onto the log. For now, the man had left her with no choice except to stay.

Mason took a seat next to the woman he'd never expected to see again. She sat with her hands in her lap—slim, graceful hands, but stained with oil, the nails bitten off to the quick. They were not the hands of a woman who'd had an easy life. Somehow, he liked her for that.

"Are you all right, Ruby?" he asked.

"I will be. But you're not supposed to know my name. And I'm not supposed to know yours. That's how this business works."

"My name is Mason. Mason Dollarhide. Now we're even. Am I to understand that you'll be my regular delivery person?"

"That's what I was told. But if I get myself fired, you won't be seeing me again."

"That would be a disappointment. I'll try to see that it doesn't happen. How many pilots are working this operation?"

"Even if I knew, I wouldn't tell you."

"And I don't suppose you'd tell me how far you have to fly to get back to your home base."

"You should know better than to ask."

He did know. Safety depended on discretion. The less he knew about her, the better. But the loaded Jenny wouldn't hold enough fuel for a long round trip, so it was probably close by. Miles City had an airstrip, but it wasn't private. Maybe his suppliers had a facility of their own, somewhere hidden.

The question was, would it be safe to let her fly there?

Ruby fell into silence, gazing toward the east, where the morning clouds had taken on the soft pinks and violets of early sunrise. He studied her profile against the sky: the chiseled cheekbones, the stubborn chin, the soft curl of auburn hair lying against her cheek. Her tan flight clothes were probably a man's. But there was nothing mannish about the way they fit her curvy body. Looking at her, Mason felt the tug of desire in his loins. He had yet to slake his lust with a woman. But he knew better than to mix business and pleasure—and this lady was business—important business.

She stirred, turning to fix him with those melting eyes. "I don't know what your game is, mister, but you've paid for your delivery, and that's all you're going to get. Take your goods so I can leave. People will be waiting for me—my father and . . . others."

"Yes, I understand." He could imagine those others. He'd spoken with Leo Colucci on the ranch house phone to arrange delivery of his first shipment. Julius Taviani had put the two in touch. If Ruby was spending time with the likes of Colucci, she was in dangerous company. Should he warn her? But she looked old enough to know the score. Maybe it was already too late. Maybe she was already sleeping with the bastard.

She stood, brushing off the seat of her pants. "I'm feeling much better now. Let's get those boxes unloaded."

He rose to stand beside her. "You hit hard enough to break your goggles. Before we start, do you mind if I check your eyes for any injury?"

"Be my guest. Just get me out of here." She stood facing him, defiance in her expression and in every line of her body. Mason turned her toward the light and brushed back her hair.

"Hold still. This won't take long." He took a flashlight out of his pocket. She gazed up at him, her expression one of suspicion. Looking into her dark eyes, he sensed fear coupled with courage, vulnerability coupled with strength. An ordinary woman—especially one so beautiful—wouldn't be flying planes to rendezvous with smugglers. Despite his misgivings, Mason found himself wanting to know more about her.

But first things first. In prison, he'd spent time in the infirmary. Among other things, he'd learned how to check for a possible concussion. When he directed the beam into her eyes, the pupils reacted, shrinking uniformly, a good sign.

"Did I pass inspection?" The question carried an edge.

"I'm no doctor. I could be wrong, but everything looks fine."

"I told you so."

He pocketed the flashlight. "I can't resist asking. What makes a woman get into a dirty, dangerous business like this one?"

"Why does any woman get into a dirty, dangerous business?"

"You didn't answer my question."

"Because this job pays better than the air shows—a lot better."

"What does your father think of what you're doing?"

"He's the one who got me into it. Come on. Let's get this plane unloaded."

The plane had overshot the cave entrance. Mason decided to unload where it had stopped. He could carry the crates back to the cave by himself after the plane left. There wouldn't be that many. He'd hoped for more, but there was a limit to what the small plane could carry.

Ruby started with the forward cockpit, passing each box of bottles, emblazoned with the red Canadian maple leaf, down to Mason on the ground. The rest of the shipment was lined up behind the pilot's seat to balance the load. The work was finished in a few minutes.

"I'm going to need more," Mason said. "Will you be bringing me the next order?"

"Maybe. Maybe not. It's a risky job. I could crash or be fired—or be replaced by a better pilot."

"Do you know how soon it will be?" Mason was just beginning to realize how much he wanted to see her again.

"I just fly the plane. The less I know the better." She'd climbed back into the rear cockpit and was strapping on her helmet. "Right now, you'd better hope we can start this engine. Otherwise you'll be stuck with me, and I'll be out of a job."

Except for the complications, that might not be so bad, Mason reflected. But for both their sakes, he needed to get her back in the air. She was probably supposed to keep the plane running while they unloaded the cargo. But the rough landing had cut the engine.

She appeared to be checking the controls. "Do you know what to do?" she asked.

"I watched you and your father at the air show. I'm assuming that starting a plane is something like cranking a Model T."

"A little, maybe. Just listen and do what I tell you."

Trying to remember what he'd seen and heard, Mason stood next to the propeller. "Ready," he called.

"When I say 'contact,' you spin the propeller. Do you remember which way?"

"I remember." He waited for her cue. When it came, he gave the prop a hard spin and jumped back, out of the way.

Nothing happened. They tried again with the same result. The engine wouldn't even turn over.

With a broken sigh, she climbed out of the cockpit, holding a small canvas tool bag. "I'll have to open her up." She climbed onto the lower wing and opened the cowling door that covered the engine. "Let's hope it's nothing serious. I didn't bring any spare parts because of the weight. Oh, blast, I don't need this."

The sun's golden rim had barely risen above the mountains. On the land below, the shadows were still long and deep. Ruby stretched upward and peered into the dark recesses of the engine.

Mason stood close by, watching her from the ground. "I'm a fair mechanic myself," he said. "I'd be happy to take a look."

"I'm the one who knows this engine," she said. "But if you'd come up here with your flashlight and hold it while I check, that would help."

Mason climbed onto the wing and slipped the flashlight out of his pocket. To get the light where she needed it, he had to stand close behind her and shine it over her shoulder. The contact with her body, warm through her clothes and fragrant with her womanly aroma, sent electric tingles racing over his skin. His arousal stirred. With a silent curse, he shifted back a step, breaking the physical connection between them. But he could still feel her nearness going through him like a shimmering current.

"Can you see the problem?" he asked.

"Not . . . yet. Something could've gotten jarred in the landing. A nut or a wire, maybe. I'm checking all the connections." A moment later, her breathing quickened. "There—I may have found it. Shine the light in closer . . . no, closer, right there."

Mason leaned closer and did as she'd asked. He struggled to ignore the sweet pressure of her body against his. But as she braced against him, leaning to tighten a bolt in the engine, his imagination began to wander forbidden paths . . . caressing her . . . kissing that lush, moist mouth . . .

What happened next was a blur. Did she lose her footing on the wing, or did Mason's fantasies get the better of him? All he knew was that she seemed to miss a step and was scrambling for balance when he caught her with an arm around her waist and swung her against him.

Neither of them moved. Mason could feel her trembling. He knew he should let her go, but she fit into the circle of his arms as if she belonged there. He ached to kiss her. Would she let him? Would she respond?

"It's all right, Ruby . . ." he murmured, his arms tightening around her. "You're safe. I won't let you fall."

She stirred against him. That was when he felt it—something

hard jammed against his ribs. "Let me go," she said in a cold voice. "Now."

Mason dropped his arms and stepped back on the wing, his free hand clutching a wire for support. That was when he saw the pistol she was aiming at his chest. The weapon was small, but big enough to do the job. Smart girl, carrying something to protect her from woman-hungry jackasses like him.

"You can put that gun away, Ruby," he said. "I was only trying to keep you safe. I would never take advantage of a woman like you."

But how many women and girls had he taken advantage of in past years? One of them had been the mother of his son. And there'd been so many others that he'd lost track. All of them had been willing—some more than willing. But he'd only been thinking of his own pleasure. Maybe it was time someone taught him a lesson.

She released the hammer on the gun and slipped the weapon back into her pocket. "I don't know what kind of woman you think I am," she said. "But right now, I need help getting this plane off the ground, and you're the only help I've got."

"Tell me what to do," he said.

"I think I've fixed the problem with the engine. We won't know until we try to start it again."

"Fine. When you're ready, I'll be at the propeller."

He swung down off the wing while she closed the cowling, climbed back into the cockpit, and fastened her seat belt.

"Good luck." Standing at the ready by the propeller, he gave her a smile and a wave. "It's been nice doing business with you, Ruby."

She didn't return his smile. All her attention was focused on the controls and the instrument panel. She needed the plane to fly. Mason understood that, even if it meant he might not see her again.

At last she was ready. As the risen sun flooded the land with light, she gave him the signal and the call. Mason threw his strength against the blades, giving the propeller a powerful spin. The engine sputtered, then caught and roared to life.

Mason stepped out of the way as she taxied to a takeoff position. She'd landed the plane with a heavy cargo. She was leaving empty. But the ground was rough and dangerous. Anything could go wrong.

He prayed in silence as the biplane lumbered down the makeshift runway, rocking and bucking all the way. Only as the wheels left the ground did he begin to breathe normally. If she ever came back, he vowed, she would find the way cleared to provide safer conditions.

He watched the plane until it was nothing more than a dot in the western sky. Then he turned to moving his merchandise into the cave. He was still working out the details of the distribution, but quality Canadian liquor would be in high demand. He should have no problem selling it for a healthy profit, enough to buy a bigger shipment next time—if he could arrange a bigger delivery.

Mason paused to rest his back and gaze at the empty sky. The irony hadn't escaped him. He and Ruby were part of a complex criminal enterprise with ties to the underworld. They had both compromised their honor for the sake of money. True, what they were doing was harming no one. But it was nothing to be proud of.

So why did thinking about her make him want to be a different kind of man, not just rich but respectable and respected—a man like Webb Calder?

Maybe, when his fortune was made, he'd find a quality woman, set her up like a queen, and give her all the things she deserved. Even marriage and a family wouldn't be out of the question. But that woman wouldn't be Ruby. She'd hinted that she already belonged to somebody else—probably Colucci or a man like him, who could drape her in silks and diamonds as long as she was willing to pay the price.

But that was none of his business, Mason told himself. And right now, he had work to do.

Resolving to forget the beautiful pilot, he picked up another crate of illegal whiskey and lugged it to the cave. Later today he would bring a team of horses and start leveling the runway.

*　*　*

As she eased the plane into its descent, Ruby could see the farm below. Its shabby barns and outbuildings housed a growing bootleg operation, but aside from the landing strip and a few vehicles in the yard, there was little that might be noticed from the air. A large sign painted on the side of the barn advertised a crop-dusting service. It was there to justify the activity around the place and the presence of planes and a runway.

Her first successful run had been a nerve-racking experience. The client had been so unsettling that she'd had to restrain herself to keep from punching him. Everything about the man seemed to challenge her control, as if he expected her to melt in his arms like a helpless doll. When she'd slipped on the edge of the wing and he'd caught her, the heat between their bodies had taken her breath away. That was when she'd drawn her pistol—as much to save her from herself as to threaten him.

A glance at the fuel gauge showed her that the tank was almost empty. The can of spare fuel she usually carried had been jettisoned to allow for more cargo. A few more miles and she'd have run out. She would mention that to her father. Surely Art would back her insistence on carrying enough to top off the tank before the return flight.

In the dark morning hours, Art had delivered one shipment, returned to the base, and left with another loaded plane. These three deliveries, counting her own, would be the last of the current batch.

Her father planned to be waiting for her at the airfield when she landed. They would turn her plane over to the ground crew, collect their pay, and be driven back to Miles City, where they'd enjoy a celebratory breakfast and a few days of rest before going back to work.

By now the sun was up, giving her a clear view of the runway. Ruby's spirits rose as the wheels touched the ground. She had completed her mission. Her father would be proud of her.

She taxied the plane to the hangar, stopped outside, and climbed out of the cockpit. She couldn't see her father anywhere.

Instead, waiting outside the wide double doors, looming tall in his black tailored suit, was Leo Colucci.

As Ruby jumped to the ground, he dropped the cigarette he was smoking, crushed it under his boot heel, and strode toward her. She was instantly on alert. Something was wrong.

"Where's my father?" Her heart was pounding.

He laid a proprietary hand on her shoulder. "It's too soon to worry, Ruby, but he's overdue. We were expecting him back an hour ago."

She stared up at him. "My father's a good pilot. He probably just had engine trouble."

"Let's hope so. I've looked into equipping our planes with radios, but it's not practical, especially not in this rugged country, so there's no way of knowing what's gone wrong." His fingers tightened on her shoulder. "All we can do is wait and hope he shows up. Meanwhile, you must be hungry. We've got coffee and doughnuts in the kitchen."

"I'll stay here for now." Ruby couldn't imagine relaxing in the kitchen while her father was missing. "Oh—I have something for you." She drew the envelope of cash out of her jacket. "I haven't counted it, but I'm assuming the amount is right."

He took the envelope, opened it, and counted the bills. "Fine for now. But after this you count the money before you turn over the cargo. Understand?"

"I understand." But how could she be worried about money at a time like this?

"How was the delivery?"

"Fine, except for a rough landing and having to tinker with the engine."

"The client—was he all right with you?"

An image flashed in Ruby's mind. Those stunning green eyes meeting hers. "He was fine," she lied. "I didn't ask his name."

"His name's Mason Dollarhide. He's new, which always makes me wary, but an important man recommended him. Evidently they were friends in prison."

This information was new. "Dollarhide was in prison?" she asked.

"He served five years for bootlegging out of his barn and hiring locals to help. One of them turned him in for the reward. Let's hope he's learned his lesson."

"Yes, let's hope." Ruby's eyes were fixed beyond the runway, where she hoped to see her father's plane appear in the blue, coming in for a landing. *Please . . .* she prayed silently. *Let him be safe.*

But the empty sky only mocked her prayer. As she felt the weight of Colucci's hands on her shoulders, her instincts whispered that it was too late to hope. Her life would never be the same again.

CHAPTER SEVEN

*R*UBY WAITED AT THE AIRSTRIP UNTIL MIDDAY, ANXIETY POOLING cold in the hollows of her heart. With no sign of her father, she finally agreed to be driven back to the boardinghouse in Miles City.

"Get a good meal and some rest," Colucci said as he escorted her to the car and helped her into the back seat. "If your dad shows up, or if we learn anything, we'll call you."

He gave her shoulders a comforting squeeze—something he would never have done if her father were there. Ruby suppressed a shudder as he released her.

"Please let me take a plane and look for him," she pleaded, not for the first time. "He could be hurt or stranded somewhere."

Colucci shook his head. "I've already told you no. With one pilot missing, we can't risk you, too. All we can do is wait."

"And if the worst has happened—if he doesn't come back?"

"Then you'll be more important to us than ever. We'll need you. Don't even think about quitting." He closed the door and signaled the driver to leave.

Ruby sank back into the seat, closed her eyes, and tried to focus her thoughts. Art was a skilled pilot. But flying a strange route in the early dawn hours, with an illegal cargo for an unknown client, was full of risk.

Tragedies happened. She'd learned to accept that when her husband came home from the war. Losing her father would be unthinkable. But that didn't mean it couldn't happen—and whether it happened or not, Colucci had made it clear that she wouldn't be allowed to leave.

The boardinghouse had no lunch service, but the kitchen was open. Ruby considered making herself a cheese sandwich but realized that she was too anxious to eat. There was only one telephone. A candlestick style with the receiver cord mounted on the top, it stood on a low table at the foot of the stairs. Her father had the number. So did Colucci. When the house was quiet, as it was now with most of the tenants at work, she should be able to hear the phone ring from anywhere.

Her small room was at the top of the stairs, with her father's room next door. She pressed her ear to the wall, tapping on the plaster and listening for a response, as if by some miracle he might have made it back to town. But that was only wishful thinking. No one was there.

She was exhausted, but to lie down on the bed would be to risk falling asleep and missing a phone call. Stripping off her flight clothes, she splashed herself clean in the basin, brushed out her hair, and dressed in a simple white sailor blouse and gray twill skirt. She'd taken off her boots and was putting on her sturdy, high-topped shoes when, from downstairs, came the sound of the ringing telephone.

Stumbling over her untied shoelaces, Ruby dashed down the stairs and seized the earpiece from its cradle. Would it be good news or heartbreak? Either way, she had to know.

"Hello?" Struggling to catch her breath, she spoke into the mouthpiece.

"Miss Weaver?" She didn't recognize the man's voice.

"It's *Mrs.* Weaver." Her heart was pounding.

"Mrs. Weaver, this is Agent Hoover with the Bureau of Investigation. We have your father, Arthur Murchison, in custody."

"My father?" Her pulse slammed. "Is he . . . all right?"

"He's not injured, if that's what you're asking. But he's being detained for a violation of the Volstead Act. When a U.S. Marshal arrives, he'll be formally arrested."

Ruby's throat tightened, leaving her speechless for the moment. Her father was alive—blessed news. But he was in serious trouble. The Volstead Act, passed by Congress in 1919, lent teeth to the Eighteenth Amendment, which had put Prohibition in place. Barring some miracle, Art could be going to prison for several years. By the time his sentence was served, he would be an old man.

"Mrs. Weaver, are you there? Talk to me." The agent's voice was sharp, his speech rapid, firing words like bullets from a machine gun. His manner grated on Ruby's raw nerves. For all she knew, he was about to have her arrested, too. She might be wise to catch the next train out of town. But she couldn't desert her father when he needed her.

"I'm here," she said. "I want to see my father."

"That can be arranged. But only if you cooperate. You and I need to talk."

"Talk where?" Was this some kind of trap? "How do I know I can trust you?" Ruby asked.

"You don't have a choice. Go out the back door of the boardinghouse. There'll be an automobile waiting for you. Do you understand?"

"As you say, what choice do I have?" She was liking the agent less and less. "It may take me a few minutes, but I'll be there."

He ended the call with a click. Back in her room, Ruby tied her shoes, pinned up her hair, and collected her cash and other small belongings in her handbag. Head high, she left the room, marched downstairs and through the kitchen to the back door.

The black car, a newer model with an enclosed cab, waited in the shadows next to the trash bins. The driver flashed an official-looking ID and opened the door without a word. His young face was expressionless, his manner almost military, except for the spotless gray suit he wore. Ruby sat erect on the edge of the back seat, her hands clasping her purse. Her father was alive—that was what mattered most. But what else was going to happen? They could both end up in prison, even dead.

The rear windows of the vehicle were covered; but the ride

wasn't a long one. The feel of the road and the faint sounds from outside told Ruby they were still in town.

The auto made a right-hand turn into a dark space and stopped. Ruby heard the rumble of a heavy overhead door sliding into place. Seconds later, the driver came around the car to open her door.

She stepped out into what appeared to be a garage or a small warehouse. Peering into the near darkness, she saw several vehicles as well as piled wooden crates—some of them bearing the maple leaf symbol of Canada. Were they seized contraband? Ruby was given no chance to ask.

The only light came from a dim bulb hanging above a closed door. The driver beckoned Ruby toward the door and opened it for her to pass into the kitchen beyond.

The room was simply furnished and spotlessly clean, with a new electric refrigerator—a motor mounted atop an icebox—standing against one wall. Three men in suits sat drinking coffee at a table covered with a red-checked oilcloth.

Young and clean-cut, the three remained seated as Ruby entered. Her eyes were drawn to the man at the head of the table. He was slight of build, with a head of dark, wiry hair and riveting eyes. As soon as he spoke, Ruby recognized the voice of Agent Hoover, the man who'd telephoned her.

"Thank you for joining us, Mrs. Weaver. Take that empty chair. We have some questions to ask you."

"I'll stand," Ruby said. "And there's no need to thank me. I'm only here because you said you have my father. Let me see him. If he's all right, I'll tell you anything you want to know. If you've lied to me, or if he's been harmed—"

"Watch your tongue, Mrs. Weaver." Another man at the table interrupted her. "You obviously don't know who you're talking to. Agent Hoover here has just been appointed director of the Bureau of Investigation. He's a very important man, and I can assure you he doesn't lie."

"Thank you, Agent Hargrave," Hoover said. "Now please stop wasting my time and sit down, Mrs. Weaver."

"Not until you tell me where my father is."

Hoover's annoyance showed in his scowl. "Your father is in our custody. He is safe and well. But if you don't cooperate, I can promise you'll never see him again."

"Then tell me what you want from me."

"Sit down and listen." He indicated the empty chair at the foot of the table. One of the men stood and pulled it out for her. Knees quivering, Ruby allowed herself to be seated.

"I'm a busy man." Hoover machine-gunned his words. "But I've taken the time for a visit because Montana has become a hotbed of the smuggling trade, and it's my job to stop it. It's come to my attention that airplanes are being used here and elsewhere to transport and deliver illegal alcohol. Your father was arrested while making such a delivery. The maximum prison sentence for such an offense is ten years at hard labor."

"Please—" Ruby broke, all defiance gone. "My father is a good man. And he's no longer young. Ten years would kill him."

"Just listen, Mrs. Weaver. Your father is willing to cooperate and tell us what he knows, which may get his sentence reduced. But his usefulness to us is limited because he can't go back to flying for the mob. If we were to release him, the thugs he was working for would suspect him of colluding with us. Even if they let him live, they would never trust him again. And we wouldn't be able to trust him either. That's where you come in."

Hoover took a cigarette out of a silver case, lit it with an engraved lighter, and exhaled a spiraling column of smoke. "You strike me as fairly intelligent for a woman, Mrs. Weaver. Have you guessed where this discussion is going?"

Ruby took a chance. "You're looking for an informant."

"That's right. Your father can give us names, but that's not enough. We can't arrest people without evidence. And even then, that wouldn't stop the smuggling. What we need is to know when a shipment comes in and also when and where deliveries are to be made. If we can stop enough transactions ahead of time and catch people in the act—not only the smugglers but their buyers—we can cut off profits and shut down the whole network."

"And how do I fit into this? My employers don't tell me anything I don't need to know."

"You keep your eyes and ears open. Make friends with people who can tell you what's coming. Flirt if you have to—I imagine you know how. We'll arrange a way for you to pass us your information."

"And now for the big question," Ruby said. "If I do my job, what happens to my father?"

Hoover took a long drag on his cigarette and tapped the ash into a porcelain teacup. "You tell her, Hargrave. I've said enough."

"You understand, we can't just turn him loose," the agent said. "We'll arrange to fake his death—probably burn his plane with an unclaimed body from the police morgue. Then we'll keep him in custody until your work is finished."

"Exactly what do you mean by custody?" Ruby asked.

"Minimum security in the state prison at Deer Lodge. His own room. Decent food. Access to books and writing materials."

"And no hard labor—absolutely."

"Absolutely."

"And if I keep my end of the bargain, all charges against him will be dropped and you'll send us somewhere safe. Can you guarantee that with a contract, in writing?"

Hargrave glanced at his boss.

"All right," Hoover said. "But we'll have to define the conditions—for example, what would constitute default on your part. And if we give you a document, you'll have to keep it somewhere safe. You can't risk having it found. If you back out of the agreement, Mr. Murchison will be formally charged, go to trial, and serve his sentence. Agreed?"

Ruby sighed, knowing she'd crossed a line, and there could be no going back. "Agreed—but only after I've seen my father and made sure he's all right."

"Fine. He's in the back room. I'll have Agent Jensen bring him out." Hoover nodded to the blond man, who rose and vanished down the hallway.

"How did my father get caught?" she asked as they waited.

"His client was turned in by a neighbor," Hargrave said. "The client gave us the pilot and the delivery window. We had agents waiting when the plane landed."

And of course my father gave you my name. The words remained unspoken.

Now she could hear muffled footsteps coming back down the hall. Ruby had hoped to see her father alone, but she knew better than to ask. She'd be lucky to exchange a few words with him.

A moment later, he was ushered into the room, looking like a child who'd misbehaved and been punished at school. His hair and clothes were rumpled, his cheek bruised. His wrists were secured in front by steel handcuffs.

Poor, proud, naive man. All he'd wanted was a chance to make a better life for the two of them. He should have weighed the risks. He should have known something like this would happen. But it was her fault, too. She should have held firm against this adventure. Now it was too late. They were both trapped.

His gaze met hers. The look of desperation in his eyes broke her heart.

"I'm sorry, Ruby," he said. "You know I meant for this to turn out well."

Leaving her seat, she pushed past the agent to embrace him. He felt frail in her arms, older somehow. "I know you did," she said. "I'll be here for you. You can count on that."

He shook his head. "Don't waste your life being here for me. Find a good man to take care of you. Have a family while you can. Live the life I want for you."

Tears sprang to Ruby's eyes. She choked on her reply as the agent pulled her father away from her and marched him back down the hall.

She turned toward the table where Hoover sat watching her. "Satisfied?" he asked.

Gulping back the emotion she knew that she mustn't show, Ruby nodded. "Tell me what to do," she said.

A week later

Mason had sold his first shipment of Canadian whiskey. Follow-ing phoned directions from Colucci, he had met his buyer on a back road after midnight, transferred the crates from Mason's horse trailer to the hollowed-out interior of the man's 1921 Dodge Roadster, and pocketed the cash payment. As a precaution, both men had been wearing hats and been masked with bandannas over the lower parts of their faces. All Mason had seen of his cus-tomer was his pale blue eyes and a heavy gold ring in the shape of an eagle.

Hopefully, the sale would be repeated soon, as well as others; but he'd been told that next time the meeting arrangements would be different. That was Colucci's formula for not getting caught—don't follow a predictable pattern.

Mason had already ordered his next shipment and put aside most of his profits to pay for it. At this rate, getting rich would take time, and Mason wasn't a patient man. He wanted bigger shipments and more customers. Colucci, who kept a tight rein on distribution and sales, was starting him out small. Maybe if he called the prison and asked, Julius Taviani would steer more busi-ness his way.

Meanwhile, he owed himself a small celebration.

Blue Moon's only restaurant, known as Jake's, was not what you'd call high-class. But Jake was a first-rate cook. The food was as good as any you could get in Miles City for double the price. There was also a back room for pool and card games; and the "nieces" Jake employed as waitresses were known to entertain pay-ing guests in their rooms upstairs.

Mason had been so busy improving the cave and airstrip and managing the ranch that he hadn't spent much time in town. His mother, who almost never left the house, had her groceries deliv-ered, so there wasn't much excuse for errand running. What he'd needed in the way of tools, hardware, and other supplies, he'd bought in Miles City to avoid suspicion from the locals.

But forget all that. Tonight he was driving into Blue Moon for a steak dinner. Maybe he'd get into a poker game if there was one going on or shoot a few rounds of pool. As for Jake's girls—he would pass for now. He'd slaked his lust on his last visit to Miles City. The lady had been accomplished, and the encounter had gone all right, but it had been purely physical, leaving him vaguely dissatisfied. Whatever was missing, he wasn't going to find it upstairs at Jake's—not even if he tried to picture the haunting face of that beautiful pilot.

As he left the house, he said a dutiful good night to his mother. Amelia seemed indifferent to his comings and goings. Most nights, toward her early bedtime, Sidney would bring her a cup of tea. She would drink it, totter off to bed, and sleep deeply, with her dog lying next to her on the rug, until well after sunup. Mason could guess what might be in the tea, but he didn't really want to know.

It was in his best interest to keep his mother calm and contented. Now that he'd streamlined the ranch management, keeping stock numbers down and leaving the physical work to two longtime hired cowboys, that was easy enough. As for the money he'd found and replaced in the bank, Amelia had never appeared to notice it was gone. The two of them had settled into a truce of sorts. For now, at least, it didn't make sense to upset the apple cart.

As he drove into town, he looked forward to putting his cares behind him, enjoying a hearty meal, and maybe a relaxing game of cards. On a Saturday night like this one, Jake's became the social hub of Blue Moon. Maybe he would run into old friends, or even meet an attractive woman who knew the score.

Jake's was bustling tonight. Autos, buggies, and even a few saddled horses waited outside the roadhouse, the line extending down the street for nearly a block. Mason saw a battered Model T pull out of a parking spot. He gave the driver room to get clear, then swung into the place next to a classy-looking Dodge Touring Car. Good timing.

He was hoping that his luck would hold, but when he stepped through the door of the restaurant, he saw that all the tables were full. But someone was bound to leave soon. He shouldn't have long to wait.

He gave his name to the tired-looking waitress, then found a quiet corner to wait. From where he stood, he could see the entire dining room, which had booths around the outside and movable tables in the center. Servers were bustling back and forth between the customers and the kitchen.

Webb Calder sat at a corner booth with two men. One was Webb's longtime foreman, Nate Moore. The other man, a blonde who sat with his back toward Mason, was unfamiliar.

Webb had a son slightly older than Joseph. Chase—that was his name. The lad hadn't come to dinner with his father. Maybe he had a girl somewhere. He was old enough to be sowing some wild oats. So was Joseph—and even as Mason thought about his son, he spotted the boy, sitting with his parents at a table across the room.

Over the years, he'd caught occasional glimpses of Hannah—enough to make him aware that she'd matured into a ripe, golden-haired beauty. But he hadn't spoken to her since the moonlight rendezvous twenty years ago when he'd taken her innocence and left her with his child. He knew better than to speak with her now.

Blake, Mason's half-brother and childhood playmate, was close to a decade older than his wife. His age showed in the gray at his temples and the weathered creases that framed his eyes. A rugged man—a good man who'd lived a life of hard work and family responsibility. That was more than Mason could say for himself.

Mason stood in plain view of their table, but the three were paying no attention to him. They appeared to be arguing. Their words were lost in the babble of conversation that filled the room. But even from a distance, Mason could sense the tension between them. He knew one possible cause for it—Joseph's hope for a different future than the one his parents had planned for him. Britta had told him how much the boy wanted to fly—and Mason had witnessed that burning desire for himself. But what about duty to family? What about safety and security? One small mistake, and Joseph could end his promising young life in a plane crash.

Mason's musings, and the discussion at the Dollarhide table, were both interrupted when Webb Calder and his two companions stood and pushed in their chairs. Webb paused to lay several bills on the table. Then, with the two men following, he led the way out of the dining room.

They didn't appear to notice Mason, although they passed near to him on their way out. Mason couldn't help noticing how they walked—like lords, confident of their power and their places at the top of the social order. Webb led the way, head high, people moving out of his way. Nate Moore followed his lifelong boss. Mason caught a clear view of the third man—a stranger with a well-groomed moustache and striking, pale eyes.

When the man reached up to brush a fly from his ear, Mason noticed the heavy gold ring on his right-hand middle finger—a ring in the shape of an eagle with outspread wings.

Mason's reflexes went cold as he remembered the Dodge Touring Car next to where he'd parked outside. There could be no mistake—this was the man who'd bought his first shipment of Canadian whiskey. And he appeared to be working with Webb Calder.

Blake had turned in his chair and was glaring, not at the Calder party but at his brother. As Mason stood his ground, Blake rose and wove his way through the crowded tables. Reaching Mason, he muttered one word.

"Outside."

Mason followed him out through the door, onto the boardwalk. He'd known that a confrontation between the two brothers was bound to happen. This wasn't the time or place he'd have chosen, but it was what it was—and he had as much right to be here as Blake did.

As they stepped into the shadows, Blake turned on him. "I was hoping you wouldn't have the nerve to come back here."

"This is my home, Blake. My ranch is here. My mother is here. And I've paid my debt to society. This is where I belong. So you might as well get used to the idea."

"I figured you'd say something like that. So there's just one thing I've got to tell you. Leave my family alone—especially my son, and don't think for a minute that he'll ever be yours. Five years ago, you almost got him arrested, or worse. You were making him into a criminal—and you didn't even care."

"Would you believe me if I said I was sorry? Of all the things I did, and paid for, exposing those boys to danger is the one I regret most."

"Regret wouldn't matter if you'd gotten them killed." His eyes burned into Mason's. "I'm only going to say this once. If you try to speak with my son or put any of your wild ideas into his head, so help me, I'll have you tarred and feathered. And the whole town, even the Calders, will help me run you out on a rail. Do you understand?"

The anger that surged in Mason was the kind that would have sent his fists slamming into his opponent if he'd been in prison. But this was his brother, and his family was nearby. Mason held himself in check—for Joseph and Hannah, if for no other reason.

"I'm not a fool, Blake," he said. "I don't want trouble. I only came into town to get dinner. But thanks to you, I've lost my appetite. So go back in and join your family. I'll treat myself when I can enjoy my meal in peace."

With that, he turned away and walked out to his car. The Dodge Touring Car was gone. Mason had glimpsed it driving off, following Webb's Packard out of town on the road to the Triple C. Questions sprang to mind. Was Mason's customer using the Calder ranch as a secret base for distributing bootleg whiskey—or was Webb himself involved? Maybe Webb's own supply was dwindling; or maybe the Triple C was running low on cash.

Dismissing the questions, he started the car, swung it around in the dusty street, and headed back to the ranch. As long as his customers kept buying and paying, what happened to the liquor after it left his hands was none of his business, Mason reminded himself.

Neither was the means by which it was delivered to him—although his wish to see Ruby again had deepened into a craving. There were plenty of beautiful women in the world. She was one of them. But the skill in her calloused hands and the sorrow in the depths of those dark eyes had stirred him in an unexpected way. As for the courage required to take her life in her hands, piloting a craft of wood, wire, cloth, and glue, propelled by a temperamental engine, into the far reaches of the sky, that simply astounded him. He knew almost nothing about her except that she was widowed, brave, and subtly sensual. He burned to know more.

Even if it meant finding out that she was Colucci's woman.

With the trail lit by a midnight moon, Joseph rode his horse down the side of the bluff. He'd discovered the shortcut a few weeks ago. The way was narrow, steep in spots, but shorter than the main switchback road and less visible from the house. For a young man sneaking out to see a girl, that was important.

His parents didn't know he had a girl. But then, there were a lot of things they didn't know, especially about this girl.

Annabeth Coleman's family lived on a small farm beyond the border of the Dollarhide property. Her father raised a few scrawny cows and sold the milk for enough to feed and shelter his five ragged children. Her mother's reputation was the subject of whispers in town, but that wasn't Annabeth's fault. She couldn't help having been born into a poor family—any more than she could help her stunning blue eyes, her mane of honey gold hair, or her voluptuous sixteen-year-old figure.

She was waiting by the pasture gate when Joseph rode up, her thin nightgown blowing around her bare legs. Joseph's pulse skipped at the sight of her. As she ran to him, he bent down to catch her hand and pull her up behind him on the horse's bare back. She sprang into place, her arms gripping his waist, her knees spooning against his thighs.

"Let's go before we get caught," she said.

He nudged the gelding to a lope. Her clasp tightened around him as they flew across the fields. Joseph could feel her breasts against his back. The awareness that she was naked under her nightgown triggered a familiar tightness beneath his trousers.

Earlier that summer, he'd come across her bathing at a wide

place in the creek, her clothes laid out on the bank. He'd spent guilt-ridden minutes watching her from behind the screen of willows, transfixed by the beauty of her ivory breasts, the nipples shrunk to beads by the cold water. As his body sprang to readiness, she'd looked directly at him and laughed. It appeared she'd been aware of him all along.

That first encounter had been little more than a tease, with her ordering him to turn his back while she dressed. But from there, things had progressed according to Mother Nature's plan. Now, all he could think of was having her again.

After reining to a stop on Dollarhide land, he lowered Annabeth to the ground. Dismounting, he ground-staked the horse and followed her through a thicket of willows toward the sound of a gurgling spring. She was barefoot, her steps heedless of rocks and brambles. Summers without shoes had left her feet as tough as leather. As she slipped through the willows, he lost sight of her for a moment. When he emerged into the clearing, she was lying on the grass in a pool of moonlight, her wispy nightgown barely covering her body.

Laughing, she held out her arms to him. "Come here, Joseph," she said.

He fumbled with his belt and trousers, letting them fall over his boots. She opened her legs to welcome him in. Wild with teenage lust, they bucked and thrust in the moonlit grass, breathing in ecstatic gasps.

But Joseph was no fool. As he felt his climax surging, he prepared to do what he'd always done before—stop moving and pull out. This time she prevented him. Her legs locked around his hips, holding him inside her. "No!" she moaned.

Too late, he lost control.

Muttering, he rolled off onto his back. "Blast it, Annabeth, what did you go and do that for? We're not ready to deal with having a baby."

She snuggled against his side. "I'd be all right with it. We could get married and live on your ranch. Think of the great life we could have there. We could help out around the place and raise our family. Then, when your folks passed on, you'd be in charge of it all—the ranch and the mill."

He sighed. "What if I don't want to be in charge? What if I want a different life?"

"Like what?" She sat up and pulled down her nightgown.

"I want to be a pilot. I want to fly airplanes."

She snorted. "That's the dumbest idea I've ever heard! Where would we get money? And what would I do if you crashed? I'd have to go back to my family."

Joseph groped for a reply that would satisfy her. He'd fancied himself in love with Annabeth. But he'd never thought of her in terms of marriage. They were too young for that kind of responsibility—especially if a baby was involved.

Joseph's own father had run out on a girl he'd gotten pregnant. Blake had stepped in, married Hannah, claimed her son, and saved them from a future of poverty and shame. But a happy ending like theirs wasn't going to happen a second time. If Annabeth was pregnant, Joseph knew he would have no choice except to take responsibility—even if it meant the end of his dream.

For now, there was nothing to do but wait.

Standing, he pulled up his trousers, fastened his belt, and reached down to give Annabeth a hand up. "Come on," he said. "It's time to get you home."

CHAPTER EIGHT

Ten days later

RUBY FINISHED HER SECOND DELIVERY OF THE NIGHT, LEFT HER plane with the ground crew, and settled on the front porch step to wait for her ride back to town. By now the sun was rising. Meadowlarks were calling from the weedy, abandoned fields that surrounded the old house. A pair of ravens rose from a dead tree in the front yard and flapped into the sky.

She was getting better at her job, the landings and takeoffs smoother, the business concluded and the cargo unloaded with cool efficiency. She had cultivated an impersonal manner with her clients, avoiding questions and eye contact. Since she could be sending them to prison, familiarity would only make things more painful.

She had passed on any and all information she picked up to Agent Hargrave, her contact in the Bureau of Investigation. What they did with that information was beyond her control. But if they'd taken anyone into custody, she hadn't heard. Maybe they were waiting for her to earn more trust from her employers, or hoping for a bigger cache than what a small plane could carry.

She had yet to make a second delivery to Mason Dollarhide's ranch. But she'd noticed that the place was on the docket for the next shipment. She would have to report it, of course. If it got him caught, it would serve him right. One would think that a man who'd served five years for bootlegging would have learned his lesson.

But she couldn't help remembering her body's response to their contact as he helped her check the stalled engine, and how his piercing green-eyed gaze had stirred a sensual heat in her—a heat she hadn't felt since her husband left for the war.

What did it mean? Only that she would need to be on her guard with him. Her future and her father's life hung on her ability to freeze her emotions.

"How about some coffee?" The young man handed her a steaming cup and sat down beside her. Mack, whose last name she'd chosen not to learn, was the new pilot. Younger than Ruby, he'd barely gotten into the war before it ended. His flying skills were above par, but he had a lot to learn about the business. He was just beginning to make deliveries.

"Thanks." Ruby sipped the strong, black coffee while Mack lit a cigarette. He had sandy hair and a good-natured, freckled face. She knew that he wanted to be friends, but how could she warm to him when, at any time, she might have to betray him to the law?

"The cook told me what happened to your father," he said. "I'm sorry."

"Thanks. I'm sorry, too." Art's plane had been found wrecked and burned, the incinerated body in the pilot's seat presumed to be his. Ruby had put up a convincing show of grief and moved on.

"It could happen to any of us," she said. "Tomorrow it might be me, or it might be you. This is a dangerous business, Mack. You're young and smart. You didn't ask for my advice, but I'll offer it anyway. Get out now, while you can—leave town if you have to—before you're arrested or killed."

He blew a smoke ring and watched it drift upward. "I don't plan to do this forever. As soon as I have enough money to buy some land with a house, I'll be done here. There's a girl I want to marry as soon as I have something to offer her."

Should she tell him the truth—that if he stayed, even if he wasn't killed in a crash, Colucci and his cohorts would never let him walk away? Would he listen?

"I have a question," he said. "If it's as dangerous as you say, why are you still here?"

"That's easy," Ruby replied with a half-truth. "I'm here because I have nothing to lose."

Later that morning, Ruby was driven back to Miles City to rest and wait for the next big shipment. Mack had stayed behind to help the ground crew overhaul the planes, including the Jenny they'd bought to replace the one that Art had flown.

Colucci had insisted that she move from the boardinghouse to a room on the third floor of the Olive Hotel. The food was better, and the private bath was heaven, but the change made it harder to stay in contact with Hargrave and his fellow agents. Outgoing calls from her room phone could be monitored—the operators could easily be paid off. She'd taken to calling from a pay phone in the lobby or slipping into vacant rooms to use the phones there. The agents rarely called her. Most of the incoming calls were from Colucci or others at the farm.

The driver let her off at the hotel's front entrance on Main Street. Tired and dressed in her rumpled flight clothes, she headed straight upstairs to her room. She would bathe and get a few hours of sleep, then maybe order a sandwich from room service before she checked in with Agent Hargrave.

The key was pinned inside her pocket. She fished it out, used it to open the door, and walked into the room. There she stopped cold.

On the bed lay a large, rectangular box from an exclusive women's wear shop here in Miles City. The first possibility that sprang to mind was that it had been delivered by mistake. The second possibility was one she didn't even want to think about. But as she raised the lid on the box and saw the card with her name on the envelope, Ruby had no more questions. Heart sinking, she put the card aside and lifted away the tissue paper that covered the box's contents.

The fragrance that rose to mingle with the stale air in the room was subtle and sophisticated, whispering of money and the elegance it could buy. One by one, Ruby lifted up the layers in the box. On top was a dress of beaded beige silk, cut in the latest knee-length fashion with a flirty row of fringe along the hem. Under it was a matching silk slip, and tucked beneath were underthings so fine and sheer that they seemed to float—lace-trimmed drawers and silk stockings with satin garters. Tucked into the corners of the box were high-heeled satin slippers in her size and a beaded headband to match the dress.

The card lay on the bed. Feeling vaguely ill, she forced herself to pick it up, open the envelope, and read the message inside.

> *Dinner tonight at 7:30. Command performance with a special guest. I will call for you. Can't wait to see you looking the way you were meant to look.*
> *Leo*

Ruby couldn't recall having called Leo Colucci by his first name, and she wasn't inclined to start. What she wanted to do was throw the box and its contents out into the alley below, then catch the next train out of town.

But she couldn't do that. Not while her father was a prisoner and his welfare depended on her. And not when she had a chance to pick up some vital intelligence. She would do her job— wear the clothes, go to dinner, and take mental notes on everything she saw and heard.

She could only hope that Colucci—and his guest—expected nothing more than a dinner companion.

The woman in the full-length mirror was a stranger in a glittering wisp of a dress that skimmed her body and showed off her silk-clad legs. She'd twisted up her hair, secured it with the headband, and added the dangling earrings she'd found in the bottom of the box. They were cheap rhinestone imitations, thank goodness. She could wear them with a clear conscience.

Only her work-worn hands and bitten, grease-stained nails betrayed the person she really was—but also her eyes, perhaps, their depths reflecting the trepidation that made her stomach clench at the knock on the door.

Colucci stood framed in the doorway. Dressed in his usual three-piece suit and tie, he loomed above her, his size making her feel overpowered, like a gazelle face-to-face with a lion. His handsome, fleshy face wore a confident smirk.

"My, don't you look stunning," he said. "I hope you're enjoying my gift."

Ruby bit back a too-clever retort. "It's nice," she said. "Hardly what I'm used to—a bit like playing dress-up."

"A woman as beautiful as you deserves more playtime." Colucci placed a possessive hand at the small of her back and guided her out into the hallway. "I'm going to see that you get it, starting tonight."

The implication of his words sent a shudder all the way to Ruby's knees. How far was she prepared to go in her role as an undercover informant? Not that far, she was certain.

He offered his arm as they descended the carpeted stairs. Wobbling a little on her high heels, Ruby took it. Together, they went down to the lobby and crossed it to enter the dining room.

The man at the corner table who rose at their approach was no stranger. As before, Capone took Ruby's hand and brushed a courtly kiss across her knuckles. "How lovely you look, Mrs. Weaver. Please sit down. I hope you won't mind—I took the liberty of ordering the leg of lamb for all of us."

"That's fine. It's good to see you again." Ruby took the chair that Colucci held for her.

Capone's sharp eyes studied them as Colucci took his seat. What was the man thinking? He was almost certainly evil, but he hadn't gained the power he enjoyed by being stupid. And he could be charming. For all his reptilian heart, Ruby found herself liking him more than she liked Agents Hoover and Hargrave.

"I heard about your father, Mrs. Weaver," Capone said. "Such a loss. I'm so sorry. A great pilot and a fine man."

"Yes, he was," Ruby said. "I miss him every day. And how is your family, Mr. Capone?"

"In good health, by the grace of God. And what about you, Leo?" Capone fixed Colucci with a penetrating look. "I understand your wife is about to deliver number four. Maybe you'll be lucky enough to get a boy this time."

"God willing." Color flooded Colucci's face. Clearly he hadn't expected his boss's revelation. Capone's meaningful glance toward Ruby told her he'd spoken deliberately to give her a warning. Whatever her relationship with Colucci, if it was to be more than business, she needed to know that she was dealing with a married man. Beyond that, the choice was hers. But Capone had respected her enough to do her a favor, and she was grateful.

She returned his look with the slightest nod as the waiter arrived at the table with their meals. The roasted lamb, served with baby potatoes, asparagus tips, and a minty sauce, was hot and well prepared. The dark liquid in Ruby's glass, which she assumed to be fruit juice, turned out, at the first sip, to be wine. Capone chuckled at her startled expression.

Ruby's gaze scanned the dining room, which was crowded at this hour. At each of the three entrances stood a thuggish-looking man with a telltale bulge under his suit jacket. Capone, it appeared, had brought along his bodyguards, something he hadn't done the last time he'd come here. Evidently, he was moving up in the organization, high enough to have acquired some enemies.

"To what do we owe this visit, Mr. Capone?" she asked, remembering her mission. "Is there something special going on?"

"Actually, I'm passing through on my way to Seattle." Capone speared a small potato with his fork. "I thought I'd take a break from the train, stop off here, and see how your air-delivery operation is going."

"You've seen the numbers," Colucci said. "Aside from the crash that killed Ruby's father and cost us a plane, it's going well. All we need to ramp up the business is a couple of bigger, newer, and safer airplanes—like those De Havillands the post office has bought to carry the mail."

"You've got the pilots you need?"

"You're looking at the best one. And the new guy, Mack, is

going to be a cracker once he learns the ropes. Besides, we can always hire more if we need them. There are plenty of barnstormers who'd be interested in the money."

"If you can trust them."

"I'll make sure of that," Colucci said.

"Well, if it turns out you can't, you know what to do." Capone sipped his wine. A chill passed down Ruby's back.

"We were talking about planes," Colucci said.

"Yes, the planes." Capone sliced his meat into bite-sized pieces. "Go ahead and do some shopping. If you find something that will work, send me the specs and prices, and we'll take it from there. How does that sit with you, Mrs. Weaver? Would you like a new plane?"

"Of course. But I'll need some training to pilot it."

"That can be arranged. Meanwhile, keep those Jennies flying. We're counting on you."

The talk drifted to plans for new markets and more product, as they called it. Ruby pretended to focus on her meal, but her ears were alert to every spoken word. She would have plenty of new intelligence to pass on to Hargrave—maybe enough for the feds to make some arrests.

Could she trust them to free her father when she'd done what was asked of her—or would the agents walk away and leave her to deal with the situation? Even the signed release document from Agent Hoover might not be honored. She could no more count on him than she could on the likes of Capone and Colucci.

After dessert, Capone excused himself and went out to his private railroad car, flanked by his bodyguards. Ruby allowed Colucci to escort her back upstairs to her room. Braced for a confrontation, she faced him at the door.

"Thank you for a lovely evening and for your generous gift," she said. "Keep me posted about the new planes. I'll see you when the next shipment comes in."

She took the key out of her bag and slipped it into the lock. Colucci leaned into the door frame.

"You can thank me by inviting me in, Ruby," he said.

This was the moment for strength. "I know what you're expecting, Mr. Colucci," she said. "And I realize you're my boss. But you have a wife who's expecting a baby. And I have a firm rule against crossing the line with a married man."

Colucci didn't move. "That's not how it works. Men like me and Al Capone, we have our wives and families. They're like, sacred, untouchable, apart from the lives we lead. And then we have our girls—girls we pet and pamper and play with. They're treated like queens. I could give you everything a woman might want, Ruby—clothes, jewelry, an apartment, a nice car . . ."

"So you're asking me to be your mistress—is that it?"

"There are worse things to be. Look at you—you've got nothing. I could give you a world you've only dreamed of."

"It's a world I don't want," Ruby said. "Find yourself another woman. I'm your pilot, not your girl."

He leaned closer, trapping her between the locked door and the frame. His breath was hot and damp against her face, his voice a throaty growl. "I'm not a man to take no for an answer," he said. "You'll change your mind. When you do, let me know. Just don't make me wait too long."

She braced herself to fight off his kiss, but he turned away with a rough laugh. "Sleep tight, Ruby. I'll see you in your dreams."

As he walked away, Ruby unlocked the door, slipped into the room, and secured the lock behind her. Knees shaking, she leaned against the door. In the silence, she could hear heavy footfalls going back down the hall toward the stairwell.

At least he'd walked away like a gentleman, she told herself. But no sooner had the thought crossed her mind than she heard the crash of a giant fist slamming into the wall, followed by a splintering sound.

The urge to open the door and look out swiftly fled. There could be just one explanation for what she'd heard. Leo Colucci had expected a different outcome to the evening. He was giving vent to his frustration.

Once the noise had faded, she moved away from the door and

began pulling the dress over her head, fighting the temptation to rip it off. She never wanted to wear it again. One by one, she laid the gauzy garments in the fragrant, tissue-lined box and placed it on the dresser bench. Maybe, with luck, one of the maids would steal it.

Colucci had just shown her who he was—a dangerous, mercurial man who could become violent if he didn't get what he wanted. Not that she was surprised—she'd never felt at ease around him. Now that he'd made his intentions clear, the safest course would be for her to run—change her name, leave Montana for someplace where Colucci would never find her. But her situation gave her no choice except to stay. Until Colucci and his like were under arrest, and her father set free, she was trapped.

The worst of it was the guilt. As Colucci's mistress, she'd be privy to secrets that could bring down the whole Montana bootlegging operation and free her father. Was she being selfish, saying no to a man who made her skin crawl? Maybe Colucci was right. Maybe she would be forced to change her mind. But not yet. Please, God, not yet.

She would have a few days' rest until the next shipment came in—maybe time to make a furtive trip to Deer Lodge to check on her father. But what was she thinking? Art was supposed to be dead. If it became known that he was alive, she would be exposed and probably killed. So would her father.

For now, unless she chose to sleep with Colucci, there was little she could do except perform her job as expected, keep her eyes and ears open, and report on what she learned. But she was walking a tightrope—a rope that was getting more fragile with every step. Sooner or later it would break—and she would have no one she could depend on, no one to save her. Her life would count for nothing. She was alone.

After the loss of her sister and her parents, Britta Anderson had sold the family home in town. She had moved into the quarters that were built onto the old log schoolhouse as a residence for the teacher. The rooms were small, and there was no plumbed-in bathtub. But conditions were no worse than they'd been when she was growing up on the family farm.

Tonight, she sat on the back porch in the rocker she'd brought from her old home. Her father, a skilled carpenter, had made it for her mother when their first child, her late brother, Alvar, was born. There was no way Britta could have left it behind, even though it was unlikely she would ever rock a baby of her own.

When the weather changed, she would take the chair inside. But for now, it was a pleasure to sit in the peace of the late night, with the stars overhead and the town slumbering around her.

On the next street over, stood the sheriff's office and the city jail. Like the school, the facility had been built with attached living quarters. Sheriff Jake Calhoun lived upstairs from the jail with his little girl.

Tonight, with most of the block in darkness, she could see a distant light in the upstairs window. Did the handsome sheriff have company? she wondered idly. Could something be wrong, or was he just restless? Not that it was any of her business. She'd had a few dreams about the man, but she'd sworn off any interest in him when he'd married pretty Cora. Even with Cora gone, that hadn't changed. There were younger, more attractive women waiting for Jake to pick and choose. She had missed her chance, and she had too much pride to try again.

A coyote streaked across the schoolyard and vanished into the shadows. Britta rose and moved the chair back under the shelter of the porch roof. It was getting late. She would change into her nightgown and read in bed until she got sleepy. That was one of the luxuries of being single. She could do whatever she wished.

She'd gone inside, put on her nightgown, let down her braids, and was about to switch off the parlor light when she heard an urgent rapping on the door. A woman alone couldn't be too careful. Britta disliked guns, but she kept a baseball bat propped next to the door frame. Holding it ready, she called, "Who's there?"

"It's Jake. I need your help." The voice was familiar, but its worried tone was nothing like she'd heard before. Pulse racing, she opened the door.

He stood on the threshold, dark hair disheveled, clothes rumpled, as if hastily pulled on. His four-year-old daughter, Marissa, lay like a golden-haired doll against his chest. She was wrapped in a light cotton blanket, her breathing labored, her eyes closed. "She's burning up with fever," he said. "I can't reach the doctor, and I don't know what to do. You were the first person I thought of."

One look at the child and Britta forgot her awkward past relationship with Jake. She forgot that she was wearing nothing but her thin cotton nightgown. There was nothing on her mind but a sick little girl who needed help.

"Bring her in. Lay her on the bed. I'll have a look." Britta had no medical training except her own practical experience. But right now, there appeared to be no one else available.

Blue Moon's only doctor was Blake Dollarhide's sister, Kristin. She lived on a ranch with her family, nearly an hour's distance on a rough road. She came into town three days a week to see patients. But now she was out of reach, and this child needed help.

"I tried to telephone the doctor." Jake followed Britta into the bedroom. "There was no answer. Either she's away, or the phone line's down."

Britta turned down the coverlet on her narrow single bed, grateful that she'd changed the sheets that morning. Marissa's sky-blue eyes fluttered open, then closed again as her father laid her on the pillow. Britta filled a basin with cool water, unwrapped the cotton blanket, raised the child's nightgown, and began sponging her hot skin with a washcloth in an effort to make her more comfortable.

Resting her ear against the small, hot chest, Britta could hear the rasp of congested breathing. It could be bronchitis or even pneumonia. Whatever it was, it was serious and might be deadly.

Jake laid his hand on his daughter's forehead to check her fever. "There has to be something we can do."

Britta could understand the anguish in his voice. He'd lost his wife two years ago. This precious little girl was all he had left.

"I'm no doctor," she said. "But I was raised on a dirt farm by a mother who doctored us with whatever she had. Willow bark tea was the thing for fevers. I've got aspirin—it's the same thing, salicylic acid. But I don't know how much is all right to give her. We could start with a small dose. But maybe the tea would be safer. Our mother used to give us all we'd take, and it never harmed us. We'll need some fresh bark."

Jake smoothed his daughter's hair back from her face. She whimpered at his touch. "There are willows growing behind the jail. If you've got a knife, I'll cut some bark."

"There's a knife in the kitchen. I'll get some water boiling. Meanwhile, I'll break up an aspirin tablet and crush a piece with some sugar. Maybe she'll take that—and maybe we can steam her for the congestion."

Jake was already on his way out. Britta fired up the stove and put a pan of water on to heat. Then she tried getting Marissa to swallow a bit of the crushed aspirin and sugar mix. It was a struggle, with the little girl pushing away and trying to spit it out. Britta had no idea whether she'd swallowed enough to help. At least she was familiar with the tea and how her mother had used it. But would scant knowledge, based on childhood memories, be enough?

She was sponging the feverish little girl again when Jake reappeared with his hands full of bark strips. "I tried phoning the doctor again. No answer." He laid the bark and the knife on the kitchen counter.

"Here." She handed him the cool, damp washcloth. "You can do this while I brew the tea. Talk to her, or even sing to her. She'll be less frightened if she knows you're close by."

"You didn't have much cut wood. I brought some from my place. It's piled outside the back door in case you need it."

"Thank you." It would be like Jake to notice that something was needed.

On her way to the kitchen, Britta passed her flannel robe, which hung on its hook by the bathroom door. She slipped it on over her nightgown and tied it at the waist. At least now she'd be covered. Not that modesty mattered much at a time like this.

The water had begun to boil. Britta rinsed a handful of bark and dropped it into the pot, then added more. Would it be strong enough? She remembered the bitter taste of it. That would tell her she'd made it the way her mother used to. She raised a spoonful of the boiling liquid, gave it a moment to cool, and tasted it cautiously. Still too mild. She added more bark.

From the bedroom, she could hear Jake singing an old-time lullaby to his little girl. His muffled voice was gruff and slightly off-key. She still loved the sound of that voice. For a time, back when she'd hoped that he would wait, she'd imagined him tucking their children into bed and singing them to sleep.

But she was a fool to think of that now. Jake had been looking for a wife. Buried in grief for her family and the burden of responsibility, Britta had turned him away. So he'd wed pretty, loving, Cora, who had filled his heart and given him this beautiful child.

She dipped another spoonful of tea, blowing on the surface to cool it. This time the taste was as strong and bitter as she remembered. She might want to add some honey, something her mother wouldn't have done. Inga Anderson hadn't believed in making anything easier for her children. Life wasn't like that, she'd always said.

Inga had been right, especially about her own hard life. But this was different, Britta told herself as she poured some tea into a cup, stirred in a few drops of honey, and gave the mixture a moment to cool. She said a silent prayer before carrying it into the bedroom. If Marissa didn't take it willingly, she would have to be forced, and even then, the tea might not be enough to help her.

Jake sat on the edge of the bed, cradling his daughter in his arms. His worried expression tore at her heart—a painful reminder that she still had feelings for him. But that was water under the bridge, as her mother used to say. Nothing mattered now except saving this little girl.

"Hold her steady. Let's hope she'll take this." Britta waited until Jake had cupped his daughter's chin in his palm, his free arm cradling her body. The little girl's face was flushed, her skin dry and feverish. Her eyes opened wide as the spoonful of tea neared her mouth. She pressed her lips together and shook her head.

"This medicine is to make you better, Marissa," Jake said. "You need to swallow it."

She pulled a face. "No," she muttered. "Medicine is nasty."

"It's fine. Look, I'll show you." Glancing up at Britta, he nodded. Understanding, Britta spooned the tea into his mouth. He hid a grimace as he forced himself to swallow. "See, it's all right. And it will make you feel better. Now be a brave girl and drink it."

Her eyes closed, then opened again, their look drowsy and feverish. "Sing to me some more," she murmured.

"Will you drink the tea if I sing to you?"

She nodded.

"Promise?"

"Uh-huh." Her gaze shifted to Britta. "Her, too."

"You want me to sing with your father, Marissa?"

The girl nodded.

"All right, as long as you keep your promise."

Jake began to sing the lullaby again.

"Hush-a-bye, don't you cry. Go to sleep, my little baby."

Britta joined him in the old song. She didn't have a great voice, but she could carry a tune.

"When you wake, you shall have all the pretty little horses . . ."

As she sang, Britta gently spooned the warm tea into Marissa's reluctant mouth. The child resisted some at first, letting the tea dribble down her chin onto the clean towel that had been laid over her. But then she began taking each spoonful as it was given. Her small face wrinkled in distaste, but she did as promised and emptied the cup.

"Good girl." Her father gave her a gentle squeeze. She was still feverish; the home-brewed medicine would take time to work—if it worked at all. "Do you think she's had enough?" Jake asked Britta.

"For now. We can give her more later if we need to. If the fever breaks, she'll start sweating—that's a sure sign. But it might take time—it could be hours."

"I feel so damned helpless—she's never been this sick before. I always assumed I'd know what to do. Thank you, Britta. Maybe you can give me some of that tea in a jar. Then I'll take her home and watch her so you can rest."

"She'll be better off here, where we can both watch her. The doctor is scheduled to be in town tomorrow. You can take her in then. Meanwhile, we can at least try to keep her stable. There's a rocking chair on the back porch. I'll bring it in so you can sit with her."

"I'll get it." He laid his daughter back on the pillow, stepped outside, and was back in a moment with the chair, which he placed close to the bed. When he leaned over her, Marissa opened her eyes. Her arms reached up to him. He gathered her close and settled into the rocker with the little girl across his lap.

"You might as well lie down and get some sleep," he said to Britta. "I can wake you if anything changes."

"I couldn't sleep if I wanted to. Would you like some coffee? You have one free hand."

He yawned, supporting his daughter against the curve of his left arm. "Sure, if it's not too much trouble. Maybe it'll help keep me awake."

In the kitchen, Britta measured the coffee and put the pot on the stove to boil. When it was almost ready, she prepared a tray with two cups and a small plate of oatmeal cookies she'd baked earlier. The memory lingered that Jake drank his coffee black. Leaving both cups the same, she carried the tray back to the bedroom.

Stopping in the doorway, she sighed. How long had she been gone? Fifteen minutes? That was all the time it had taken for Jake to drift off. Marissa lay curled in the curve of his arm, her small, golden head resting against his chest. Her eyes were closed.

Setting the tray atop the bureau, Britta stole around the bed and brushed a fingertip down the little girl's cheek. Still hot. Still dry. There was still a rumble of congestion in her breathing. But at least she'd drunk the tea, and now she was getting some rest.

As she stood looking down at the pair, a hopeless love welled in her. Jake Calhoun was the only man she'd ever wanted. But he hadn't cared enough to wait for the end of her mourning. True, he'd made her no promises. Their romance had barely begun before it ended. But she'd already begun to dream of a future when he stopped coming to her door.

The fact that he'd chosen a girl who was Britta's complete opposite only deepened the sting. Petite, feminine, and fragile, Cora had been made for adoration. What man could have resisted her?

Now Jake was back—but only because he needed her. When he found another woman to marry, it would be someone like Cora. Britta's doorway to forever was closed and tightly locked.

Turning away, she picked up the tray and carried it back to the kitchen.

CHAPTER NINE

MASON STOOD AT THE FOOT OF THE NEWLY CLEARED LANDING strip. His eyes scanned the eastern horizon, where the dark sky showed the first thread of light above the peaks. Unless something had gone wrong, his next shipment of Canadian liquor should be arriving any minute. This time he would be better prepared.

Kerosene-doused bonfires had been laid every twenty-five paces along the landing strip, to be lit when he heard the plane coming. But with daylight approaching and no sign of the craft, the fires might not be needed. It would be a waste to light them too soon.

Would Ruby be making the delivery? Mason had told himself that nothing mattered except getting the shipment. But he hadn't been able to stop thinking about her. Concern for Ruby's safety had been the reason he'd brought the team of draft horses out here with harnesses and a heavy chain to clear the landing strip of brush, holes, and rocks and smooth the surface as best as could be done with primitive equipment.

No one had asked him what he was doing. The ranch's two hired hands had long since learned to do their jobs and mind their own business. As for Mason's mother, she seemed to be retreating into her own world, caring less and less for what happened around her. She probably needed to see a doctor. Maybe he could ask Sidney to take care of it.

Holding his breath, he listened for the thrum of an engine. But all he heard was the sigh of the breeze and the piping call of a bird. Where was that plane?

The cash for the transaction was in a fat manila envelope, stuffed into the inner pocket of his vest. As he checked to make sure it was in place, his fingers brushed the brass buckle that had survived the cave fire.

Restless, he took it out and polished it on his sleeve. He'd almost forgotten about the buckle—though he would never forget the body he'd found. But the evidence could be important if the man's family showed up, or if he turned out to be wanted by the law.

Switching on his flashlight, he studied the buckle. It could be a rodeo trophy, an old one. Shining the light closer, he read the worn inscription—*Preston, Idaho, 1896*. Could there be a name? He turned the buckle over. No name. But a pair of initials were etched into the metal: *R.T.*

Something stirred in Mason's memory—a long-buried hunch that swiftly fled as a distant sound reached his ears—the approaching drone of an airplane engine. His springing hopes told him that the pilot might be Ruby.

Dropping the buckle back into his pocket, he hurried to light the bonfires.

He was touching a match to the last one when he realized something.

The sky was silent. The engine had stopped.

As the propeller slowed, Ruby checked the gauges, opened the throttle, and tried again and again to restart the engine. Nothing. The Jenny was dead in the air and losing altitude.

She would have to glide to a landing. She'd done it once before, but that had been in broad daylight, onto a field she'd known to be safe. And she hadn't been loaded down as she was now, with all the heavy cargo that the plane could hold.

Why did it have to happen now, on the last flight in this damned plane before the newly arrived De Havilland could be prepared for loading?

The only sound was the wind rushing past her ears. But now, ahead and far below, she spotted the bonfires along the landing strip. She could just make them out, like a string of luminous beads in the dark distance. Using the rudder bar, she steered a course toward them.

Mason Dollarhide had laid the line of fires to guide her in. But even with the lights to mark the way, the landing would be tricky. She could overshoot the runway or come in too sharp and land nose first. The plane's heavy cargo could take it down faster than expected. Minutes from now, given the slightest miscalculation, she could crash and die.

Ruby willed her nerves to freeze. With her feet controlling the rudder, she eased the stick back to raise the Jenny's nose a few degrees to slow the descent. Would it be enough? Was the plane's angle too sharp?

But there was no time to wonder. She'd done all she could. Bracing for the worst, she steered for the line of bonfires.

Heart in his throat, Mason scanned the sky for the plane. He couldn't see it, couldn't hear it, but he knew it was up there in the silent dark. And the pilot had to be Ruby.

Had she seen the fires? Would she be able to follow them? He could do nothing to help her. He could only trust skill, courage, and luck to get her safely on the ground.

Suddenly, as the sky paled, he spotted her. The plane was in line with the landing strip, but she was coming in too fast, with no way to stop.

He felt the wind on his face as she shot past him, a few feet above his head. With the plane in the grip of gravity and inertia, she was going to overshoot the landing strip and plow through the prickly scrub at the far end. If that didn't stop the plane, the momentum would be enough to tear off its wheels and rip out its belly.

Heart bursting, Mason raced down the landing strip. Far ahead of him, the plane had crashed to earth. In the early dawn light, he could see it moving forward, tearing through the brush like a runaway locomotive.

By the time he reached the plane, his lungs were burning.

Through the settling dust, he made out Ruby, in her helmet and goggles, slumped in the rear cockpit. She didn't appear to be moving.

The plane was tilted at a sharp angle. Mason clambered up a slanting wing to reach her. Wooden crates stamped with the familiar maple leaf were piled in the front cockpit, partly covered by a canvas tarp. They would have to wait.

Reaching Ruby, he pulled off her goggles. Her eyes were closed, but when he touched her throat to unfasten the leather helmet, he felt a pulse. At least she was alive. But as he peeled off the helmet, he saw the swollen bruise above her left temple. From beneath the plane came a faint dripping sound. If gasoline was trickling out of the line onto the hot engine, the plane could catch fire and go up like a torch. He had to get her out of the cockpit.

"Ruby." He brushed her cheek with a fingertip. "Can you hear me?"

She shuddered. Then, to Mason's relief, her eyes opened. "The plane—"

"The plane's in one piece but it's leaking fuel." Even as he spoke, Mason could smell the gasoline vapors.

She groaned. "Oh, no . . . I'll be in so much trouble."

"Forget the plane. You're hurt. We've got to get you out. Come on, I'll help you."

"I can do it." She shifted, gingerly moving her limbs as she reached down to unfasten her safety belt. "No, I'm fine. Just— ow!" She yelped and laid her free hand on her shoulder. "That hurts."

With luck, the shoulder would just be dislocated, but he couldn't wait to find out. "Give me your free hand," he said.

"Just get back and give me room. I'll . . . manage." She sounded groggy, barely aware of the danger. Unable to wait any longer,

Mason wrapped his arms around her torso and hauled her out of the cockpit, onto the wing. She screamed in pain as he pulled her into his arms and jumped to the ground. For an instant he stumbled backward. She was heavier than he'd expected, her curvy body solid muscle beneath the khaki jumpsuit she wore. Barely regaining his balance, he staggered away from the plane—just in time. With a rumble of exploding gas, the Jenny burst into a ball of flame.

Still holding Ruby in his arms, he carried her away from the searing heat and set her down on a heavy log he'd used to clear the brush from the landing strip.

Clasping her arm against her side, she stared at the burning plane. The pop of bursting glass bottles mingled with the roar of the flames. The valuable cargo would be nothing but ashes and broken glass, but there was nothing to be done.

Mason stepped back, giving her time to catch her breath and process what had happened. When she didn't speak or turn around, he sat down beside her on the log.

"We've got to do something about that shoulder," he said. "You need to let me feel for the injury. It'll hurt, but that can't be helped."

She glared up at him, distrust blazing in her dark eyes, but after a moment's hesitation, she nodded.

His fingers explored her shoulder through the thin khaki shirt. She grimaced and whimpered as he found the loose connection between the bones.

"Hurts?" he asked.

She nodded, her lips pressed tight against the pain.

"It's dislocated. I can pop it back into place."

"Why should I trust you? You're not a doctor."

"No. But I've treated injuries like this."

"Where? In prison?"

Mason's throat jerked.

"I know about you," she said. "You served five years for bootlegging. And now you're back at your old game. Some people never learn."

"I learned plenty," Mason said. "That's why I'm doing things differently this time. Come on, let's take care of that shoulder. If we don't do it now, it could swell and get worse." He shifted to face her on the log. "Ready?"

Having no better option, Ruby nodded. She held out her arm. He felt for the dislocation, took her hand, and braced against her side. Ruby turned her head away, not wanting to see what he was about to do.

"On the count of three," he said. "One, two . . . *three.*"

She stifled a scream as the pain shot down her arm and rocketed down her back. There was a popping sensation as the joint snapped into place.

"Good as new." Mason Dollarhide lowered her arm. "It'll be sore. You might not be able to fly for a while."

Clutching her arm against her body, she watched the fire consume her plane—the one she and her father had flown in their barnstorming days. By now, little more than the frame and the metal parts remained. The engine had fallen loose and lay on the ground. Parts of the wooden liquor boxes were charred and scattered. Broken glass lay everywhere.

As her situation sank home, she sagged forward, curling over her knees like a child. Salty tears flowed from under her eyelids and dripped onto her lap. The bruise on her head had become a swollen, throbbing lump. She felt dizzy and slightly nauseous.

Getting another plane shouldn't be a problem. Jennies were easy to buy, and the new De Havilland should be ready soon. But what would she do if she wasn't fit to fly? Would she be out of a job? With no other way to help her father, would she be forced to give Leo Colucci what he wanted?

Her shoulders began to quiver, then to heave as sobs racked her body. It was as if her life over the past few weeks had caved in on her—the crash, the threats from the government agents, her father's arrest, Colucci's possessive eyes, and the game of deception she was forced to play, even now.

The man who'd saved her life was an enemy. It would be her job to betray him to the authorities and put him back behind bars, probably for an even longer sentence—long enough to ruin his life.

"Are you all right, Ruby?"

She sat up. "I'll have to be, won't I?"

"How's your shoulder?"

"It hurts. But I can tell everything's in place. I suppose I should thank you."

"That's good enough for me. There's some water back near the cave. Maybe we can put something cold on that bruise. It's not far. Are you all right to walk?"

"I'm just fine," Ruby lied. If this man knew how lightheaded she felt, he might try to keep her here. She couldn't let that happen.

Her vision swam as she let him pull her to her feet. Her first steps wobbled. He slipped a hand under her elbow to support her.

"You're sure you're all right?"

"I'll be fine once I get my legs working."

His arm tightened, pulling her in against his body. She could feel his solid strength holding her upright. "Don't worry about getting home," he said. "I've got a car. I'll drive you. Just let me know where to go."

"Miles City will be good enough. You can let me off on Main Street." She knew better than to give him any hint of her living arrangements.

"The car's at the end of the road. It's a half-mile walk from the cave. If you can't—"

"I can walk. I'll be fine."

"My sister's a doctor. Her ranch is an hour away on the far side of Blue Moon. We could let her check that bump on your head."

"Unless she understands the business you're in, I'd call that a dangerous idea. You can't trust anybody, not even family. That's how you get caught."

Fighting pain and lightheadedness, Ruby focused on matching her steps to his. Through the haze of morning light, she could see a jutting rock outcrop with a scattering of gear outside. That would be the cave Mason had mentioned. She couldn't see the entrance, but this was no time for curiosity.

After giving her a drink of cool water from a canteen, Mason soaked his handkerchief and gave it to her to hold against the bruise on her head. The water was soothing but not cold enough to ease the swelling. After a few minutes, she squeezed out the handkerchief and gave it back to him. By now her head was beginning to clear. The ache was still there, throbbing like a drumbeat in the background of her brain. Waves of light passed over her vision. She probably had a mild concussion. It wouldn't be the first time. She knew the signs. But right now, she had more urgent concerns.

Mason Dollarhide was a risk. He knew who she was. He'd met her father, and he knew men who would be in prison with him now. A word to the wrong people, even by chance, could put her and Art in danger. The longer she stayed with him, the more he was liable to learn about her. And since she was duty-bound to report his activities to her federal handlers, she was as much a danger to him as he was to her.

The sooner she could put some distance between them, the better off they'd both be. Meanwhile, she needed his help. And all she could do to protect herself was watch every word she spoke and every move she made.

By the time they reached the Model T, parked where the road ended south of the ranch, Mason could tell that Ruby's strength was flagging. She was leaning against him, occasionally stumbling over her feet. She needed a doctor, but she'd refused to be taken anywhere except to Miles City.

He'd tried to keep her talking. But any efforts at drawing her into a conversation had been met with one-syllable replies, which was frustrating because he had questions and was hoping for answers. How soon could he get another shipment? Who could he contact to get more and bigger deliveries? And then there was the question that had chewed on him from the night of her last delivery—the question he had no right to ask. What was her relationship with Leo Colucci?

He helped her into the car and offered her the canteen. The deep drink she took seemed to revive her. Still, as he cranked the engine and climbed into the driver's seat, he couldn't help worrying about the risks she was taking. In a dangerous world with dangerous people, anything could happen.

But Ruby had made her choices, just as he'd made his. He had no business trying to save her. He had his own ambitions, his own problems. After their encounter this morning, only one course of action made sense. Leave the woman in Miles City, drive away, and forget her—before he was tempted to risk his future and ruin his life.

"I remember your father." Mason made conversation as he drove. "Where is he now? Is he doing the same job you're doing?"

"Not anymore. He's—" Ruby caught herself. Her stomach clenched as she reminded herself of the lie she had to tell. "He's dead. Killed in a crash."

"I'm sorry. He struck me as an excellent pilot and a good man."

"Yes, he taught me everything I know about flying. I miss him every day." She swiftly changed the subject. "I'm sorry you lost your cargo. I feel responsible, since I crashed the plane."

"It wasn't your fault. Did you have a mechanic check the engine before you left?"

"Yes. And I double-checked it myself. But those Jennies have had a lot of use. Things can go wrong. My father would have brought the plane down safely. But with the extra weight of the cargo, I couldn't manage it. I don't have his experience."

"Planes can be replaced. At least you'll live to fly again. But you should stay grounded until you've had time to recover from that bump on the head."

"When I'm ready, I'll know."

"I mean it. You could pass out in the air."

"You sound like my father." It was time to shut the conversation down. The rule was a sensible one—when doing business, don't exchange personal information with anyone who can give you up to the wrong people. "Please, just drive," she said.

He slowed the car as they passed through Blue Moon; the town was just awakening for the day. Then he picked up speed as the road opened up toward Miles City. The morning sky was streaked with clouds of mauve and amber that faded with the rising sun. Traffic was light on the road—here and there a farmer hauling produce or chickens to market, or a traveler rushing to catch an early train.

Ruby could almost have found the ride pleasant, except for the throbbing pain in her head and her worry about what would happen after she made her call to the farm. By now she would be overdue. Concerns would arise, not only for her but for the plane and the cargo. There would also be concern that she'd been arrested and forced to tell the authorities what she knew.

Colucci would be furious. But she couldn't control what was going to happen. She could only react. And she couldn't allow herself to trust anyone. Not the criminals she worked for, not the government agents who would abandon her—and her father—if anything went wrong, and certainly not the man beside her, driving the car.

"You're awfully quiet," he said, breaking the silence between them. "I know it's none of my business, but I can imagine how worried you must be."

"Worried?" She gave a bitter laugh. "I've just destroyed a valuable plane, lost several thousand dollars' worth of cargo, and the people I work for aren't known to be very forgiving. Why should I be worried?"

"You work for Leo Colucci, right?"

His words stunned her into silence, not because Mason knew she worked for Colucci, but that he would mention it to her.

"He's my contact," Mason said, "the man I'll need to call to order a new shipment. I could put in a good word for you—make sure he knows the plane's engine failure wasn't your fault and that you did everything you could to land safely. Would that help?"

"Don't be naive," she said. "The only way you can help is to let me off in Miles City and forget me. I'll deal with Colucci myself."

"Is he your boyfriend?"

His words slammed her. "He's my boss. Trust me, the less you know about him the better."

"Does that mean you can't pull some strings to get me bigger shipments?" Mason's voice held a teasing note. Was he joking? Ruby couldn't tell.

"Don't even ask," she said. "Just let me off at the Olive Hotel on Main Street and drive away. For your own safety and mine, you don't know anything about me."

"Understood. How's your head?"

"It hurts, but I'll be fine."

"You should see a doctor."

"What could a doctor do that I can't do myself? I just need to rest."

They were coming into Miles City. The hotel was on the next block. Mason pulled up a couple of car lengths short of the main entrance.

Ruby glanced up and down the boardwalk. It wasn't crowded at this hour, but she still appeared wary. "Turn right at the next corner and go around the block to the delivery entrance," she said. "I don't want to be seen getting out of your car."

Mason followed her directions. By the time he pulled into the alley leading to the rear of the building, Ruby was already reaching for the door handle. "No need to help me," she said. "I have a room inside. I know the way, and the key's in my pocket."

"Are you sure you'll be all right?" He pulled the car into a spot where it wouldn't block any traffic. Right now the place was quiet, but workers and delivery trucks would be arriving soon.

"I'll be fine," she said. "I'd just rather not be noticed. Thank you for the lift, Mr. Dollarhide. And good luck with your business."

She flung the door open and stepped out into the alley. Before Mason could react, she was headed for the back door, which opened next to the loading dock above a short flight of steps. He could see that she wasn't going to make it. She swayed and wove like a drunkard, struggling for balance with every step.

Mason sprang out of the car and sprinted after her—but Ruby had a head start. Before he could reach her, her legs buckled and she collapsed at the foot of the steps.

He scooped her up in his arms. Her eyelids were closed. They fluttered open as he carried her inside.

He'd expected to walk into the kitchen and get some help. Instead, he found himself in a shadowy hall with a staircase leading up to the second floor. It appeared that this passageway had been designed for discreet access to the hotel.

She cast her gaze around the dim space. "My room's upstairs," she murmured. "Put me down. I can walk."

"Don't push your luck." Mason started up the stairs, still holding her. "What's your room number?"

Ruby gave him the number. Being carried by Mason made her feel like a helpless child. But in its own way, being in a man's arms was strangely comforting. Her body began to relax and soften. Tingles of awareness rose from the core of her body to trickle along her limbs. She released a long breath.

His arms were solid muscle, and his shirt smelled of smoke from the fires. Where her head lay against his chest, she could hear the drumming of his heart.

They reached the top of the stairs. The long corridor was empty except for a tired-looking maid pushing a laundry cart. She gave them a curious glance before disappearing into one of the rooms. Was she just doing her work? Or did that work include a call to Leo Colucci, who had spies everywhere? If Colucci got word that his pilot—the woman he wanted to claim—had been seen with a man, that could mean trouble for her and for Mason.

Ruby went rigid against him. "My room's here, on your left," she muttered. "Put me down and go. We mustn't be caught together."

"I'm not leaving until I know you're all right." He lowered her feet to the floor so she could get the key out of her pocket and open the door. Following her inside, he closed the door and locked it behind him.

"No!" She turned on him, frantic. "You have to leave. I need to make a phone call."

He stood his ground. "If it's to Colucci, I already know you work for him. He'll want to know about the crash. So go ahead and call. When you're done, I'm going to phone the front desk and have them send up a doctor."

She shot him a murderous look. "I don't need a doctor."

"Make your call. I'll try not to listen." He turned away and walked toward the far side of the room to stand next to the window. Moving the blind aside a few inches, he peered down into the alley.

Ruby sat on the bed, lifted the telephone from the nightstand, and forced herself to make the call. She braced for the sound of Colucci's voice. But it was Mack, the young pilot, who answered.

"Ruby?" He recognized her voice. "Where are you? Everybody's been worried."

"I'm all right. I'm in Miles City. But the plane crash-landed and burned. The cargo was a total loss. I've got to tell the boss. Is he there?"

"He's out at the hangar, probably watching for you. I can give him your news. He'll probably want to phone you when he gets back to the house."

"Thanks, Mack." Ending the call, Ruby felt the tension drain from her body, leaving her exhausted. She lay back on the coverlet, her head sinking into the pillows.

"Better?" Mason had come around the bed.

Ruby nodded. "I still have to face Colucci. But at least I won't have to give him the news. For now, I just need to rest. You can forget about calling the doctor."

"Not on your life. You didn't even make it to the steps out there." He picked up the phone and made a quick call. "The concierge knows a doctor who's close by and should be able to

get here sometime before lunch. Meanwhile, let's get you comfortable."

He soaked a washcloth with cold water from the bathroom
basin and laid it over the bruise. Then, sitting on the end of the
bed, he lifted her foot, loosened the laces on her military-style
boot and worked it off. He did the same with the opposite boot.
Closing her eyes, Ruby allowed him to strip off her woolen socks
and massage her bare feet. His powerful thumbs pressed the tension from her arches and the base of her toes. The sensation was
heavenly. She recalled rubbing her husband's feet to soothe him.
But she couldn't recall a time when anyone, especially a man, had
treated her with such tenderness.

A moan of pleasure escaped her lips.

"How did you learn to do this?" she asked, beginning to drift.
"Who taught you?"

There was a beat of hesitation. "Trade secret."

"Was it a woman?" The words swam in her head. Words she
might never have spoken in her right mind. "It was, wasn't it?
What else did she teach you, Mason Dollarhide? Anything you'd
care to pass on?"

"Just rest, Ruby. If you fall asleep, I'll wake you when the doctor
comes."

"Come on . . ." She was sinking, letting go. "Your secret is safe
with me. . . ."

Mason lowered her bare feet to the coverlet and laid the spare
blanket over them. Ruby's eyes were closed, her breathing deep
and regular. Would it be safe to let her sleep like this? He would
stay nearby and watch her to make sure.

As he stood by the bed, looking down at her sleeping face, a
wave of compassion swept over him. He had never known a
woman like her—so bold, so intelligent, and yet so vulnerable.
She deserved to be cherished and protected like the treasure she
was, not have to fight for survival in a brutal world where life was
cheap and profit was everything.

Mason had long since stopped counting the women he'd been with. He'd enjoyed them all. But had he really loved any of them—even the innocent young mother of his son?

Maybe he'd been waiting for a different kind of woman—a woman like Ruby.

Driven by a reckless impulse, he leaned over her, intending to brush a chaste kiss onto her forehead. What he found instead was her mouth. His pulse soared. But he knew that he'd crossed into forbidden territory. With exquisite restraint, he held himself in check, allowing only the lightest contact. Her lips were salty and chapped from the wind. He fought the urge to savor them, then plunder her mouth with his tongue.

The hunger that burned in his body was familiar—but this time he knew better than to follow his instincts. When she stirred, he pulled away and stepped back. Theirs was a business relationship, and this wasn't the time or place to change things.

After she'd settled back into sleep, he moved away from the bed and walked to the window. In the alley below, a delivery truck, loaded with crates of fresh vegetables, was making its way toward the dock. Workers were scurrying to clear the way. There was no sign of anyone who might be the doctor.

Turning away from the window, Mason bumped his leg against a cardboard box that had been left on the dresser bench. The box tumbled to the floor, knocking off the lid and spilling the shimmery contents onto the rug.

Mason dropped to his knees and began putting everything back in order. He picked up a flapper-style dress, sheer silk made heavy by glittering sequins and beaded fringe. As he laid it in the box and gathered up the matching high-heeled shoes, the awful truth began to dawn on him. These luxury items were in Ruby's size. And something told him she hadn't paid for them herself.

He collected the more intimate pieces—the beige silk slip that matched the dress, the underwear, the silk stockings, and garters. A slow anger was burning away his denial. Why wear glamorous underthings if nobody was going to see them . . . and take them off?

With everything inside the box, he slammed on the lid and put it back on the bench where he'd found it. Silent curses swirled in his mind. He'd wondered whether Ruby was Colucci's girl-friend—or, to call a spade a spade, his mistress. Now he had the answer to his question.

CHAPTER TEN

MASON COULD HAVE WALKED OUT OF THE ROOM AND LEFT CO-lucci's woman to wake up on her own. Pride tempted him to do just that. But he was concerned about Ruby. He'd heard about people with head injuries who went to sleep and never woke up. He resolved to stay, at least until the doctor arrived, which he hoped would be soon. Now that he knew the truth, he could scarcely look at her without imagining her wearing that dress with the silk stockings and the wispy drawers, in Leo Colucci's arms.

Ruby stirred, whimpered, then sank back into sleep. What would he say to her if she were to wake up? Nothing, he decided. Her relationship with the mobster was none of his business. As for that fleeting kiss he'd given her, she would never know about it.

As he settled into a padded armchair, a leaden mood crept over him. After the tension-filled night, which had ended with nothing gained, it was as if his energy and excitement had drained away, leaving him hollow inside. With the slow passing of time, he fell into a doze.

A loud rapping on the door jarred him awake. Ruby had opened her eyes and was struggling to get up. Mason pushed himself out of the chair. "That would be the doctor," he said. "Stay where you are. I'll get it."

He strode to the door and opened it. The man who stood on the threshold was well over six feet tall, with wavy hair, a fleshy build, and heavy, handsome features. He was dressed in a tailored suit, his shirt collar loose, without a tie.

Mason had never seen him before, but he knew at once that this wasn't the doctor. The man had to be Leo Colucci.

Ignoring Mason, Colucci strode into the room. Ruby's eyes were like a cornered doe's, wide and nervous. She sat up and slid her legs over the side of the bed.

"Are you all right, Ruby?" Colucci demanded.

"Just a sore shoulder and a bump on the head. The doctor should be here soon to check me." Ruby kept her voice level. "You probably know that I crashed the plane and lost the cargo. This gentleman, my customer, pulled me out of the cockpit and drove me here. You owe him your thanks."

As Colucci turned toward him, Mason thought fast. Ruby had just given him an opening. He'd be a fool not to seize the advantage.

"It's a pleasure to meet you in person, Mr. Colucci," he said, extending his hand. "Mason Dollarhide. We've spoken over the telephone."

"Yes, I know." Colucci accepted the handshake. "The old man spoke highly of you. He's the reason I agreed to work with someone I hadn't met."

"I want you to know that the crash wasn't your pilot's fault," Mason said. "The engine stalled in midair. She had to glide the plane down. If the landing strip had been longer, she would have made it fine. But the extra weight of the cargo—"

"I understand," Colucci said, cutting him off. "When she's ready to fly again, it will be in a more reliable airplane. Meanwhile, as Ruby said, I owe you my thanks. I'm guessing you'll need a replacement for that lost cargo."

"The sooner the better," Mason said. "But I could sell a lot more than I'm getting. I've got an ideal setup for receiving—a natural cave for storage and an airstrip that's on ranch property but remote enough to be out of sight. All I need to grow the business is more product."

Colucci looked unconvinced. "I'll keep you in mind. I'm still building up the supply lines. But at least I can replace your missing cargo in the next few nights. The pilot will be a young man.

He's new but already proving himself. Someone will let you know when to expect him."

The conversation was interrupted by a polite tap on the door. Mason opened it for an elderly man with thick glasses and a cane. The black bag he carried identified him as the doctor.

"You can go, Mr. Dollarhide," Colucci said. "I'll take over from here and make sure the lady is looked after. We'll be in touch."

Mason had little choice except to make a polite departure. For the briefest instant, his gaze met Ruby's across the room. Her expression was like a cornered animal's, pleading, almost frantic. But she wasn't his problem, he reminded himself. He turned away without a second look and walked out of the door.

When Joseph discovered four Triple C steers among the Dollarhide cattle in the north pasture, he knew without being told what had to be done. With the help of his well-trained horse, he cut the four branded animals out of the herd and headed them back toward Calder land, riding behind to hurry them along.

If the Calder hands missed their steers and came looking for them, things could get ugly fast. There was probably a fence down somewhere. Joseph would find it, herd the steers through the gap, and take time to mend it with the tools that were part of his everyday range gear.

The days were getting shorter now. On the mountains, the aspens were turning to gold below the timberline. The first flocks of geese were starting their journey south, their long V formations crossing the sky.

On a day like this, being outdoors was a pleasure. Joseph didn't mind cowboying. Anything was better than spending time in the sawmill. But inside him, the deep discontent was still churning.

A few mornings ago, as he rose before dawn to start his chores, Joseph had heard the drone of an airplane flying low over the house in the direction of the Hollister Ranch. Rushing to the porch, he had tried to spot the plane, but he was too late. The sound had faded into the distance. After a few seconds it had stopped altogether.

Was Mason Dollarhide up to his old tricks, getting his contraband liquor shipped in by air this time? After the trouble his natural father had gotten him into five years ago, Joseph wanted nothing to do with Mason and his shady ways. But the throb of the engine as the plane passed overhead had set his blood on fire.

As punishment for his airborne adventure, Joseph had been confined to the ranch and sentenced to mucking out the stables for a week. In addition, Blake had forbidden him to mention flying or airplanes in his hearing—ever. Joseph knew when to toe his father's line. He'd been on his best behavior since the punishment ended. But that couldn't change his desire to become a pilot. Somehow, when the time came, he would find a way.

Now he was coming up on the property line, one of the few places where the Triple C and the Dollarhide Ranch came together. Along most of their borders, the two rival ranches were separated by other holdings—Angus O'Rourke's ramshackle place in the foothills and lower down, the horse pastures owned by Logan Hunter, the man who'd married Blake Dollarhide's sister, Kristin. But here the demarcation was marked only by a barbed wire fence. To cross onto Dollarhide land, the four steers must have come through the fence in this area. The break shouldn't take long to find.

Fifty yards ahead, Joseph could see the fence. But somebody was already mending the downed wire. As he rode closer, herding the steers toward the opening, he recognized Chase Calder, son of Webb Calder and heir apparent to the Calder ranching empire.

Seeing Joseph with the missing livestock, Chase waved and moved the wires aside so the steers could pass through the damaged fence. Returning the wave, Joseph herded the animals back into their pasture. Then, turning his horse, he rode to where Chase was righting the tilted fence post before reattaching the loosened strands of barbed wire. Both young men were tall and dark, but Chase was older, his build huskier, while Joseph's body was still filling out. Years ago, the two had been good friends. They'd since grown apart, drawn by separate lives and the bitter rivalry between their fathers. Still, their relationship was cordial enough for Joseph to dismount and offer his help.

"Could you use an extra pair of hands?" he asked. "I can steady that post and hold the wires for you."

Chase looked up and grinned. "Thanks. And thanks for herding those steers back home. I had other plans for the morning, but this emergency couldn't wait. Your help just may have saved my day."

Wearing his gloves, Joseph thrust the post deep into the hole and held it upright. "By any chance would those other plans include a girl?" he teased.

"They might." Chase filled in around the post with dirt and rocks, packing it tight. "I just hope she'll be waiting when I finish this job."

"Anyone I know?" Joseph had met a pretty brunette at a dance a couple of weeks ago—Lucy Merriweather was her name. Lucy had mentioned that she and her father were guests of Webb Calder's. Maybe Lucy was Chase's new love. If so, that was too bad. Things had cooled between Joseph and Annabeth since the night she'd brought up marriage. If Chase hadn't staked his claim, he wouldn't mind romancing Lucy himself.

"Is it Lucy you're seeing?" he asked.

Chase laughed. "Nope. Lucy's a bit too prim and proper for me. You'll never guess who it is."

"I hope that means you're going to tell me. I need to know which girl I should leave alone."

Chase picked up a loose section of barbed wire and pulled it into a taut line. "All right." He paused, heightening the suspense. "It's Maggie O'Rourke."

Joseph couldn't suppress an outraged gasp. "You mean Culley O'Rourke's little sister? Chase, she's just a kid—what, fifteen maybe? And she wears her brother's hand-me-downs."

"You've never seen what she looks like under those baggy old clothes. She's a beauty."

Joseph held the wire in place while Chase hammered it to the post. "The O'Rourkes aren't exactly your class of people," he said to Chase. "Does your father know about this?"

"No, and he's not going to find out."

"So you're not interested in Lucy?"

"If you can impress the girl, she's all yours."

"I know she and her father are staying at your place. How long will they be around?"

"It might be a while," Chase said. "Lucy's father, Nigel, has been hired to build an airstrip for my dad. Once it's done, along with the hangar, Dad plans to buy a couple of planes. Then we'll be able to fly in and out of the ranch."

Joseph's pulse broke into a thundering gallop. This was like his first glimpse of a dream. Whatever the cost, he had to pursue that dream. "If your dad's getting planes, he's going to need pilots," he said.

"We'll have to hire somebody at first," Chase said. "But next year, Dad's going to send me to flight school. Then I'll be able to pilot the planes myself."

Chase's words triggered an emotion in Joseph—a feeling so painful and fierce that it felt as if his guts were being tied in knots. Why did things seem to happen so easily for some people? Here was Chase, accepting the privilege that Joseph had dreamed of, yearned for, and would have to fight for.

But he couldn't give in to envy, Joseph told himself. All he could do was try to use this small opening.

"I'd like to know more about the project," he said. "Who knows, maybe an airstrip would be a good thing for our ranch, too. Is there any way I could meet Lucy's father? That way, maybe I could get to know Lucy as well."

Chase tightened another wire and hammered it into place. His silence was beginning to dampen Joseph's hopes when, at last, he spoke.

"I guess you could come to dinner tomorrow night, as my friend. My father might grumble, but he'd be a gracious host. Your father, on the other hand, wouldn't like it at all. He might not even allow you to visit us."

"My father wouldn't have to know," Joseph said. "I could make something up, like going to see a girl. Or I could just leave. I'm not a twelve-year-old kid anymore, even though my father treats me like one."

"All right, I'll ask my dad." Chase finished attaching the last wire, bagged his tools, and strode to his horse. "I'll call and leave you a message. Either way, you'll know what it means."

"Thanks." Joseph watched him ride off in the direction of the O'Rourke place. He tried to remember little Maggie O'Rourke from the last time he'd seen her in town—a slip of a girl with fiery eyes and a wild mane of black hair. She could be a beauty, Joseph conceded. But she was so young and most likely innocent. What could Chase be thinking?

The Calder dining room had gone almost twenty years without a woman's touch, and it showed. Mounted hunting trophies—bear, bison, and moose—decorated walls that wanted a good whitewashing. The linen tablecloth was worn, the china plates chipped here and there, the silver tarnished. An open wine bottle stood in the middle of the table, in defiance of prohibition laws. A drop that had trickled down the outside of the bottle left a crimson stain on the cloth.

All the same, Joseph was impressed. An air of power made up for any lack of elegance. It was a power that emanated from Webb Calder at the head of the table, like the aura surrounding a Viking chieftain or a medieval king.

Chase sat on his father's left with Joseph next to him. Mr. Nigel Merriweather and his daughter sat facing them on the other side. Nigel, whom Joseph had glimpsed with Webb at Jake's restaurant, claimed to have emigrated from Britain after the war. He was lean and pale, with the studied air of an aristocrat. His affected manners and speech struck Joseph as overdone, like the massively ornate gold ring he wore, in the shape of a bird; but the man did appear to know a great deal about airplanes, especially British planes. Joseph had come here to learn, but the daughter distracted his attention again and again.

In this drab, masculine setting, Lucy Merriweather bloomed like an English rose. Her lavender gown seemed to float around her slender figure. Its color set off her porcelain skin, dark hair, and sparkling hazel eyes. Her smile—and she smiled often, mostly at Chase—showed dazzling white teeth.

Clearly she had her eye on the heir to the Calder fortune. Her father probably had the same idea. Maybe Webb did, too. Lucy was the very picture of a suitable rich man's wife. But Chase's thoughts were elsewhere—on a ragged Irish girl as wild as the birds that woke the morning with their cries.

Joseph was doing his best not to stare, but with Lucy sitting directly across from him, it was hard to take his eyes off her. He was scarcely aware of the delicious beef stew and fresh bread he was eating. Only one thing was clear in his mind. This was no time to be timid. If he wanted this chance, he had to be bold enough to take it—even if it got him slapped down.

Lucy was laughing at a joke Webb had made. Her laugh was charming and genuine. Joseph couldn't take his eyes off her. She was the most enchanting girl he'd ever seen. The fact that her father was in the airplane business was the icing on the cake.

Not that it mattered. Lucy's father could have been a junk dealer or a traveling snake oil salesman, and Joseph would still have been smitten. But when he looked across the table at Lucy, he saw his dream—a dream that would never be his unless he reached for it.

"When do you expect to have the airstrip finished, Mr. Merriweather?" Joseph asked, putting down his fork.

Nigel sipped his wine. "We'll do as much as we can this fall. But it probably won't be finished until spring. That's when we'll buy our first plane and hire a pilot."

"I'd be interested in seeing how you get the land ready for the planes and how you build the hangar," Joseph said. "In fact, if you need a worker, I could make myself available. I've been interested in flying for a long time. I might even become a pilot myself."

Webb cleared his throat. "I can't imagine your father would let you get involved in this project, Joseph—especially here with us on the Triple C. You're his only son. He needs you at home, to run the ranch and that accursed sawmill. He can't spare you to go gallivanting off to build airstrips and fly planes."

"My father doesn't own me."

Webb chuckled, an unpleasant sound. "That's where you're wrong, boy. And it's what you'll learn as you grow older. You think I had any say about what I wanted to do with my life? You think Chase does? Hell, he'll do what I tell him to, won't you, son?" He gave Chase a stern look. "And you'll do the same with your old man, Joseph. It's called life. Understand?"

"Yes, sir." Joseph cringed inside like a whipped dog. He'd never had a reason to hate Webb Calder, not the way his father did. But he hated the man now.

It was Chase who broke the tension. "Dad, I promised Joseph I'd show him the filly I'm raising. May we be excused?"

"Fine." Webb's eyes narrowed. "After that, I believe your friend will be ready to get into his car and head for home."

Ignoring his father's words, Chase smiled at the girl across the table. "Would you like to come, too, Lucy? I know you like horses."

"I'd love to." Lucy stood, then glanced across the table at her father. "Is it all right, Papa?"

Nigel hesitated, then gave her a nod. "I suppose it would be more enjoyable than sitting here with a couple of stuffy old men. And I'm sure these two young gentlemen will treat you like the lady you are. Right, Chase?"

"Certainly, sir," Chase said. "Come on, let's go."

Chase led the way out of the dining room, opening the front door to let Lucy pass through ahead of him. Joseph followed them across the graveled yard to the nearest stable, one of several on the property. This stable housed the most prized horses among the Calders' vast remuda.

The stable had recently been wired with electricity. Chase opened a door and switched on the light. Horses were drowsing in their roomy box stalls, shifting and blowing. The air smelled of hay and fresh manure.

If Joseph hadn't had his eyes on Lucy, he would have taken more time to admire the splendid animals. In the largest stall, he recognized Cougar, the majestic, claybank stallion that Webb Calder rode on the range. Several other mares and geldings here were Cougar's offspring. There were even two fine quarter horses, raised and trained by Logan Hunter, the rancher who was married to Joseph's aunt Kristin.

Chase had moved ahead with Lucy to a stall at the far end of the stable. Joseph lengthened his stride to catch up with them. Looking over the gate, he could see a bay mare nursing her leggy four-month-old filly—a yellow claybank, probably another of Cougar's babies. The mare and her young one made a charming pair.

Petite Lucy stood on tiptoes, stretching in an effort to look over the gate.

"I can't see them," she complained. "Could somebody give me a boost?"

"Sure," Joseph said, thinking that he and Chase could lift her together. But when he looked around for Chase, there was no sign of him.

Lucy gave him a flirtatious smile. "Chase had someplace to go. So I guess you'll have to be the one to help me."

The truth struck home, triggering giddy flutters in Joseph's chest. All this had been a plot to get him alone with Lucy. And Lucy had been one of the plotters.

This was a dream come true.

Bending, he scooped her up, lifting her high enough to see over the stall gate. She was featherlight, her curves settling nicely into his arms. A moment passed before he realized that she wasn't looking at the horses. She was looking at him, her gaze softly mischievous, her mouth barely a fingerbreadth from his own.

Joseph had intended for the meeting of their lips to be brief, almost chaste. To kiss Lucy the way he'd kissed Annabeth would have been way out of line. Lucy was a lady, and he couldn't afford to be hasty with her. But as her baby-soft lips met his, and he felt her response, a shock of arousal passed through his body. With a whimper of pleasure, she wrapped her arms around his neck. Her fingers twined in his hair. He could feel her heat as the kiss deepened. His pulse hammered. His breath was as harsh as a runner's.

Flushed and panting, they separated. As he lowered her feet to the straw floor, the promise of that kiss and all it held left him dizzy with hope. Beautiful Lucy held the key to his dream. If he played his cards right, with no mistakes, she could be his. And his father wouldn't have anything to say about it.

But his future could depend on her father's goodwill. It would be wise to tread carefully. "I think I'd better see you back to the house, Lucy," he said, offering his arm. "I'd like to see you again if your father would allow it. He should know that I come from a good family. We have a ranch, a sawmill, and plenty of money, if that's a concern to him."

"I know about your family." She took his arm and let him walk her out of the barn. "So does my father. He'd probably allow you to call on me. But he's working with Webb Calder, and Webb doesn't like Blake Dollarhide—or his son."

"I'm not my father. I'm nothing like him."

"I'm sure that's true." Her clasp tightened on his arm as they crossed the yard. "This isn't a good time to speak to my father. He wants to stay in Webb's good graces. But meanwhile, we can find ways to be together. The harvest festival will be coming soon. There'll be a dance in town. I could meet you there. And maybe we'll get other chances. I want to be with you, Joseph. I've been thinking about you ever since we danced together."

They were nearing the house. Joseph burned to take her in his arms and kiss her one more time. But they were standing in full moonlight, and now Chase was walking across the yard toward them.

"I'll take over from here," he said, offering his arm to Lucy. "I hope you two had a good time."

Lucy giggled and accepted Chase's arm.

"I'll be on my way," Joseph said. "But I owe you a favor, Chase."

"I'll remember that when the time comes." Chase's grin flashed in the moonlight as he turned to escort Lucy back to the house.

Joseph watched them disappear through the front door. He could have sworn there was air under his feet as he walked back to the car. He'd viewed lovely Lucy as a lady. But she was more than that. She was a warm, passionate woman.

He could hardly wait to see her again. But he couldn't allow his eagerness to make him reckless. Lucy was too important for that. And her father's goodwill was equally important.

He started the old Model T and drove out toward the gate. Damn Webb Calder for dashing his hopes at dinner tonight and making him look like a fool in front of Lucy. But he would show all the people who tried to stomp on his dream of becoming a pilot. Webb, his father . . . Someday he would show them all.

Marissa lay slumbering in her bed, her cherubic face lit by a shaft of moonlight that fell through the window. She had made a full recovery from the fever. Once more, she'd become her lively, small self, playing, laughing, singing, and jumping into her father's arms to give him kisses.

Britta stood in the doorway, next to Jake, watching the little girl sleep. To thank her for her help, he'd invited her over for a roast beef supper, delivered by the restaurant. It was a nice gesture, but now, as they stood together, looking in on the little girl she was coming to love, Britta was reminded again of what she would never have.

Jake was grateful to her, that was all. When he chose a new wife, it would be someone young and gay and pretty. Not a shy, bumbling moose of a woman who was only at ease with her students. Even when he'd shown some interest, Britta knew he hadn't loved her. If he had, he would have made more of an effort to win her. He would have waited.

She turned away from the bedroom door. "Thank you for the meal, Jake," she said. "I'll repay you by clearing the table and washing the dishes."

"Don't bother," he said. "The restaurant will send somebody to collect the dishes and wash them. They do the same thing when I've got a prisoner in the jail downstairs—only, the food is more likely to be beans or mutton stew."

"Then I suppose I'd best be going."

"Stay, Britta," he said. "It's a nice evening, and I don't get much company up here."

"Something tells me you could have all the company you like, Jake." It was a waspish thing to say, and Britta regretted the words as soon as she'd spoken them.

"Then something told you wrong. I happen to be choosy about the company I keep." His hand found the small of her back and guided her out through the parlor doors to the landing that served as a porch, with stairs coming up from the rear of the jail to provide a private entry.

The sky was clear, with a glory of stars overhead and a moon that cast long shadows across the yard. He stood behind her, his breath warm on the backs of her ears.

"I never got a chance to tell you how much I admired you for taking that plane ride," he said. "Not one woman in a hundred would be brave enough to do that."

"You'd be surprised what women would be brave enough to do," she said. "We're brave in ways that you men don't even notice. Bringing children into the world and raising them. That's an act of courage in itself, one I've never experienced. Maybe that's why I went up in the airplane. I had nothing to risk, and no one to mourn me if I died."

"Your life isn't over, Britta. You're still young. And you have the most generous, loving heart I've ever known." His fingers toyed with her braid, which she always wore tightly coiled atop her head. "Your hair was down the night of Marissa's fever. I was too worried to pay much attention, but I remember that it was glorious." He tugged at the pins that held the coils in place. The braid fell loose, hanging down her back, almost to her waist.

As his fingers unraveled the plait, Britta felt the heat stir and rise from the depths of her body, the low pulsing, the hunger between her thighs. Was that what Jake had in mind? She knew it was wrong, but she knew that she still loved him. What if she never got another chance?

Would that be enough? Would it be all she deserved in this life?

His hands lifted the curtain of her hair. Britta felt the soft pressure of his lips on the back of her neck. Resisting, she pulled away and turned to face him.

"Don't play games with me, Jake. If that's what you want, find a woman who's willing to settle for your offer. But I won't let you use me. I'm worth more than that."

"I know what you're worth, Britta." His voice was thick and husky, his eyes hooded in moonlit shadow as he pulled her close and kissed her tenderly on the mouth.

She melted against him in surrender, his kiss heating her blood. But as her arms went around him, a voice from below broke them apart.

"Woo-hoo! If it isn't Miss Anderson! Having a good time, are you?"

A trio of sixth-grade boys—Britta's students—stood in the yard below, grinning up at her. Before either she or Jake could speak, they scattered, vanishing into the dark.

Britta knew them to be mischief makers. Worse, the mother of one boy was a vicious gossip. By midmorning the delicious story, with embellishments, would be all over town. She would be a public disgrace. She might even lose her job.

"Britta, it's all right—" Jake reached for her, but she backed away.

"No, it isn't all right! You can't imagine—"

Breaking off, she spun away from him, stumbled down the outside stairs, and fled across the yard for home.

CHAPTER ELEVEN

Two weeks later

MASON WATCHED THE DAWNING SKY, HIS EARS KEEN FOR THE SOUND of an approaching plane. Since his encounter with Colucci, he'd received two shipments of Canadian whiskey, both of them delivered by a boyish, ginger-haired pilot flying a Jenny. Now it was time for a third.

He'd known better than to ask the young man about Ruby, although he probably knew her. Was she all right? Was she flying again? Would he see her this time?

But the answers to those questions were none of his business. He'd seen the glittering dress, read the possessive look in the mobster's eyes, and faced the truth—if he wanted to do business with Colucci's organization, Rule Number One would be hands off the boss's woman.

His business was picking up, with supply and demand growing. New customers were either referred by Colucci or picked up by word of mouth and carefully vetted. He'd bought a used Oldsmobile, newer and more reliable than the aging Model T, with room under the seats for a hidden stash. He kept it out of sight and used it only for business, so it wouldn't be connected with him at other times.

He had dealt twice with Webb Calder's friend. The few words

they'd exchanged hinted that he might be British. But the man remained a mystery. Satisfying as it might be to learn that Webb was involved in the illegal liquor trade, Mason knew that probing deeper could prove a risk to his own safety. There were no friends in this business, only contacts. And confidence was an invitation to betrayal.

The air was chilly. Mason thrust his hands into his pockets to keep them warm. He could hear the rush of wind along the rocky escarpment that hid the cave. The morning birds were waking in the scrub to greet the dawn with their piping calls. But there was only one sound he wanted to hear.

As he was about to abandon hope for the day, he heard it—the sound of an engine, coming closer. But something was different. The drone of the Jenny had become so familiar that he could recognize the plane sight unseen. But this engine sounded different—smoother and more powerful.

Colucci had mentioned that Ruby would be flying a new plane after her recovery. Could she be on her way to him now? His pulse raced at the thought of seeing her again.

But this was business, Mason reminded himself. If the incoming pilot was Ruby, they would make contact, exchange payment, unload the crates, and say as little as possible. Then she would climb back into the plane and fly home. Home to her lover.

He hurried to light the fires he'd laid along the landing strip.

Piloting the De Havilland DH-4 was a dream. With the Rolls-Royce Eagle in-line engine humming in her ears and the controls responding to her slightest touch, Ruby could almost forget that she was flying a load of illegal cargo for unsavory clients in a dirty, dangerous business.

First designed in Britain for the war, the DH-4 was a wood-framed biplane like the Jenny. The prototype had been built as a light day bomber and reconnaissance craft with two seats—one with controls for the pilot and one for an observer, with mounts for a Vickers machine gun in front. In the refurbished peacetime model Ruby was flying, the front cockpit had been converted to a fortified cargo bay. Compared to the Jenny, it was faster, stronger, and more maneuverable, with longer range and higher altitude capabilities.

Ruby had never been told where the long-nosed plane had come from. It had been waiting one morning when she'd been driven in from town. For all she knew, it could've been stolen from the U.S. Mail and repainted. Maybe Al Capone had had a hand in procuring it. She only knew that flying it gave her confidence, as well as a sense of freedom she no longer felt on the ground.

At least there'd been no need to fend off Colucci since the crash. His wife had given birth to a baby boy. The proud father had gone home for the christening and the festivities to follow. He'd left a posted schedule for the pilots and ground crew and an armed assistant to see that everybody performed their duties. This morning it was Ruby's turn to deliver a shipment to Mason Dollarhide.

On approach, Ruby's nerves sent prickles down her back and along her arms. Mack had assured her that the airstrip had been smoothed and lengthened. He'd had no problem getting in and out in the Jenny. But it wasn't the landing that triggered the quivering sensation below Ruby's ribs. It was a memory—lying on her bed, drifting awake to the gentle contact of Mason's lips on hers.

She had kept her eyes closed and willed herself not to move. But the response had shot through her body like summer lightning, setting off shimmers in the depths of her body.

When he moved away, she had drifted back into sleep. She'd awakened to find Colucci at the door and Mason behaving like a cold stranger.

When the plane touched down on the airstrip, which version of the man would be waiting for her?

But this was business and no time to be a romantic fool—especially when she could be called on to set him up and betray him to the feds.

She could see the bonfires that marked the landing strip. Even heavily loaded, the plane performed like a well-trained steed. Using the stick and rudder pedals, she made a perfect landing and taxied to a stop in front of the cave, where Mason stood waiting for her.

His expression was unreadable. He made no move toward her as she removed her goggles and helmet and climbed out of the cockpit. "I was hoping it would be you," he said. "Are you all right?"

"I'm fine. Otherwise I wouldn't be flying. Let's get this business over with." Walking over to him, she held out her hand for the payment envelope. His green eyes locked with hers as he slipped it out of his vest and placed it in her hands. She counted the bills, stowed them inside her flight jacket, and climbed back onto the wing, using a step below the exhaust pipe to reach the front cockpit.

Mason stood on the ground below, watching as she lifted out the first crate. She was strong, and she was doing a man's work. She deserved better, he thought. He'd known other men like Leo Colucci. Back in the city, they had wives who bore their children and were treated with respect. Away from home, they had the women they used. Women like Ruby.

She passed the first crate down to him. He took it from her gloved hands, set it down a few feet from the plane, and reached up for the next one. For the first few minutes they worked in silence, Ruby avoiding eye contact. But as the tension grew, Mason could no longer hold back his words.

"Are you sure you're all right, Ruby? I've been worried about you."

"If you mean my head and my shoulder, they're fine." She lifted another crate from the plane and passed it down.

"That's not what I mean. Is Colucci treating you okay?"

"I told you, he's my boss. He tells me what to do, and I do it." She hefted the last crate of whiskey, passed it down, and climbed off the wing, rubbing her shoulder. "What are you really asking, Mr. Dollarhide? Is there something else you want to know?"

Mason put the last crate on the stack with the others. As he turned back to face her, something worked its way loose in him, like the first break in a dam. The words spilled out before he could stop them.

"You're better than this business, Ruby. And you're a hundred times better than Colucci. A man like that will only ruin your life. Get away while you can, before the filthiness drags you under—like it already has me."

She stared at him. "Is that what you think—that I'm sleeping with Colucci? If it is, you're wrong. As I told you, he's my boss. My work boss. That's all."

Was she telling the truth? Mason wanted to believe her. But why should it matter? Who was this woman to him?

"I saw the way he looked at you in that hotel room, Ruby," he said. "It was like he owned you—or at least wanted to. And if you don't leave while you can, he'll take you—by any means necessary."

She took a step toward him, her dark eyes burning their challenge into his. "What's it to you? Why should you care what happens to me?"

In the heavy beat of silence that followed, Mason crossed the line that divided wisdom from desire. His hands caught her waist, pulling her against him. His mouth found hers in a crushing kiss. She resisted, but only for the briefest moment. Then her lips softened and parted. Her body responded, arms circling his neck, her curves molding to his hardened frame. Her breath came in gasps that were almost sobs. The taste of her, the womanly scent of her, like fresh earth, and the feel of her firm breasts against his chest, ignited a fire between them. He was crazy with wanting her, and he sensed that her hunger matched his own. But there was no place for the way he wanted to make love to her—not the thorny, rocky ground, not the cave—and the sun was coming up. They needed to get her plane back in the air and the contraband liquor out of sight.

It was for the best, Mason told himself as he eased her away from him. Her eyes were moist, her lips softly swollen from their kisses. Something in her look told him that this would have to be goodbye. Mason couldn't argue with that. Seeing her again wouldn't do her any favors. As men went, he wasn't much better than Leo Colucci.

"I need to go," she muttered.

"Yes, you do." He fought the urge to pull her into his arms again. "No need for words. What happened . . . happened. But if you're smart, you'll get into that plane and fly away. Go to another town, another state, anywhere but back to this life and that man."

She shook her head. "I can't. There are things you don't know. Obligations I have. My father—" She broke off, as if she'd been about to reveal too much.

"Your father is dead, Ruby. He would want you safe."

"Yes. But that can't be helped. Goodbye, Mason."

She climbed into the cockpit and donned her helmet and goggles. Without being asked, Mason spun the propeller to spark the engine, then stepped back as she taxied the plane to the far end of the landing strip and turned it around.

As the sun rose above the mountains, the plane soared into the sky. Mason watched its flight until it vanished into the clouds. For a moment he allowed himself to imagine a different future—Ruby at his side, no bootlegging, no Colucci, no secrets, just a simple, happy life, raising a family on the ranch. But that would never happen. He had broken too many laws. So had Ruby. Sooner or later, there would be a price to pay. Maybe they were already paying it.

If there had ever been a chance for them, it had passed them by.

For Ruby, the delivery to Mason's ranch had been the final run at the end of a grueling five days. Colucci would be returning next week. Meanwhile, she had earned some time off. As the driver let her off behind the Olive Hotel, she was already looking ahead to a room service meal, a hot bath, and a long night's sleep. But first she needed to contact Agent Hargrave.

After climbing the back stairs to her room, she tossed her purse and her travel bag onto the bed. Had anyone seen her come in? Could one of the maids be watching for her, ready to report her movements to Colucci? She needed to make a phone call, and she didn't want to do it from her own room.

Slipping out of the room again, she locked the door, pocketed the key, and walked to the far end of the hall. Most of the doors were closed, but a few vacant rooms had been left open for cleaning. After checking the corridor again, she stepped into the nearest one and picked up the receiver on the phone. The operator connected her with the number she requested.

The voice that answered after several rings was Hargrave's.

"Is that you, Mrs. Weaver?" He never called her by her first name. "Are you on a safe phone line?"

"I'm in a vacant room of the hotel. It's as safe as I'm going to find."

"And you've made your deliveries on schedule?" He always asked her that question.

"Yes. The new plane—the DH-4—is wonderful." She gave him a list of her customers by location, including Mason's ranch, which was no secret. Hargrave had never told her what the agents did with the information she gave them. She was kept in the dark about their activities. It made sense that they didn't trust her. Still, given the risks she took, she found it annoying that they didn't keep her better informed.

That didn't stop Ruby from wanting to know more. Today, with Colucci at a safe distance, she felt bold enough to speak up.

"How long do you expect me to keep working for you, with nothing to show for it? I don't know if I've helped you at all. I don't see anybody being arrested or any business being stopped because of what I've passed on."

Hargrave sighed. "That's because you don't see the whole picture. We could keep shutting down those small operations forever. More would just take their place. But you're giving us a pattern. We can use that pattern as evidence, to catch the man we call the Big Fish—the man running the whole illegal bootleg show in Montana."

"But who is he? If it's Leo Colucci, I can tell you everything you need to know. You can have him arrested when he steps off the train from Chicago."

"Colucci's small stuff. But he's a link. We're giving him plenty of line in the hope that he'll lead us to the Big Fish."

"What about Al Capone? Is he big enough?"

Hargrave's laugh was humorless. "Capone's out of our league. He's got his fingers in more pies than you can imagine. So far, thanks to his lawyers, he's been too smart to get nailed. But we've got our best agents on him in Chicago. The bastard will get what's coming to him—it's just a question of when."

"I see." Ruby took a deep breath. "One more question. What about my father? Is he all right? Will I get to see him, or even talk with him on the phone?"

"Not now. Any kind of communication with him would be too risky. But the warden reports he's doing fine. His health is good. He gets along with the other prisoners. He's even made a few friends."

Friends. The word, which should have cheered her, struck Ruby with an unexplained chill.

"What friends?" she demanded. "I understood he wouldn't be housed with other prisoners."

"It's nothing to be concerned about, Mrs. Weaver. Your father wouldn't be happy sitting around alone, doing nothing. He's been helping out in the prison library. The warden reports that he's doing an excellent job."

Ruby gulped back a sense of dread. Hargrave was right, she told herself. Her father had always loved books. Art would enjoy working in the library. And surely he would be safe there. All the same, something didn't feel right.

"But how much longer will he have to stay in prison? I've done everything you asked of me. I can't help it if you haven't caught your so-called Big Fish."

"Let me remind you of something, Mrs. Weaver. You and your father were both committing crimes when we caught him. We could've had you both tried and sentenced to long, hard prison terms. Instead, we gave you a chance to help us. And you have. But that doesn't mean we owe you any favors. You've no right to demand anything from us. Overstep yourself, and your father will be on a chain gang tomorrow. Do you understand?"

"I—" Ruby broke off at the sound of a creaking laundry cart coming down the hall. "I've got to go!"

She hung up the receiver and replaced the phone on the bedside table. An instant later, the laundry cart came rumbling through the door, followed by the sour-looking maid—the one who always seemed to be watching her.

"This isn't your room, missy," she said. "What are you doing in here? Did you get lost?"

Ruby managed a nervous laugh. "No, sorry. I've locked myself out of my room and can't find my key. I was just about to call the front desk and have a bellhop come to open the door. But now that you're here, you can do it for me. I know you have a master key to all the rooms."

The woman sighed. "All right. But don't start thinking I've got time to be at your beck and call. I've got work to do."

Ruby followed the maid back down the hall, chatting. "I'm so sorry. I left my purse on the bed when I went out. The key is probably in it. I won't let this happen again."

"The next time it does, you're on your own." She unlocked Ruby's door. "There."

"Wait." Ruby rushed into the room and pulled a dollar bill out of her purse. "Here's something for your trouble."

The tip was more than generous enough for a few seconds of work. The woman frowned at the bill, tucked it into the neckline of her dress and, without another word, walked back to the room where she'd left her laundry cart.

After locking the door behind her, Ruby sank onto the edge of the bed. Given the woman's behavior—always lurking nearby—

she had to be working for Colucci. What if she'd been just outside, listening to the phone conversation, then going back to get the cart and make her entrance? What if she'd heard everything, knew everything, and was waiting to tell Colucci?

Ruby's instincts screamed at her to run—grab a few essentials and catch the next train, any train that would get her out of Miles City. But if she were to flee, what would happen to her father? Art had protected her all her life. Now it was up to her to protect him.

Maybe she would be all right. Maybe the maid hadn't overheard her phone call. But she couldn't assume she was safe. There was always a chance that Colucci would find out she was working for the feds. If he confronted her, she could only brazen it out, deny everything.

And if he ordered her killed . . . what then?

As she shifted her weight to stand, her foot brushed the dress box she'd shoved partway under the bed. The box was a constant reminder of dressing up for Leo Colucci, his hands touching her, his eyes devouring her. All she'd wanted was to get it out of sight.

Even now, she battled the urge to take the box down to the alley and dump it in the trash. Or donate it to the brothel at the far end of the alley. Some poor girl would put its contents to good use. But the awful truth Ruby faced now would be that she might need the clothes herself, to buy mercy from the man who controlled her life.

Early that morning, she had stolen a moment in Mason's arms. When he'd kissed her, sensations she'd buried since the war, and her husband's tragic return, had surged through her body. For those few, precious seconds, she'd felt like a whole woman. She'd almost felt hope.

But she couldn't go back to Mason. Not now, not ever. Tell him the truth, and he would despise her for it. Keep the truth from him, and the danger could get him killed or arrested.

Her father was out of reach. She had no close friends. Whatever was to come, she would have to face it alone.

* * *

Mounted on his bay horse, Joseph led the way along the canyon trail. Lucy followed on the roan she'd borrowed from the Calder stables. Arranging to meet hadn't been easy. Joseph had been busy on the fall roundup; and Nigel Merryweather usually kept his daughter under close watch.

But young love would find a way. The two had managed to leave a few notes in the old, dead tree that stood at a backroad crossing. They'd even managed to see each other briefly in town. Today, however, was a gift. Nigel was meeting with some contractors, and Joseph's father had gone to Miles City to deposit the bank draft for the cattle he'd sold. Joseph and Lucy had a few precious hours to spend together.

"Where are you taking me?" Her laughter rang out as they wound their way along the trail. It was a beautiful day. Under a crystalline sky, the foothills were ablaze with the scarlet hues of oak and maple. Higher up on the slopes, stands of aspen had turned to patches of brilliant gold.

Joseph looked back over his shoulder, relishing the sight of her in her yellow dress, the skirt rucked to the knees to accommodate the western saddle. He ached with wanting her. But Lucy wasn't like Annabeth. She was a lady. And going beyond a few kisses would be a serious mistake.

"Joseph, where are you taking me?" she demanded again.

"It's a surprise. Wait and see." He'd never taken Annabeth to the spot in the hills where a trickling spring formed a charming pool amid the rocks, framed by ferns and mosses. Now he was glad he'd saved it for Lucy.

Years ago, the summer he was fourteen, he'd come here sometimes with his three friends to relax on the rocks and swim in the chilly water. But the four boys had gone their separate ways after that awful night when they guided bootleg smugglers to the Hollister Ranch. The feds had moved in with guns. Chase Calder had been hit and almost died trying to warn his friends. Culley O'Rourke, whose father had betrayed them for the reward, had failed to show up. Buck Haskell had turned tail. And Joseph had been saved by Logan Hunter, who would later marry his aunt. The blame for the whole mess fell squarely at the feet of Mason Dollarhide.

But all that had happened five years ago. By now, other, younger, boys must have taken over the pond. But today those boys would be in school. Joseph and Lucy would have the place to themselves.

"Oh, this is lovely!" Lucy exclaimed as Joseph swung her down from the horse. "And so romantic, like a scene from a fairy tale."

"And you're my fairy queen!" As her slippers touched the ground, Joseph gathered her into his arms. His kiss was long and deep, her innocent response igniting a firestorm in the depths of his body. He drew back, aware that his hardness against her might feel frightening. She was childlike in many ways—but all woman in her passion. It would take every ounce of his willpower to keep himself under control.

"Let's go sit on that flat rock, next to the pond. We can talk there."

Her laugh sounded slightly nervous. "Good. I was afraid you'd want to go swimming."

"Not in that water. It's ice-cold." Joseph brushed off the surface of the rock before she sat down. "I'd hoped to bring some food for a picnic, but it was all I could do to get away without being caught by my sisters. They're little tattletales."

"You're lucky to have sisters, Joseph." She tossed a pebble into the water and watched the ring of ripples fade away. "Being an only child is dismal, especially since my mother died. I'm all my father has, and he rarely lets me out of his sight. You've seen that for yourself."

Joseph reached for her hand, cradling her soft, white fingers in his. "I love you, Lucy." He had never spoken those words to any girl, not even to Annabeth.

She seemed to hesitate. His heart dropped. "I love you, too, Joseph," she said. "But that doesn't mean things are going to be easy for us."

"Your father—"

"Yes, my father. He brought me here for a reason—hopefully to wed Chase Calder."

That was no surprise. Joseph couldn't blame Nigel for wanting to marry his daughter into a wealthy family. But he didn't have to like it. "Chase already has a girlfriend," he said.

"I know. My father found out about her. He says she's dirt-poor, the daughter of a cattle thief, with no education. Not a suitable match at all."

"Do you love Chase?"

"Of course not. You know who I love. But my father says that doesn't matter. According to him, love can be learned."

Joseph swallowed his disappointment. There was still hope for him. "What if Chase doesn't want to marry you?"

She stared down at the water, avoiding his eyes. "Then I'll be expected to win his father."

Her words struck Joseph like a punch to the solar plexus, knocking the breath out of him. "But that's crazy," he said. "Webb is old enough to be your father, maybe even your grandfather. Is that how they do things in England?"

"England?" She stared at him. "Is that what you think?"

"Isn't that where you and your father came from?"

She shook her beautiful head. "Our blood may be English, but my father was born in New York City—in a one-room flat over a butcher shop. The man you've met, Nigel Merryweather . . ." Lucy took a deep breath. "That's the persona he created for himself. He has a talent for that sort of thing, and he's put it to good use."

Joseph struggled to mask his shocked expression. So the man who called himself Nigel Merryweather was nothing but a con artist. Lucy had just given him a powerful, and dangerous, piece of information. But why?

"What about you?" he asked. "Are you really his daughter?"

"Yes. He and my mother were never wed, but he took me in when she died and raised me to be a proper lady. I owe him for that, as he often reminds me."

Joseph checked the impulse to put his arms around her. He sensed that she was asking for comfort. But her revelation had come as a shock. He needed to know more.

"So, does your father really know how to build an airfield?"

"Only what he's read. But he can be very convincing. The airfield will be built, but for a lot less than Webb Calder will be paying. My father is passing himself off as a rich engineer with an estate in Canada. He's been proving it with the Canadian liquor he brings in as a gift for Webb. I have no idea where the liquor is coming from, but he's also been selling enough to provide us with spending money."

Joseph had an idea where the bootleg liquor might be coming from. But that wasn't his problem now. He took a deep breath and asked the most puzzling question of all. "Lucy, this is dangerous information. It could get you and your father in a lot of trouble. Why are you telling me?"

She turned toward him. "Because I trust you. I know you love me, and I've nowhere else to turn."

He seized her hand. "You know I'd do anything for you. What do you need? Are you in some kind of trouble?"

"Not the kind you might think. I haven't done anything wrong. But there's something I haven't told you."

"Tell me, Lucy. You can tell me anything."

Tears welled in her eyes. "It's . . . Webb. The other night he came into my room. He kissed me, and . . . put his hands on me. When I threatened to scream, he backed off. But he was laughing. He said he'd be back—and something about making it worth my time." She was trembling, on the verge of breaking down in sobs.

Joseph's grip tightened on her hand. He'd known the Calders all his life. Never had he imagined that Webb would take advantage of a young girl. But then he remembered Webb's past—his illicit courtship of a young immigrant wife. Now Chase had made a move on young Maggie O'Rourke, who was barely out of her childhood. Maybe the trait was passed down from father to son.

Or more likely, it was the Calder arrogance, the belief that they could take whatever they wanted.

"Who knows about this, Lucy?" he demanded. "Have you told your father?"

"I did. He was actually pleased. He said that Webb's attention could work in our favor, especially if I let him get me . . . with child." It was as if she could barely speak the words. "I can't stay there, Joseph. I've got to get away."

I could marry you, Lucy.

The words were poised on the tip of Joseph's tongue, but caution and common sense held them back. He was too young to wed. And what about his dream of becoming a pilot? Marriage would mean the end of his freedom. He'd be stuck on the ranch, caring for his family. There had to be another way to help her.

"Do you have anywhere to go?" he asked.

"I've got an aunt in Texas. If I could get there, she'd take me in and help me find work. But it's a long way, and train fare is expensive. My father doesn't give me any money—I think he knows I might try to run away. It's not that he cares about me. He worships the wealth the Calders have—and he's capable of using me to get a piece of it."

"My family isn't poor," Joseph said. "Between the ranch and the sawmill, we Dollarhides probably have more cash in the bank than Webb does. Of course, it isn't *my* money. My father controls it, and he hangs onto every cent."

"Heavens, Joseph, I would never ask you for money," Lucy said. "But if you insist on helping me, I promise to pay you back as soon as I get work. I'll send you money every month until the loan is paid off—with interest of course."

"Don't worry about interest. How could I leave you at the mercy of men like your father and Webb Calder?"

"The Harvest Dance is this Saturday. If you can get me the money by then, I can leave that night." She lowered her gaze. "Of course, you can always say no. This is my problem, not yours, Joseph."

"That's not true," he said. "I love you, Lucy. If I were older, I'd ask you to marry me. But that will have to wait." He drew her into his arms. "Will you wait for me?"

"Of course, I will! And I'll write every week." She raised her eager face for his kiss. Joseph's heart drummed with a fragile happiness. But even as he lowered his lips to hers, one thought nagged at him, refusing to be still.

What if he'd talked his way into a promise he couldn't keep?

CHAPTER TWELVE

*C*OLUCCI WAS BACK AFTER HIS SON'S CHRISTENING. SO FAR, THERE'D been no mention of Ruby's telephone call. Hopefully, the hotel maid had missed overhearing. But Colucci could be holding back, playing her like a cat with a mouse. That would be like him.

The strain was beginning to tell on Ruby. A rare glimpse in the mirror showed bloodshot eyes framed by shadows in a tense, tired face. She was grateful for the work that kept everyone busy at the farm and saved her from facing Colucci alone. A new shipment had appeared by camouflaged truck from its mysterious secret source. There would be no rest until every crate had been delivered and every cent of the money collected and turned in.

The two pilots were the busiest of all. Ruby and Mack would be living on coffee and sandwiches for most of the week, working on the planes, loading cargo, and catching a few hours of sleep when they could. Most of the flying was done in the hours before dawn, when there was barely enough light to see the landing strips. It was dangerous work for tired eyes and overtaxed brains. Having a third pilot would ease the workload. But there'd been no mention of bringing on more help.

Colucci had made out the roster. Ruby had been assigned to the Jenny—possibly a sign of Colucci's displeasure. In the morning Mack would be taking a turn at the DH-4 and making the delivery to Mason at the Hollister Ranch. That was just as well, Ruby told herself. She and Mason were poison for each other. If she never saw him again, it would be safer for her and for him.

In the hour before dawn, Ruby and Mack finished their coffee, made a final inspection of their loaded planes, and prepared for takeoff. Ruby's destination was familiar, a long but easy flight. Mack had practiced takeoffs and landings in the DH-4, but this would be his first delivery. Ruby could sense his excitement as he climbed into the newer plane to take off ahead of her.

Ruby gave him a wave. "Enjoy the flight!" she called.

He grinned, settled into the cockpit, and with a hand from the ground crew, started the engine. Ruby watched him taxi onto the runway and glide into the air. Then she pulled down her goggles and prepared to make her own flight in the Jenny.

The dawn air was chilly. Mason had lit a small fire to signal the plane and take the edge off the cold. Would Ruby be making the delivery? He remembered their last time together and that blistering kiss. It had been a mistake, giving in to the temptation of that lovely, sensual mouth. He knew better than to let it happen again. But how could he be sorry? How could any man regret the way he'd felt as he held her in his arms?

As he thrust his hands into his vest to warm them, his fingers touched the belt buckle in his pocket—the one he'd found in the ashes after burning out the cave. He'd almost forgotten it was there.

After scanning the sky and finding it empty, he took the buckle out of his pocket and studied it in the flickering light of the fire. He'd puzzled over it before, but the mystery remained.

The date of the rodeo suggested that the wearer was no longer young. But it was the initials, *R.T.*, that struck a hidden chord. Why couldn't he remember?

Mason's thoughts were interrupted by the drone of an approaching plane. Even at a distance, he recognized the sound of the Rolls-Royce engine. The plane was the De Havilland. His pulse quickened. He dropped the buckle into his pocket, lit a stick of kindling from the fire he'd made, and used it to ignite the miniature blazes he'd laid along the runway.

He could see the plane now, a speck against the fading dawn sky, growing larger by the second. It was coming in low—too low, as if carrying too much weight in the front cargo bay. Worry tightened a knot in Mason's stomach. By now, Ruby would be experienced with the plane. She would know what she was doing. Still, he'd seen enough landings to recognize a steep descent. He didn't like what he saw.

His throat jerked tight, cutting off a cry as the plane swooped in low and fast. It met the earth at a sharp angle and plowed nose first into the runway, raising a cloud of dust as it crumpled like a paper toy.

Ruby! She was the only thing on his mind as he raced down the runway, plunging toward the wreck. But as he reached the plane, he could tell that the pilot, slumped over the controls, wasn't a woman. It was the young man who'd delivered cargo here before.

Even as he unfastened the seat belt and lifted the inert body to drag it out of the cockpit, Mason knew that the fellow was dead. Above the rim of his shattered goggles, his crushed forehead, embedded with glass from the windscreen, gave mute evidence of what had happened. Mason cursed as he hefted the slight weight. The pilot was small, not much more than a boy. He was somebody's son, perhaps somebody's brother, friend, or sweetheart as well. Mason had liked him. He had been friendly and cheerful, even at that godawful hour of the morning. He had never offered his name.

Tragedies happened in life, especially in a dirty business like this one. But the young pilot's death had been so wrong. Such a waste.

The fuel line was leaking. He could smell the fumes. If the engine was hot enough, it could touch off another explosion. But if Mason wanted to keep doing business with Leo Colucci, he would have to try to salvage the cargo.

After laying the pilot's body at a safe distance from the wreck and covering it with a spare tarp, he ran back to the plane and climbed into the cockpit. Unloading cargo with a single pair of hands was awkward. The crates had to be lowered from the front cockpit onto the wings, and from there to the ground. The whole time, Mason could smell the gasoline fumes. The fuselage and wings of the DH-4 were fashioned of wood, with cloth glued over the surface. Once ignited, the plane would become a torch.

As he worked, Mason swore a string of the vilest curses he could imagine. He cursed Colucci. He cursed the business and the twist of fate that had killed the young pilot. He cursed the cargo—the contraband liquor that was worth more than human lives. Last of all, he cursed himself for ever thinking that boot-legging was an easy shortcut to riches, and the fact that he was in too deep to walk away.

By the time Mason had unloaded the crates, a breeze had come up, cooling the engine and blowing the gasoline fumes away from the wrecked plane. With that danger passed, he lugged the cargo into the depths of the cave and moved the dead pilot under the shelter of the entrance. After wrapping the body in the tarp to protect it from scavengers, he mounted up and rode back to the house. It was time to phone Colucci and give him the bad news.

Ruby returned from her flight to find Colucci waiting for her alone in the kitchen. Handing her a cup of hot, black coffee, he told her about Mack's death. The news brought a surge of tears. She'd allowed herself to feel a sisterly affection for the young pilot. Here at the farmhouse, he'd been the closest thing she had to a friend. She would miss him.

"Damned lousy timing," Colucci muttered. "Dollarhide saved the cargo, but the plane's a total loss. I told him to burn it and bury the body someplace where it won't be found."

"What about Mack's people?" Still standing, Ruby sipped her coffee. "I know that he had a sweetheart. He probably had a family as well. Shouldn't someone be notified?"

"That's not my problem, or yours," Colucci growled. "When you sign on for this business, you don't have people anymore. Sooner or later, if they don't hear from him, the boy's family—if he has any—will figure out what must've happened."

Ruby knew better than to point out that what he said wasn't true of Colucci. He had a family. But she knew better. She would mourn her young friend privately. But the immediate concern was, with most of the current shipment left to deliver, there was only one plane—the Jenny—and she was the only pilot.

"I can't do it all," she said. "You're going to have to find a second plane and pilot."

"Capone's going to be sore about that," Colucci said. "He pulled strings to get us that De Havilland. I can probably find another pilot, and there are Jennies on the market. But that will take time. For the next few days, you'll be flying double shifts. That's the only way we can keep to our delivery schedule."

"Can't you change the schedule? If I'm too exhausted to keep a clear head in the air, you could end up with no plane and no pilot."

Colucci's gaze darkened. "Drink more coffee if you have to. The schedule is set, and you'll do as you're told."

"What if it's too much? What if I say no?"

The flat of Colucci's hand struck the side of her head, setting off explosions in her brain. Flashes of light seemed to pass in front of her eyes. The cup she'd been holding shattered on the floor.

As her vision cleared, she saw Colucci glaring down at her, his face a florid mask of rage.

"I let you tell me no just once, Ruby." His voice grated between clenched teeth. "With me, one *no* is all you get!"

His hand caught her wrist. Whipping her around, he dragged her out of the kitchen and into the hall toward the bedroom he used when he stayed at the farm. Ruby twisted and struggled, kicking and scratching. But his grip was like iron, and any pain she inflicted only heightened his rage. They were alone in the house. If she screamed, no one would hear—or even dare to come to her rescue.

"You need me, Colucci!" she gasped as he kicked open the bedroom door. "I'm the only pilot you've got. If I'm not fit to fly, you'll be in a bad way! You'll have nobody to deliver the goods!"

He paused, panting like a winded bull. Had she reached him? Or was he beyond any kind of control?

As if in answer to a silent prayer, came the one sound that could stop him—the urgent ringing of the telephone.

The phone was in the kitchen, and no one was there to answer it. With a muttered snarl, he flung Ruby aside and stalked back up the hallway to answer it.

Ruby could hear his voice now. She could tell from his submissive tone that he was talking with someone important, maybe Capone. If she stayed, she might learn something she could pass on to Agent Hargrave. But Ruby had had enough. She got her feet under her, left the house by the front door, and rushed around to the hangar where the ground crew was loading the Jenny for the next delivery. Picking up a crate, she pitched in to help.

For now, she would work the double shift without complaint. Keeping busy would be the best way to avoid Colucci. When she was on the ground, she would make every effort to keep from being alone with him. He had a temper, but he also knew that he depended on her as a pilot. She'd be walking a tightrope—but hadn't she been doing that all along?

The harvest celebration had become a time-honored tradition in Blue Moon. The day was given over to a children's parade in the morning, picnicking and games in the afternoon, and in the evening, the most anticipated event of all—the Harvest Dance, held outdoors on a raised wooden platform, overhung with electric lights.

When Jake had invited her to go as his date, Britta had turned him down. Hadn't they created enough gossip? The boys in her class hadn't stopped giggling behind their hands. They'd even made up a song about her, which they sang at recess. When she went shopping, she could swear that the women in the store were giving her slit-eyed looks. Her job depended on her being respectable. Any day now, she expected to be called to account, maybe even fired.

Jake had been visibly disappointed, but he hadn't asked her again. Maybe he would come to his senses and ask one of the pretty young women who turned their heads as he passed.

Now, with the moon rising over the peaks, she sat in her rocker on the back porch, listening to the first notes of music that came from the dance less than a block away. She'd heard about the new dances in the city—dances with names like Turkey Trot and Black Bottom. But tonight, the old-time band was playing traditional music—waltzes, polkas, foxtrots, and two-steps.

One of the few magical moments of her life had happened on a night, five years ago, when she'd come to the dance to keep an eye on her younger sister. No one had noticed her until the tall sheriff had walked up and asked her to dance. They'd drifted around the floor, moving in perfect harmony, as if they'd been made to dance together. Then the music had ended. She'd seen more of Jake, but tragedy had struck, pulling her away from him. When she'd emerged from her grief, he was gone.

Jake had passed through his own dark place. Now he was ready to move on and find a new mother for his little girl. But Britta was older now and still smarting from the old hurts. Jake would be better off starting fresh, with someone younger. Besides, Britta told herself, there were worse fates than being an old maid.

A shadow moved under the eaves of the porch. Jake stepped into the moonlight, his Colt Peacemaker holstered at his hip.

Britta gasped, then recovered. "Why aren't you at the dance, Jake? Where's Marissa?"

"Marissa is spending the night with her grandmother," he said. "As for the dance, it's my job to be there in case of any trouble. I'm on the way now. But before I go . . ." He cleared his throat. "There's only one girl I want to dance with, and she's right here." He stood before her with a slight bow. "May I have this dance with you, Miss Anderson?"

The music was a slow foxtrot, not so different from the one Britta remembered. With a smile, she rose and floated into his arms. The magic returned as he held her, dancing her around the porch, the moonlight soft upon them. But the spell was brief. As the music ended, he stepped back. "I have to go," he said. "You can still come with me, Britta."

She shook her head. "I look a fright—my hair, my dress. And I'm still worried about the gossip. You go ahead. You and Marissa will be welcome for Sunday dinner tomorrow."

"We'll see about that." His manner had chilled. "Enjoy your evening."

He was gone then, as silently as he'd come. Britta settled back into the chair. She could still hear the music—a livelier tune this time. But the peace of the evening had fled with the man she loved.

She gazed up at the cold moon, wondering. Had she just made the biggest mistake of her life?

Joseph stood at the edge of the dance floor, his eyes scanning the crowd. Electric lights strung from wires lit the floor and the parking lot on the near side. Dressed in their best, dancers twirled, stomped, and paraded to the music. His parents hadn't come to the dance. Neither had his aunt Kristin and her husband or the Calders, but there were plenty of farm families, ranchers, and cowboys enjoying themselves. He spotted Annabeth with her new beau. She looked pretty, in a tiny-waisted sky-blue dress with patent leather shoes on her feet. Joseph felt a wave of relief that he hadn't gotten her pregnant and ruined both their lives.

But the one person he'd come to meet was nowhere in sight. Where was Lucy? Had she changed her mind about running away to Texas? Had her father learned about her plans and prevented her from leaving the house?

Looking across the floor, he could see Sheriff Calhoun keeping watch over the crowd. Maybe, Joseph thought, he could go to the sheriff, tell him about Nigel's plan to cheat Webb Calder, and have the man arrested. But it was too soon for such a desperate measure—and it still might not save Lucy from Webb's clutches. He would give her more time.

His hand touched the bundle in his vest pocket—two hundred dollars in bills wrapped in a red bandanna. Unable to come up with a better plan, Joseph had done the unthinkable. He had taken the money from the cash box in his father's desk. He had never stolen anything in his life—but since he planned to pay the money back somehow, it was more like a loan. Besides, it was for a good cause. How could he leave an innocent girl like Lucy at the mercy of a lecherous old man like Webb Calder?

But where was she? His eyes searched the crowd. He couldn't see Annabeth any longer. Her boyfriend was alone, waiting on the sidelines. Maybe she'd gone to the privy that was set up behind the hardware store.

Autos, buggies, and wagons crowded the street and the lot surrounding the dance. Lucy would need a way to get here, Joseph reminded himself. She'd mentioned that Chase might bring her, but he wasn't here. Maybe he'd dropped her off and gone to meet his girl.

She would also need a ride to Miles City to catch the midnight train. Joseph had offered to drive her in his father's Model T, which he'd borrowed for the dance. But she'd pointed out the risk of his father finding out and telling Webb where she'd gone. Joseph would already be giving her the money. He'd be in enough trouble when Blake checked the cash box. She'd assured him she could find another way. Once she had the money, she could find a cab or pay somebody to drive her.

He was wondering how long he dared wait when he felt a light touch at his elbow. He turned around to see Lucy smiling up at him.

"I was afraid you weren't coming," he said. "How did you get here?"

"I found a way," she said. "Have you got the money?"

"Right here." He touched his vest. Her eyes gleamed as she held out her hand.

"One more thing," he said. "I don't know how soon we'll be together again. I'd like one dance with my girl."

"All . . . right." She seemed hesitant but moved into his arms as the music started. They glided around the floor, but Lucy was rigid and anxious in his arms. Partway through the dance, he stopped and led her to a shadowed corner. "I can see that you need to go, Lucy," he said, handing her the money. "Good luck. Write to me. I'll come for you when I can."

She slipped the bills inside her dress and returned the bandanna. "Thank you, Joseph," she said. "You've saved me. I'll never forget you."

She kissed his cheek and slipped away, vanishing into the crowd. Joseph gazed after her, puzzled by her abrupt manner and her words, *I'll never forget you.*

Just then, Annabeth pushed through the crowd. Out of breath, she seized Joseph's arm and pulled him aside. "That girl you were dancing with, Joseph, did you give her anything?" she demanded.

"I did. Why should you care?"

"I was coming back from the privy when I passed a parked car. That girl—she was in it with a man. I saw them kissing and heard her say something like, 'Wait for me here. I'll be back as soon as he gives me the money.'"

Joseph stared at her, speechless as the truth sank home. Lucy had taken him for two hundred dollars of his family's money to run away with an unknown man. Her story about Webb had probably been a lie. But he hadn't taken time to think. He'd been besotted enough to believe her.

Annabeth shook his shoulder. "Maybe you can still stop them. Hurry. I'll get the sheriff."

Shaking off his shock, Joseph cleared a way through the crowd and raced out to the parking lot. He wasn't sure where to look for Lucy until he saw an older Model T with Lucy inside. A strange man in a suit was frantically working the crank in an effort to start the engine.

"Stop!" Joseph shouted. The man cranked harder. The engine coughed, coughed again, and caught with a roar. The man sprinted around the car for the driver's seat.

Sheriff Calhoun had come out to the parking lot, following Annabeth. "Hands up," he shouted, drawing his Colt. "Back away from the car."

The next part happened so fast that Joseph was helpless to stop it. The stranger pulled a pistol out of his coat and fired two shots at the sheriff. As Jake Calhoun dropped to the ground, the man vaulted into the car and gunned the engine. Tires spitting gravel, the Model T sped away, down the main street, headed out of town.

The sound of shots and Annabeth's scream brought people pouring out of the dance. Someone bent over the fallen sheriff. Joseph heard a shout.

"He's hit bad! Somebody get to a phone and call the doctor!"

Britta heard the shots. In the next instant, she was off the porch, running. She'd heard enough gunfire in her life to recognize the sound of a big gun like Jake's Colt Peacemaker. The shots she'd heard were from a smaller-caliber weapon—which meant that Jake could have been their target.

As she took the shortcut through the block, she could hear autos tearing along Main Street, as if in hot pursuit. But she couldn't concern herself with that now. She plunged ahead.

The dance had been set up less than a block from the school. Britta reached it in minutes. The overhanging lights cast shadows over the crowd in the parking lot. She fought her way to where a knot of people surrounded a figure on the ground. Even before she saw him, Britta knew it would be Jake.

He lay in the dust, where he'd fallen on his back. His eyes were open, his face a grayish white. The sight of him tore at her heart. If she'd gone with him tonight, events might have transpired differently. But this was no time for emotion, only action.

"I'm here, Jake," she said.

His lips moved, but no words emerged. He was probably in shock. A lanky figure was crouched over him, struggling with a couple of handkerchiefs to stanch the wounds in his shoulder and hip. It was Joseph.

People were standing around him, some watching, some offering advice. Heedless of modesty, Britta pulled off her muslin petticoat, ripped it in two, and dropped down beside Joseph. He turned his head to look at her. His face was streaked with tears. "This is my fault, Aunt Britta," he said.

"That doesn't matter now. Where's the doctor?"

"She's not here. Somebody went to telephone her. I'm afraid to move him until she comes. It could make the bleeding worse."

"She could be a while." Britta thrust a piece of the torn petticoat at him. "Here, bunch this up and press it hard on that hip wound. All we can do is try to stop the bleeding and get him stabilized. Have somebody bring a blanket to keep him warm—and some water."

Jake was losing blood. Too much blood. With a silent prayer, Britta focused her strength on applying pressure to the wound. All that mattered now was saving him.

CHAPTER THIRTEEN

DR. KRISTIN DOLLARHIDE HUNTER ARRIVED THIRTY-FIVE MINUTES later in the Ford Model TT truck that served as a makeshift ambulance. She had driven at breakneck speed over the washboard road from her ranch. The vehicle was coated with dust.

By then, most of the crowd had moved off. The dance band was still playing. There were couples on the floor, but a pall had fallen over the celebration.

Britta and Joseph had managed to stanch Jake's wounds, but he'd already lost a dangerous amount of blood. From every indication, the bullets were still buried in his flesh. He drifted in and out of consciousness, muttering incoherent words and phrases.

"Get him to my surgery. Now," the doctor ordered, referring to her office at the far end of town. There was a stretcher in the back of the truck. Joseph found someone to help ease the wounded sheriff onto it and lift him into the truck bed. Britta could have ridden in the cab with the doctor. Instead, she climbed into the back to huddle beside the stretcher, gripping Jake's hand.

"Hold on, Jake," she murmured, hoping he could hear her. "I'm here. I won't leave you."

Joseph sat across from her, helping to balance the stretcher for the ride. While waiting for the doctor, he'd told Britta what he'd done and what had happened. "This is all my fault," he said again. "If he dies, I'll never forgive myself."

The doctor's office was in a remodeled home with the surgery room in back. Laid out on the operating table, his bloodied clothes cut away, the sheriff was sedated with ether while the doctor probed for the two bullets.

Gloved and masked, Britta had been pressed into assisting. Away from the office, she and Kristin were longtime friends. But this was a life-or-death situation. Kristin the doctor was giving orders to be obeyed without question.

This was no time for emotion. But every time Britta glanced at Jake's pale face, she felt a wrenching tug at her heart. Why hadn't she summoned her courage, faced the gossip, and gone to the dance with him?

What if she'd been so afraid of public opinion that she'd missed her last chance to tell Jake she loved him?

The sterilized forceps probed deep, then deeper. The bullet from the shoulder wound had come to rest beneath his collarbone. By a near miracle, it had missed vital organs and blood vessels. With some careful maneuvering, it was out.

But the lower wound was another story. Britta watched the perspiration bead on her friend's forehead as she probed the wound, following the trail of the bullet. As a former military doctor, she'd treated soldiers during the Great War. She was acquainted with all kinds of gunshot wounds. Now Britta could see that she was worried. Jake was in the best possible hands, but the signs didn't look good.

Britta found Jake's hand and gripped it hard as the probe went deeper. A shudder passed through his body as the doctor found the bullet, worked it free with the forceps, and brought it out. With a long exhalation, she dropped the slug into a metal dish. Britta sponged her perspiring forehead with a pad of gauze.

"What now?" Britta ventured to ask.

"All we can do is clean him up, dress his wounds, and hope for the best."

"Will he be all right?" Britta spoke through the tightness in her throat.

"The bullet didn't penetrate the abdominal cavity. But as nearly as I could tell, it nicked the hip joint and struck the spine. We won't know how much damage it did until he wakes up."

Britta went cold. "Are you saying he might be paralyzed?"

"Don't borrow trouble," the doctor said. "All we can do is wait and hope."

Sick with worry and remorse, Joseph was waiting in the front room when his aunt Kristin walked in. She'd removed her mask and gloves but still wore her blood-spattered surgical gown.

He rose from the armchair to meet her. "Will the sheriff be all right?" he asked.

She looked exhausted after nearly two hours in surgery. "He'll probably live, if that's what you mean. But one bullet did a lot of damage. We won't know the full extent until he wakes up. We've moved him into the bedroom. Britta is with him now."

Joseph's eyes burned from dust and weeping. "Is there anything I can do?"

"You've already done quite enough." Her gaze was stern. "Britta told me about the girl and the money. How could you have been so irresponsible, Joseph?"

"I . . . thought I was doing the right thing," he replied, feeling more wretched than he could ever remember in his life. "She told me—"

"Never mind," Kristin said. "Britta called your mother after we arrived here and told her what happened. She said she'd tell your father. He'll be walking in that door any minute. You can tell him your side of the story, and he can decide what to do with you. I'm going to get cleaned up and check on my patient." She turned and walked out of the room.

Joseph sank back into the chair and buried his face in his hands. It wasn't his fault that Lucy's secret beau had shot the sheriff, was it? If Annabeth hadn't warned him, the couple would have made a clean getaway. No one would have been shot. But who was he kidding? Annabeth had done what any responsible person would do. He had no one to blame for this mess but himself.

What was he going to say to his father?

As if the thought had summoned Blake Dollarhide, Joseph heard the roar of a large truck engine outside. Since his father had lent him the Model T for tonight, Blake had commandeered one of the new delivery trucks from the sawmill to get here.

The engine went silent. Joseph heard the slamming of a metal door and the heavy tread of footsteps coming up the walk to the front stoop. The door opened without a knock.

Blake, dressed in dusty work clothes, stepped through the door and closed it behind him. His expression was rigid, his eyes like the flash of sheet lightning before a storm—contained fury, deadly but distant, hinting at the full storm that was due to break any moment.

The look on his father's face—a look Joseph had never seen before—struck terror into his heart. He stood, trembling before his father's cold anger.

"How is the sheriff?" Blake's tone was flat, without emotion.

"Aunt Kristin says he's going to live. We'll know more when he wakes up." Joseph forced himself to meet Blake's chilling gaze. "Did they catch the man who shot him . . . and the girl?"

"Not that I've heard. I telephoned Webb and told him what had happened. He said he'd deal with Merriweather, whatever that means. As for Webb trying to molest the girl, I told him about it. He swore to God it wasn't true. I may not like the man, but I believe him. A few years ago, he courted your aunt Kristin. She said he never laid an ungentlemanly hand on her." He paused, his gaze narrowing. "That leaves your part in all this, Joseph."

"I'm sorry, Dad."

"It's a bit late for that, don't you think?" Blake's expression darkened as his anger pushed to the surface. "Most of the time, I manage to forget that you're not really my son. But some things can't be changed. You've got Mason's blood in you, and Amelia's. I've tried to raise you right, but that blood is part of who you are—a part that I can't just wish away."

Joseph felt as if he'd been kicked in the stomach. Of all the things Blake could say to him, this had to be the cruelest.

"When you got involved with Mason before, and he ended up going to prison, I hoped you'd learned your lesson. But you just robbed our family of two hundred dollars, gave it to a girl to run away, and got an innocent man shot. I've got half a mind to wash my hands of you and dump you on your real father's doorstep. He could teach you the bootlegging business—you know he's doing it again, don't you? What do you think those airplanes flying over the house are all about? Hell, if you want to fly, he could probably have you trained. Just say the word, boy. I'll drop you off on the way home."

Tears welled in Joseph's eyes and flowed down his cheeks. He'd expected to be shouted at, maybe even slapped, and sentenced to punishment. But what Blake had just said to him was ten times worse than that. He felt shame, humiliation, and stark, cold fear. He began to sob.

"I really am sorry, Dad. I only wanted to help Lucy. I didn't mean for anybody to get hurt. And I planned to earn the money and pay it back. I've made such an awful mess of things. Please . . ." he begged. "Please let me make it up to you."

Blake shook his head. A long sigh rose from deep in his body. "Anything I do for you now, I do because of your mother and sisters," he said. "I may never fully trust you again, Joseph. But I'm willing to give you a job in the sawmill. You'll have room and board at home and the salary that I pay my least skilled workers. The money you earn will go to pay back what you stole. When that debt is wiped out, then we'll talk. And there'll be no mention of flying while you're under my roof. Agreed?"

Joseph hated the sawmill—the deafening noise, the dust, and the dangerous, backbreaking work. But knowing Blake, this was the best offer he was going to get. He could go to Mason and have a very different life, probably on the wrong side of the law. Was that what he wanted? What about his mother and sisters? What about his future?

He stared down at his boots, then cleared his throat. "Agreed," he mumbled.

"How's that again?"

"Agreed," Joseph said.

Blake nodded. "Then I hope you'll show me the man you can become. Break your word, and we're done. Understood?"

"Understood." Joseph had known that Blake wouldn't let him off easy. Working full-time in the sawmill would be hell, but it was no worse than he deserved. What hurt even more was that he'd let himself be taken in by Lucy's lies. His actions hadn't only been wrong—they'd been stupid. It would be a long time before he forgave himself, and even longer before he trusted a pretty woman.

Kristin came back into the room. She'd discarded her blood-spattered surgical gown and washed her hands and face. She strode to her brother. They shared a quick embrace. "I'm sorry about all this," she said.

"It's being taken care of," Blake replied. "How's the sheriff?"

"Still asleep, but he's not out of the woods. All we can do is hope."

"I'd like to be here when he wakes up," Joseph said. "I need to tell him I'm sorry. I can drive the car home from the parking lot at the dance. Is that all right, Dad?" He glanced from Kristin to Blake.

Blake frowned and shook his head. "It's getting late. The work-day starts early tomorrow. You'll leave now, with me. We'll pick up the car and you can drive it home."

"What about the sheriff?" Joseph asked.

"You can come back and see him later. But I'm not turning you loose again tonight. You've done enough damage. Come on, let's go."

Joseph knew better than to argue. Feeling like a whipped mutt, he followed Blake out the door to the truck. His well-deserved punishment had already started.

He imagined Lucy in the car flying through the night with her secret lover. Joseph hadn't recognized the man, except that he'd been dressed in a dark suit, like a traveling salesman or a gambler. The fact that he'd carried a pistol and hadn't hesitated to use it on a lawman didn't speak well of him.

Joseph could only hope that the pair would be arrested soon. If the sheriff in Miles City had been alerted, he would have his deputies watching the train station. But what if no one had called him? The man who should have made such a call—Sheriff Jake Calhoun—was lying wounded and helpless.

After the shooting, a few citizens had given chase in their autos. But the fugitives had a head start. They were also clever and dangerous. The pursuit would be little more than a gesture. Lucy and her gun-toting companion were ahead of the pack. They could already be safely on their way to freedom.

Britta sat on a straight-backed chair watching Jake's sleeping face in the lamplight. His vital signs were good, his heartbeat steady, his breathing regular. So far, he'd shown no sign of infection. But he was weak from blood loss. Kristin had told her he needed rest, and that she shouldn't worry if he slept for a while. So she sat and hoped and prayed.

Life had given her a second chance with the man she loved. But she'd been too proud and too insecure to take it. Was she too late? Could she summon her courage and take flight, as she had when she'd climbed into the plane?

As the front room clock struck two, Kristin walked into the room. Leaning over Jake she laid a hand on his forehead, listened to his breathing, and checked his pulse. "Everything's stable," she said. "You look all in, Britta. Why don't you get some rest? Or you can help yourself to the coffee I just brewed in the kitchen. I can sit with him for a while."

"I'll be fine, and I need to be here." Britta smoothed a lock of hair back from Jake's pale forehead. "He asked me to go to the dance. I said no. I didn't want to be talked about, even laughed at. Maybe if I'd been there, Jake wouldn't have been shot."

"You love him, don't you?"

"Of course I do. I've never loved anyone else. But look at me— a big, awkward, homely old maid. Jake could do so much better."

"Jake would've married you before if you hadn't pushed him away," Kristin said. "When your father and sister died, all he wanted was to comfort you. You wouldn't let him. But he still sees the beauty in you, Britta, even if you refuse to see it yourself. Don't be a fool this time. Let him love you."

As she spoke, Jake began to stir. He groaned softly. His eyelids twitched, fluttered, and opened. For the first few seconds, his eyes shifted in confusion. Then his gaze focused on Britta's face. "What . . . happened?" he muttered. "Where am I?"

"You're at the doctor's." Leaning over him, Britta squeezed his hand. "You were shot at the dance. Do you remember?"

He frowned. "Yeah . . . the bastard had a gun, he was getting into his car with a girl. I heard shots and went down. Hurt like hell . . ." He strained to sit up, wincing at the pain in his shoulder. "Let me up. I've got a job to do."

"Lie down. You're not going anywhere." Kristin eased him back onto the pillow. "I managed to dig two bullets out of you, but you've lost a lot of blood, and you're still weak. You're lucky to be alive."

His gaze shifted to Britta. "What are you doing here?" he asked.

"She's been here all night," Kristin said. "She hasn't left your side."

"I'm sorry, Jake." Britta pressed her lips to the back of his hand. "If I'd been with you at the dance, the timing might have been different."

"You couldn't have known. Nobody could. You might have been shot, too." His hand tightened around hers. "I care about you, Britta. And when I get out of this bed, I intend to do something about it."

She gave him a smile, her heart singing. "If that's a promise, I'll hold you to it."

He raised his head slightly. "I smell fresh coffee coming from somewhere. As long as I'm awake, I could use a cup. And I'm ready to sit up and drink it." He pushed partway to a sitting position and started to turn.

His expression froze.

"What is it?" Kristen had started for the kitchen. She turned around.

"It's my legs." Jake's voice was a hoarse whisper. "I can't move them. I can't even feel them."

Mason stood on the landing strip, watching the kerosene-doused remains of the De Havilland plane go up in flames. The wooden shell and the wings would be ashes in no time. The metal parts of the plane would be buried or scattered after the ashes cooled.

Mason stepped back from the heat and thrust his hands into his pockets. The smoke from the burning plane stung his eyes. This was not the way he'd imagined the bootlegging business.

The body of the young pilot had been wrapped in a tarp and buried in the scrub, in a spot where coyotes, deer, and maybe a few rabbits and birds would be the only visitors. The boy, as Mason had come to think of him, would have no service and no marker, not even a crude wooden cross to mark his resting place. His loved ones, assuming he had any, would never know what had become of him.

Mason had delivered the contraband liquor he'd salvaged from the wrecked plane. He'd had customers waiting, although Webb Calder's English friend hadn't been one of them. Maybe he and Webb had had a falling-out.

He had buried the body right after talking to Colucci. But he'd left the burning of the plane until the whiskey was sold. Mason's customers were already clamoring for more. But, as far as he knew, Colucci was down to one plane and one pilot—and where did that leave Ruby? Surely she couldn't be expected to carry out the deliveries by herself.

Mason was worried about his supply. But he was even more worried about Ruby. Why hadn't she made the last delivery? Was she all right? Had she crashed her plane, maybe been arrested? Or had she finally come to her senses, left Colucci, and fled to safety?

For a moment he imagined her coming to him for protection—imagined taking her in his arms, prepared to fight off all threats. But that wasn't going to happen. He'd be better off addressing his dwindling supply line.

He no longer trusted Leo Colucci, if he ever had. It was time he went over Colucci's head to the real boss in charge of the operation—Julius Taviani, the puppet master.

Mason didn't know all the old man's secrets. But he was aware that Taviani had enough of the prison staff in his pocket to get him whatever he needed. Telephone calls in and out at any hour were no problem. Bundles of cash or cigarettes—common currency in the prison—were freely smuggled past the guards. Drugs, knives, and even guns could be had for the right favors. Mason knew all this because he'd often acted as an intermediary, passing on messages and goods. He wasn't proud of what he'd done, but being Taviani's right-hand man had enabled him to survive prison conditions and taught him some valuable lessons.

They had parted on good terms. Taviani had even set him up for business with Colucci. But now that he needed a favor, Mason would have to watch his words with the old man. The puppet master hadn't survived this long by trusting people, not even his friends. And he had never revealed the secret source of his Canadian whiskey supply.

Mason knew better than to ask him for that secret. But if he was to grow his business, he needed an alternative to Colucci—maybe even a direct supply. Julius Taviani had the power to give him that.

The plane was already consumed by fire. The engine parts and the metal exhaust pipe were hanging loose from the glowing fuselage. Blinking away tears from the smoke, Mason gazed at the empty sky. In an hour the sun would be up. There wasn't much chance of a plane arriving, but he would stay here until daylight. After that, he would go back to the house, catch up on the ranch work, and kill time until tonight, when the most cooperative prison guards were on duty. That would be the best time to call Taviani.

His thoughts returned to Ruby. Was she still with Colucci? Was she flying? Was she safe? But he had no way to contact her, no way to protect her if she was in danger. He ached to see her; but if he broke his connection with Colucci, there'd be nothing he could do. Odds were that he would never hold her in his arms again.

Restless, he slipped the brass buckle out of his pocket and turned it over in his hands. The metal was cold against his skin, the rodeo design on the front and the initials on the back still haunting him. The memory was just out of reach. Was it something he'd blocked because he wanted to forget?

Then, in a flash, the image came back to him.

He'd been a young boy—nine or ten—walking past his mother's bedroom after an early-morning visit to the toilet. As he passed her door, it had opened, and a man had stepped out. A tall man, a man he knew well. Mason had kept his eyes lowered, as if pretending not to see him. His gaze had remained fixed on the man's belt buckle.

The same buckle he held in his hand.

The body in the cave, the body he'd burned, was Ralph Thompson, his mother's foreman—and her lover.

Questions remained—how had Thompson died, and how did his body come to be in the cave? Asking his mother would only stir up painful memories. But one other person might be able to tell him the story.

Later that day, while his mother was napping, Mason joined Sidney in the kitchen. When shown the buckle and asked about the body, the old man sighed.

"You'd remember Ralph, of course. He was here for a long time. Then he got into trouble. He was caught taking money from the local banker to harass immigrant farmers. After he skipped town, we also discovered that he'd been skimming cash from the ranch. So, good riddance.

"We thought we'd seen the last of him. Then a few years ago, after you went to Deer Lodge, he showed up again. He claimed your mother owed him money, which was a lie. When she told him to leave, the man became violent. He was shaking her when I came up from behind and struck him on the head with a cast-iron skillet. I was younger then, and I guess I didn't know my own strength. He went down and never woke up. Your mother didn't want any trouble with the police, so we hitched up a wagon, hauled his body to the cave, and left it there. You know the rest. I hope you won't mention this to your mother."

"No need," Mason said. "And I'll get rid of the buckle. I never want to see it again."

Ruby had delivered the last of the current shipment that morning. Now exhausted, she huddled on the porch steps, drinking coffee while she waited for her ride back to the Olive Hotel in Miles City. All she wanted to do was sleep around the clock.

Heavy footsteps crossed the porch behind her. She shrank inside herself. She'd been avoiding Colucci for the past several days. But she should have known he wouldn't let her go without showing her who was boss.

He lowered himself to the step beside her. He smelled of the ham-and-garlic sandwich he'd recently eaten. "I just got off the phone with one of Capone's lieutenants," he said. "He's going to find us a new plane."

"So Capone's passed us down the line to one of his helpers," she said. "How about a new pilot? I can't take another week of making all the deliveries. I'll burn out and crash. Is that what you want?"

"You know what I want, baby." He laid an arm around her shoulders. "Play ball with me, and you won't have to fly at all."

A shudder passed through her body. Shaking his arm loose, she stood. "If I wanted to play ball, as you say, it wouldn't be with a man who hit me. I'll fly your planes. But what's between us is strictly business." She stepped away from him as her driver appeared from around the house in the Model T. "Speaking of business, I believe I've earned a raise," she said.

Colucci chuckled as the car pulled up to the porch. "You want a raise, sweetheart, you know what you'll have to do to earn it."

Safe in the back seat of the Model T with its silent driver, Ruby took a deep breath to calm her nerves. Being around Colucci was becoming unbearable. If it weren't for her father, she would have left by now. But she was trapped by the commitment she'd made to keep Art safe.

When she got back to the hotel, she would be obligated to

phone Agent Hargrave. She could tell him about Colucci's advances and plead for relief. But she knew that Hargrave wouldn't care. He would tell her it was all in the line of duty. He might even remind her that going to bed with her boss could give her access to useful information.

The only time she'd felt something besides fear, anger, and frustration was when Mason Dollarhide had taken her in his arms and melted her with his kiss. Under different conditions, she could almost have fallen in love with him. He was strong, masculine, and tender. But he was also an ex-convict and an active bootlegger, no better in his way than Leo Colucci. She would be smart to forget about that kiss—and to forget she'd ever met the man.

Still, the urge to see him was there, especially when lying awake at night, yearning to give herself to his lovemaking—to feel like a woman again.

The car was coming into Miles City. As it passed the hotel, rounded the corner, and swung into the alley, Ruby forced herself to look ahead to a few hours of well-earned rest. She owed herself that much. Maybe tomorrow, with a clear head, she could think of a way to gain some control over her situation.

Joseph had been at the sawmill since first light, loading boards on trolleys and sweeping up what appeared to be mountains of sawdust. It was still early in the day when his father showed up and beckoned him away from the billowing dust and the scream of the huge blade as it sliced lengthwise through a log.

They walked to an open area by the gate, far enough from the noise to be heard without shouting. Joseph pulled off his leather gloves. He welcomed the break, but with some trepidation. He could sense the tension in Blake. Was he in trouble for something else?

They stopped next to the Model T, which was parked inside the gate. "Have you heard how the sheriff is doing?" Joseph asked, breaking the awkward silence.

"I got a telephone call from Kristin this morning. He's going to live. But you need to see him. As you said, you want to tell him you're sorry. You're about to learn the real meaning of that word. Get in the car."

They drove down to the main road and headed into town. Only then did Blake tell his son what had happened. "One of the bullets damaged his spine, Joseph," he said. "The sheriff's legs are paralyzed. Time will tell whether the condition is permanent."

"Oh, God . . ." Joseph doubled over in the seat, feeling sick. The money loss was serious enough. But this—the consequence of his actions—was unthinkable.

Blake slowed the car. "Are you all right? Do I need to stop?"

Joseph fought to control his churning stomach. He shook his head, forcing himself to sit up. "I'm not all right," he said. "But I know what I've done, and I need to face up to it."

Blake gave him a brusque nod and kept driving.

CHAPTER FOURTEEN

JOSEPH STEPPED OUT OF THE CAR AND WALKED UP TO THE HOUSE THAT served as the doctor's office. His hand shook as he clasped the doorknob. He still felt sick, but if he was ever to be a man, he needed to own up to what he'd done.

Blake stayed several steps behind him, offering no support. Joseph was on his own.

The door opened on an empty reception room, still deep in morning shadow. But Joseph could see light and hear voices from the back of the house. He followed the sound to the spare bedroom that was used for patient recovery.

The sheriff was sitting up in bed, propped from behind by pillows. A gauze dressing wrapped his wounded shoulder. A quilt covered him from the waist down. His face was colorless, but as Joseph walked into the room, he smiled.

"I've been hoping you'd show up, Joseph," he said. "I wanted to thank you for staying with me last night after I was shot. That was going the extra mile. I appreciate it."

Joseph stared at him. With effort, he found his voice. "You mean nobody told you?"

The sheriff gave him a questioning look.

"It was my fault!" The words spilled out of Joseph. "That girl in the car—I gave her the money she had, two hundred dollars that I stole from my father. When I found out she was running away with her boyfriend, I tried to stop them. That was when you came out and got shot. What happened was all my fault." A tear spilled over and trailed down Joseph's cheek. "I'm the one to blame for everything."

The smile had faded from the sheriff's face. But he spoke in a level tone. "Joseph, when I got shot, I was doing my job. I knew the risks when I signed on to be sheriff. You may have played a part in what happened, but you didn't pull that trigger."

"But I gave her the money—money that wasn't even mine. If I'd just said no—" Joseph broke down in sobs. "I'm sorry. I'm so sorry."

"Being sorry doesn't change a thing. We take what we've learned and move on. You as well as me." The sheriff's voice roughened. "Now stop mewling, dry your tears, and grow up. That's all we can do—either of us."

Just then, Kristin walked into the room. She carried a tray with a glass of water and a tablet, probably a painkiller, which she gave to the sheriff. Blake, who'd been listening from the hall, stepped in to join her.

"Where's Britta?" he asked.

"Britta's gone to look after Jake's little girl," Kristin said. "Marissa will be staying with her grandmother for now. But she'll need to be told about her father and prepared for when she can be with him."

Joseph remembered how devotedly Britta had tended the wounded sheriff. Anyone could see that she loved him. But what would happen to their relationship if Jake couldn't use his legs?

And there were more issues to be resolved. How could Jake live in the quarters above the jail if he couldn't climb the stairs? How could he drive, mount a horse, or look after his most basic needs? How could he be sheriff?

Joseph knew better than to voice his thoughts. But in his heart, he knew one thing—events triggered by his actions had destroyed a man's life.

"What about those two runaways?" Blake asked. "Have they been caught?"

"Not that we've heard," Jake said. "The doctor called the sheriff in Miles City after I was brought here. He said he'd send his deputies out to watch the roads and the train station. But there's been no word this morning. We're still waiting. I hate to think they got away." Pain flashed across his face as he shifted against the pillows.

"Somebody should talk to Webb Calder," Joseph suggested. "Lucy's father—if that's who he really is—has been working for him. He might know who her boyfriend is and where they could have gone."

"Webb called just before you got here," the sheriff said. "When he went to look for Nigel Merriweather, or whatever his real name is, the man had cleared out in the night. So, unless he shows up, we're out of luck."

"We'll leave you to rest now," Blake said. "Come along, Joseph. Kristin, would you walk us to the door?"

She fell into step beside her brother. Joseph followed behind as they passed through the hallway and into the reception room. Short of the front door, Blake paused and turned to her. "How is Jake really doing?" he asked in a lowered voice. "What are the chances that he'll walk again?"

She shook her head. "I can't be sure of the damage to his spine without an X-ray. But I've seen injuries like this. Based on the evidence, I'd say that it would take a miracle."

"Let me know if he needs anything," Blake said, preparing to leave.

"I will. But he's a proud man. Don't expect him to ask."

Blake had just opened the door when a transport wagon, its side bearing the painted symbol of the Miles City Sheriff's Department, pulled up to the house. A big-bellied man with a star on his vest climbed out of the van and strode up the walk.

"Where's the doctor?" he demanded.

"Right here." Kristin stepped forward. "What can I do for you, Sheriff?"

"We've got an accident victim—a young woman, some cuts and bruises, maybe a concussion and some cracked ribs. Your place was the closest medical help. Can you take a look at her?"

"Of course. Bring her in. I'll see her in my surgery."

"Thanks. She's on a stretcher, probably in shock. I'll have my deputies carry her in." The sheriff signaled the vehicle with his hand, then turned back to the doctor. "I understand Sheriff Calhoun is here. Is he up to talking?"

"If you don't keep him too long. He's alert, but still weak. Joseph, would you show the sheriff back to the recovery room?"

"Sure." Joseph led the big man down the hall to the room where Jake was resting. After ushering the sheriff inside, he lingered in the hall to listen. Eavesdropping might not be polite, but if there was any news, he wanted to hear it.

"Dammit, Jake, you look like hell!" The big man swore.

"I feel like hell, too," Jake said. "But that can't be helped. Pull up a chair and tell me what's going on."

The spindly wooden chair groaned as the big man sat down. "We found your fugitives this morning," he said. "From the look of things, they doused their headlamps and steered into the woods to hide from the folks that were chasing them. It might have worked, but about twenty yards in, they crashed into a tree. The man was killed. The woman was hurt and trapped in the wreck. We found them this morning. That's her my deputies just brought in."

Joseph's breath caught in his throat. From the front room, he could hear the tread of sturdy boots as the stretcher was carried inside to the surgery.

Lucy would be on that stretcher. Lucy, who had lied to him, charmed him into stealing money, and fled with her lover. Now the man was dead, and Lucy was injured. Joseph tried to tell himself that she'd gotten what was coming to her—and that he was justified in hating her. But he didn't hate her. He didn't love her or even pity her. What he felt for Lucy was nothing at all.

"How badly was she hurt?" Jake asked.

"Mostly glass cuts and bruises. Maybe a mild concussion and cracked ribs. Once the doc patches her up, we'll be taking her to jail. I recognized her from a poster. She and her husband are wanted for extortion in Colorado. He's an English type, pretends to be rich. She passes as his daughter, but she's over twenty-one. She'll be charged as an adult."

"So the fellow who died wasn't her husband?" Jake asked.

"It appears she was running off with another man. The husband's still at large."

The sheriff's words jolted Joseph. He'd assumed Lucy was an innocent girl, fifteen or sixteen at the most. Instead, she was a married woman and an accomplished con artist. What a fool he'd been.

"Did she have any cash on her?" He spoke from the doorway. "I gave her two hundred dollars. The money belonged to my father."

"She did have some money on her." The sheriff frowned and shifted in his chair. "If it's your father's and he wants it back, he'll have to come in, present some identification, and sign a claim form. Since that money is evidence, the process may take some time."

Joseph heard Blake's voice calling him from the front room. Returning down the hallway, he passed the closed door of the surgery, where Kristin was treating the woman who'd played him for a lovesick schoolboy. For a moment he was tempted to open the door and let her know that he saw her for what she was. But his father was waiting. And why should he bother with Lucy? She had no more power over him.

At least Blake would be getting his stolen money back. But Joseph knew better than to think his punishment was over. He would serve every day of his sentence in the hated sawmill. But nothing, not a hundred times that, could undo the terrible damage he'd done.

Mason waited until his mother had drunk her tea and toddled off to bed before he placed his call to Deer Lodge. Phoning the prison was always chancy. The phones could be busy or out of order. Taviani might be occupied with business or simply not in the mood to talk. Or there might be something going on at the prison, some kind of trouble like a fight or a lockdown.

But tonight, luck was in Mason's favor. After a few minutes' wait, he heard the old man's voice on the phone.

"Dollarhide! I've been thinking about you, pal. How are things going?"

"They could be better," Mason said. "That's why I'm calling."

"Something wrong?"

"I hate to complain, but it's Colucci. I'm doing everything to grow my business. I've got the setup and all the customers I can handle. But I'm not getting the goods. You probably know about the crash of that De Havilland and the loss of the pilot. I buried the boy myself. Colucci's down to one plane and one pilot, and he's not coming through with anything. Either he needs more support, or I need a new supplier."

Taviani sighed. "That doesn't surprise me. But your needs are going to have to wait. There are other things in the wind. I might even need your help. Can I count on your silence?"

"You always have. That hasn't changed. What's happening?"

"For starters, it's Colucci. He's supposed to be putting my share of the profits into an account I set up for when I leave this place. I'm beginning to think he's holding out on me."

"The way things are going, I suspect there might be nothing to hold out," Mason said.

"No, I know better," Taviani said. "He's dealing with Al Capone on the side, giving him part of my share to keep him happy. If you're being cut out, it's because Colucci knows you're my friend."

"But it was Capone who got us the De Havilland."

"I know. But Capone never does anything without a good reason. I don't trust him. And I don't trust Colucci."

"So what are you thinking?"

"That Colucci needs to be replaced with a man I can trust—a man like you."

Mason could guess what the old man was thinking. Colucci would simply disappear—Taviani had plenty of outside connections to make that happen.

But did he want to take over Colucci's job, including all the power and risk associated with it? Mason had never aspired to that level of involvement. All he'd ever wanted was the money. But Taviani could be ruthless when people didn't follow his orders. How could he say no to the old man without making himself a target?

"There's something else," Taviani said. "Colucci's pilot, a woman, is passing information to the feds. I need to get rid of her before I make changes."

Mason's pulse lurched. He forced himself to speak calmly. "How do you know about her?"

"Her father is a prisoner here. A few days ago, he was bragging about the special treatment he gets because of his daughter. When I showed a friendly interest, the fool admitted that she was an informant, working as a pilot for Colucci."

Mason struggled to take in the new reality. Ruby had been passing everything she knew about the operation—and about him—to federal agents, probably to protect her father. Earlier, when he'd urged her to leave, she'd protested that obligations forced her to stay. Now he understood.

Not that it gave him any comfort. Ruby had lied to him. And what she'd likely told the feds could put him right back behind bars.

"Does Colucci know?" Mason's heart was pounding.

"Not yet. I get the impression he's sweet on her—too sweet to do what I need done. And he depends on her for the deliveries. I'd like to keep things that way until they're both taken care of. That's where you come in. I can hire somebody to take out Colucci. But I know the woman makes deliveries to you. You could arrange a little accident for her."

"I'm a bootlegger, not a murderer," Mason said, hiding his shock.

Taviani chuckled. "There's a first time for everybody. Take out the woman, and Colucci's job is yours. You'll have the power to hire who you want, bring in all the goods you need, and take your cut of every delivery—as long as you give me my share. So what do you say?"

Mason hesitated. He could say no, but if he refused, Taviani would find somebody else to kill Ruby. The only hope of keeping her safe would be to agree and stall for time. Ruby had deceived him and worked against him. But her life mattered more to him than he'd realized until now.

"If she's reporting to the feds, the damage is already done," he said. "Why not use her—feed her false information to pass on? She'll be no use to you dead."

"Forget that. Too many things could go wrong. Are you up for the job, or do I find somebody else to do it?"

Again, Mason hesitated. If this was a test, he was already in danger of failing. "All right," he said. "But if you want it done right, it's going to take time. You could arrange a shipment. I could do it then."

"No time for that, and I can't lose another plane." Taviani's voice had taken on an edge. "I want her gone before she can do any more damage. And I'll need proof that she's dead. However you do it, it's got to happen fast."

"What about Colucci?"

"Leave him to me." Mason could hear muffled voices in the background. "I have to go. Let me know when you've done your job." Taviani ended the call.

Mason hung up the receiver and walked out onto the front porch. The rising moon cast the trees into ghostly shadows. The night wind stirred the falling leaves and carried the scent of the season's first cold storm—coming early this year, even for Montana. He felt the touch of a damp nose against his hand. His fingers rubbed the massive head. A tail thumped against his legs. Brutus had finally made peace with him.

Was Ruby safe tonight? Or had Taviani, sensing Mason's hesitation, already sent one of his minions to murder her?

The old man was as unpredictable as a wounded leopard, killing without provocation and without remorse. No one was safe, not even Mason. If he were to violate Taviani's trust, he would never be allowed to live. He knew too many secrets.

If Ruby was in Miles City, she could already be in danger. He needed to find her, to protect her or at least to warn her. And he knew of only one place to look. Taviani would know of it, too. Colucci would have told him.

Mason's mother was asleep, and the faithful Sidney had retired to his rooms. After letting the dog inside and locking the front door, Mason took time to pocket some extra cash, buckle on his holstered pistol, and shrug into his leather jacket. Exiting through the kitchen, he raced for his car.

As he cranked the engine to a start, a coldness touched his cheek and melted on his warm skin. It was snow.

With a woolen blanket wrapped over her nightgown, Ruby stood at the window of her hotel room. On the other side of the glass, snowflakes drifted into the alley, vanishing into the darkness below. She'd hoped for a night of restful sleep. Instead, she'd lain awake for what seemed like hours, haunted by a vague sense that something wasn't right.

She'd long since learned to trust her instincts. But this time the cause was hard to pin down. Was it Colucci? She'd worried about him showing up at her door. But the snowstorm should be enough to keep him on the farm tonight. The door was triple-locked. And just in case, she kept a loaded pistol tucked under the edge of her mattress. She had every reason to believe she was safe.

But as she stood by the window and saw, through the snowy blur, a pair of glowing headlights turning down the alley toward the hotel's back entrance, her ribs jerked tight, squeezing off her breath.

She couldn't make out the vehicle. Plenty of people, especially those with something to hide, parked in the alley and used the back stairs. There was no reason to believe the car had anything to do with her. But as it vanished around the corner of the building, her unease lingered. When she heard the heavy tread of boots coming up the stairs to the third floor, she flew to the far side of her bed and drew the small revolver from its hiding place.

The footfalls stopped outside her door. There was a light

knock. She didn't answer. Maybe her caller would give up and go away. Then she heard a man's deep voice.

"Ruby, it's Mason. Answer me if you're there. I need to talk to you."

Recognizing the voice, Ruby began to breathe again. But was she really safe? All she really knew about Mason was that he was a bootlegger and an associate of Colucci's.

True, he had saved her after she crashed. And his kiss had roused a surge of passion that she couldn't forget. But that didn't mean he wasn't dangerous. She would let him in, but she couldn't afford to lower her guard.

Thumbing back the hammer on the pistol, she used her free hand to open the door. He stepped inside, his presence filling the unlit room. Still gripping the gun, she locked the door again and faced him. In the snow light that fell through the window, beads of moisture gleamed on his hair.

"What are you doing here?" she demanded. "Who sent you? Was it Colucci?"

"Put that gun away, Ruby," he said. "My visit has nothing to do with our friend Colucci. But you're in big trouble."

"What kind of trouble?"

"I'll tell you when you're not pointing that gun at me. Believe me, I'm the last person you want to shoot."

Could she trust him? Did she have a choice? She released the hammer and lowered the weapon. "Tell me," she said. "Where did you hear that I was in trouble?"

"From the man who gave me orders to kill you."

She gasped, shrinking back from him, almost tripping over the hem of the blanket.

"Sit down," he said. "I'm not going to hurt you, Ruby. I'm just going to tell you what you need to hear."

She sank onto the edge of the bed. He lifted the gun from her hand, laid it on the nightstand, and sat down beside her.

"Your secret's been discovered," he said. "I know you're an informant for the Bureau of Investigation."

Her body went rigid. "Who else knows? Colucci?"

"No, not him. Not yet, at least."

"Then who else? Who told you?"

"The man who actually runs this show—from prison."

From prison. Ruby's mind rearranged the things she knew like pieces of a jigsaw puzzle. They slid into place, fitting in ways she would never have believed until now.

Prison. Her father, working in the library. Making friends. Dangerous friends. Sharing secrets in an effort to be liked.

Nothing else made sense. But where did Mason fit into the picture?

"How can that be?" she asked. "I cooperated with the feds because my father was in prison. They faked his death and promised to keep him safe."

"But they couldn't keep him quiet," Mason said. "Your father talked to the wrong people."

"That would be like him. He's always been so trusting, so naive, like a child." Ruby could feel herself crumbling inside. "Now somebody wants me dead—and you said you had orders to kill me. Who gave you those orders?"

"Never mind that. You can't stay here," Mason said. "I've got money. I can get you on the midnight train. Go as far as it will take you. Change your name, whatever it takes. I'll just say that you got away before I could find you."

She shook her head. "I'm not leaving without my father. My handlers promised me that when the time came, they'd get both of us to safety."

"Ruby, your father gave you up to the enemy."

"But he didn't mean to, Mason. If he stays in prison without my protection, they'll put him to hard labor. He's old, and he's not strong. He'll die."

"*You'll* die if you stay." He took a breath. "The man who's giving the orders is in prison. I served time with him, some of it as his bodyguard, and I know how ruthless he can be. If he decides I'm not capable of killing you, he'll send a professional to do the job."

Mason was watching her, his gaze alert but tender in the faint light. Outside, windblown snow battered the windowpane. If things had been different, she might have moved closer or reached out and touched him. Something about Mason Dollarhide made her yearn for things she had long since left behind—warmth, safety, and the freedom to love. But that chance had come too late. Tonight she could be seeing him for the last time.

"I have a plan," she said. "I'll call my handler, Agent Hargrave, and tell him that I've been found out. The agents will come and take me to their safe house to wait for my father. You can leave before they get here. They don't even have to know you were involved."

"Are you sure you can count on their help, Ruby?" Mason said. "Now that you've been exposed, you'll be of no more use to them. They'll have no reason to protect you."

"But they promised me," Ruby argued. "They said they'd free my father and send us somewhere safe. And they're working for the United States government. I even met the man who's in charge now, Mr. J. Edgar Hoover. If I can't trust them, who can I trust?"

His hands came up to cradle Ruby's face. His piercing eyes locked with hers. "Blast it, Ruby, you're just as naïve as you say your father is. You might trust those men, but I'm not leaving you alone with them, not until I know you're going to be all right."

"But they'll know who you are—I've reported you. You could go back to prison."

"I said I'm not leaving," he insisted. "I want you safe. I'll deal with the rest. I have a plan of my own."

"But why take a chance?" she whispered. "Why risk so much for a woman who's already put you in danger?"

"I've asked myself the same damned question." He kissed her then. His mouth—hard, urgent, and seeking—answered in a way that erased all need for words. As the kiss lingered, a pulsing desire, too long denied, welled in the depths of her body, its heat pooling down into her thighs and flowing upward until every part of her shimmered like sunlight through rainbow glass.

She knew Mason was far from perfect. He was a man who'd played by his own rules and paid the price. But none of that mattered. She had wanted him from the first moment he touched her.

Her blanket fell to the bed as she raised her arms to pull him down to her. Her body was naked beneath her muslin nightgown. His hands were cool through the thin fabric, but his lips were warm, pressing the curve of her neck, moving to her throat and down to her breasts.

Ruby had never been intimate with any man except her husband. After his death, and even before, she had frozen her physical and emotional needs. Now, in Mason's arms, she was swept away by a wild hunger. She wanted his hands on every part of her, his bare skin warm and rough against hers, his hard arousal filling the dark emptiness inside her.

She tugged at his belt buckle. He reached down to help her. The holstered gun thudded to the floor with his trousers, followed by his boots and the rest of his clothes. Kissing her again, he eased her out of the nightgown and folded her under the covers.

He was an experienced lover, as Ruby had sensed that he would be. But she didn't care how many other women he'd enjoyed in the past. Here and now, he was hers—and she was his.

Taking his time, he calmed her feverish need with gentle kisses, then aroused her slowly, nuzzling her breasts, his tongue teasing the nipples into sensitive nubs. She moaned, arching her body to meet his caresses.

"I've wanted you from the time you took me up in your plane," he murmured against the hollow between her breasts. "I've dreamed of pleasuring you, Ruby. But anytime you want me to stop . . ." He brushed a trail of feathery kisses down the midline of her belly, then moved lower and lower still.

"*Oh* . . ." Her fingers tangled in his hair as the first climax rippled through her body. "I didn't know you could . . . *oh!*" Her words ended in a gasp as it happened again.

"Anything else?" His tone was teasing.

"Yes . . . oh, yes." Her legs opened for him, hips rising to meet his thrust. Slick with moisture, she welcomed him in, feeling every inch of his hard strength as he filled her. Instinctively, they moved as one, as if they'd been forged for this—and for each other. Deeper, faster, like two comets mounting the sky, they burst into starlight and floated back to Earth.

She lay in Mason's arms, her head resting in the hollow of his shoulder. He had shown her what could happen between a man and woman when their bodies and souls were in tune—something she had lost sight of during the last years of her marriage. But when he turned and kissed her, Ruby understood.

Mason had given her one last gift—something to remember after they had to say goodbye.

I love you, Mason. The words rose in her mind. But some things were better left unsaid.

CHAPTER FIFTEEN

OUTSIDE, THE SNOW WAS STILL FALLING. RUBY AND MASON HAD dressed and remade the bed. It was time to prepare for whatever was to happen next.

They had stolen a few precious moments in each other's arms. But there was no more time to spare. They needed to act decisively. But now it appeared they'd reached a stalemate.

Mason had tried once more to talk Ruby into leaving on the midnight train. But Ruby had been adamant. She would not go without her father.

Standing at the window, Mason listened as Ruby made the phone call to the government agents. Earlier, she'd explained why she never made calls from her own room, but the reason no longer mattered. She'd be safer here, with him, behind a locked door.

While she told her story to the agents, Mason checked his .38 Smith & Wesson, making sure it was loaded and ready. He wasn't expecting to need it, but Taviani's goons could be anywhere. So could Colucci's, even in the storm. And Mason didn't trust the so-called government agents Ruby was counting on to keep her safe. Anything could happen.

Ruby hung up the receiver, set the phone on the nightstand, and turned to face him. "I spoke with Agent Hargrave," she said. "He and Agent Jensen are coming right over. They're close by. It shouldn't take them long to get here."

"Did you tell them you had company?"

"No. If you leave now, they won't have to know you've been here." She raised a hand to his chest, as if trying to push him toward the door. "Go on, Mason. Don't worry about me now. I'll be fine."

He stood his ground. "I'm not leaving you, Ruby. Not until I know what they're planning to do."

"Just go. Please," she pleaded.

"I'm not leaving you." He weighed the plan that had come to him—a desperate plan that involved playing the one ace he possessed. It could be his only chance of saving them both.

She sighed. "Then at least stay out of sight. Wait in the bathroom or the closet when they come. If I don't need you, they won't have to see you."

"All right." It was a sensible option. "But I'll want to hear what's going on. And you should have a password to use if you need my help. Choose something I'll recognize."

"I understand." She was silent for a moment, thinking. "De Havilland," she said. "After that beautiful plane that crashed. I know how to use a password, but I don't expect to need it."

"I hope you're right." Ruby was too confident and too trusting, Mason thought. To cover their own reputations, the federal agents might be capable of throwing her to the wolves.

With uncertainty looming, only one thing was sure. He loved her as he'd never loved a woman before in his life. He would keep her safe at any cost.

Tension-laden minutes crawled past, marked by the ticking wall clock. It was eleven-fifteen when Ruby heard a bold rap on the door. She glanced at Mason. He slipped into the closet, leaving the door slightly ajar. If only she could have convinced him to leave. As it was, she was more worried for him than for herself. She'd come up with the password to satisfy him, but she couldn't imagine using it.

The rap on the door became more insistent. "Mrs. Weaver, are you in there?" Hargrave's voice had an irritating, metallic quality.

"Yes, I hear you. I'm coming." Ruby, now dressed in a skirt, a woolen sweater, and boots, crossed the room to open the door. Her heart was pounding but she willed herself not to hurry.

The two agents strode into the room, brushing snow off their coats and shaking it from their fedoras. Hargrave was tall with a hawkish face and a scarecrow-like body. Jensen, apple-cheeked and blond, looked like a schoolboy next to him.

"Have a seat," she said. "There's only one chair and the dresser bench, but—"

"We'll stand," Hargrave said. "So you say you've been found out, Mrs. Weaver. How did it happen?"

"My father. He told someone in prison."

"And how do you know this?" Hargrave demanded. "Who told you?"

Ruby groped for an answer. Why hadn't she thought this through? "It doesn't matter how I know. I meet people in this business. One of them heard it through the grapevine and cared enough to let me know. Now I need your help."

"So why are you here? Why not just leave town?" Hargrave's tone was sarcastic, his expression cold.

"You know I can't leave my father in prison. Please, I've done everything you asked me to do. You promised to get him out of there and send us somewhere safe."

Hargrave's expression could have been chiseled in stone. "Things have changed, Mrs. Weaver. The warden called us this morning. Your father was found dead in the prison library. His neck was broken."

"*No!*" Ruby's knees buckled. She staggered, struggling to breathe as her body contracted like a fist. Behind her, a door opened. Mason's strong arms caught her, holding her upright until she could get her breath. Together they faced the two agents.

"We know who you are, Mr. Dollarhide," Hargrave said. "Thanks to Mrs. Weaver here, we have a record of the times you've received contraband goods in violation of the Volstead Act."

"You're also in violation of parole." Agent Jensen had drawn a pistol. He spoke for the first time. "That means we can take you into custody, call the U.S. Marshals, and have you escorted back to Deer Lodge without a hearing. So I suggest you surrender your weapon."

Having no choice short of violence, Mason lifted his gun out of its holster and passed it, grip first, to Hargrave.

"No!" Ruby fought her way back from the shock of her father's death. "This man saved my life when my plane crashed. He came to warn me that I'd been discovered and someone wanted me dead. I would have left on the train tonight, but because of my father—" The words ended in a stifled sob as her new reality sank deeper.

"Save your story, Mrs. Weaver," Hargrave said. "Now that you're of no use to us, we have other plans for you. Director Hoover is getting impatient to see some faces behind bars. We have proof that you were delivering contraband liquor before we ever contacted you. After we take you into custody, the Marshals Service will be escorting you to jail, pending trial."

Horror-struck, Ruby stared at the agent. "But you promised to help me! You even signed a paper. Your boss was there. He was a witness. Call and ask him."

"Mr. Hoover is a busy man. I doubt he'd even remember. But even if we made you a promise, it would have been conditional on your finishing your assignment. As things stand, we can't protect you."

Her temper flared. "Of all the underhanded—"

Mason's hand, tightening on her arm, silenced her words. "Be still, Ruby," he whispered from behind her. "Sit down and let me handle this."

Giving in, she let him lower her to the edge of the bed where she sat rigid and quivering, her hands clenched in her lap. How could Mason help her when he was in even more trouble than she?

He faced the agents, his presence powerful and calm. "Hear me out," he said. "I have a proposal for you."

"We're all ears." Hargrave's voice dripped with sarcasm. Ruby could almost read the agent's thoughts. What could this man offer them that they couldn't simply take?

"I've read about your boss," Mason said. "I get the impression he's not a patient man. He expects—and demands—results."

The two agents exchanged furtive glances. Jensen gave a slight nod.

"I know you need to make yourselves look good and keep your boss happy. But what's Mr. Hoover going to say when he finds out you've jailed a young woman, a war widow, whose only intention was to help her father—a woman you forced to spy for you? When the public gets wind of this—and they will—the bureau is going to look like a bunch of cowards and fools. Keep her safe, put her on that train, and I'll offer you a prize that will make Hoover bust his buttons."

Ruby understood what Mason was offering—his own freedom in exchange for her safety. She imagined him walking into prison, knowing the awful conditions that awaited him. And there was nothing she could do. Only his hand on her shoulder kept her from crying out.

"We've already got you dead to rights, Dollarhide," Hargrave said. "I'm still thinking about the woman. But you're not going to talk your way out of this."

"True," Mason said. "But I'm just a small-time bootlegger. What if I told you I could give you the man who runs this whole operation?"

"If you're talking about Leo Colucci, we can pick up that goon any day of the week. We're just hoping he'll lead us to the man we call the Big Fish."

"Then you'd better pick him up fast. The man who wants Ruby dead is planning to off Colucci, too. He thinks Colucci might be holding out on him."

"And you know this how?" Hargrave was suddenly alert, like a bloodhound catching the scent.

"He told me over the phone the last time I called him at the prison," Mason said. "That was how I knew he wanted Ruby killed. I'm sure he had her father killed, too. Not that he ever dirties his own hands. He's got enough people in his pocket to run that prison like he owns it." Mason's gaze bored into the agent's. "I know because I was one of them."

"So who is this person, and how do we get him?" Hargrave demanded. "I take it we're going to need your help."

"I'll tell you his name after I see Ruby get on that train," Mason said. "When I know she's safe, I'll be willing to go back on the inside for you. But I want a written guarantee of full pardon for both of us, mailed to my half-sister, whose name I'll give you. Agreed?"

"Only on condition that you deliver him. But all right, the woman can go."

"Get your things. We don't have much time." Mason passed her a handful of large bills. Ruby's lips parted, but Mason shook his head, cautioning her not to speak.

Ruby's clothes and meager possessions fit easily in her small duffel. She would leave Colucci's gift box under the bed for anyone who wanted the glittery garments inside.

The train station was nearby. They would be walking through the snow—Ruby, Mason, and the two armed agents. Ruby huddled in her thin coat as Mason leaned close and whispered a few last words.

"Don't try to write or call. We want the old man to think you're dead. If you need anything, contact my sister, Dr. Kristin Dollarhide Hunter, in Blue Moon."

"Mason—" Love and fear for him were tearing her apart.

"Hush. There's nothing to say. Just be safe."

Agent Jensen bought her ticket at the window. By then the train's headlamp was visible through the snow. The whistle quivered on the air. As the Northern Pacific engine, trailing its passenger cars, pulled up to the platform, Mason swept her into his arms for a last urgent kiss. Breaking away, he thrust her toward the open car where a conductor waited to take her ticket and help her aboard.

Clutching her purse and duffel, Ruby stumbled to her second-class seat. Her tear-blurred eyes strained to see the platform through the snow-covered window, but the train was already moving. The whistle shrieked as the engine picked up speed and raced into the snowy night.

*   *   *

Britta stomped the snow off her boots before stepping inside the doctor's reception area. She found Jake in the spare wheel-chair the doctor had given him. He was practicing maneuvers in the middle of the room, turning, backing, moving around and behind the furniture. The doctor's office was closed today, but Jake was still here. His wounds were healing, but he was unable to leave for his second-floor quarters above the sheriff's office.

He'd insisted that Kristin go home to her family and leave him to manage on his own for the weekend. Britta had offered to check on him and bring his meals. The arrangement was a worry, but Jake was a proud, stubborn man, determined to deal with his disability on his own.

"Hello, Britta." His face was drawn, his unshaven beard shad-owing his jaw. Pain had deepened the creases around his eyes. He greeted her with a smile, but as she set the covered basket on the kitchen table, she could sense the frustration raging inside him. The simplest tasks, like getting out of bed, dressing, and relieving himself, had become almost insurmountable challenges. He wanted his strong body back. He wanted his useful life.

"I know you like my chicken and dumplings," she said, trying to be cheerful but not too cheerful. "There's apple pie for dessert. And I thought you might like some coffee. I brought you a thermos. It should still be hot." She chatted as she set the table for dinner, removing the chair on the nearest side so he could wheel into place. "After you've eaten, I'll check your wounds. I promised the doctor I'd do that."

"You're too good to me, Britta." He took his place at the table and spread the napkin on his lap. Britta filled his plate and poured him some coffee. What would he say if she brought up the idea that had come to her? Would he be outraged, even angry?

"How's Marissa?" he asked. "Did you see her today?"

"Yes, I saw her this morning." Britta took her place across from him, knowing he would want her to share the meal. "She's fine, but she misses you. She wants to see you."

"Does she understand what's happened?"

"I explained as best I could," Britta said. "I even drew her a picture. I can imagine how difficult this is for you. But you're her father. She needs you."

He took a bite of chicken as if forcing himself to eat, then put down his fork. "All right. Bring her the next time you come, then," he said. "But how can I answer her when she says she wants to go home? We can't go back to our old place—I could never make it up the stairs. Cora's mother has been good to take Marissa, but she's getting old. She isn't strong, and her little house has only one bedroom. I could never live there, and I can't stay here much longer." Desperation broke his voice. "What kind of father can't even provide a home for his child?"

His words had left Britta with an opening. She summoned her courage.

"You could move in with me, Jake," she said. "My place has no stairs, and it has an extra bedroom. You could have Marissa with you. When I'm not teaching, I could be there to cook and look after things. It wouldn't have to be forever, just until you're better able to manage and make other arrangements."

She had run out of words. In the dead silence that followed, she forced herself to meet his startled gaze. Seconds crawled by as she waited for him to respond.

At last he spoke. "What are you thinking, Britta? You've always been concerned about gossip. What would people say if I were to move in with you, even with my daughter?"

"Hang what people say! My place would serve your needs."

"But what about your job? Your house belongs to the school board. You could be fired and have to move."

"They'd have to find a new teacher first. And how many teachers would be desperate enough to come to Blue Moon?" As she spoke, Britta felt an exhilarating sense of freedom, not so different from the way she'd felt stepping into the airplane. Let people talk. Let them judge her. The only thing that really mattered was Jake.

"I'm sorry, but you must be out of your mind," he said.

"Think about it. For the foreseeable future, you're going to need a place to stay, with room for your daughter and someone to help you. And if—no, when—you're well enough to go back to work, you'll be close to your office and the jail."

Pain flickered across his face. Had she said too much? Maybe she shouldn't have mentioned his job. But it was too late to take back the words.

"Be still and listen to me, Britta," he said. "This is one of the hardest things I've ever had to say. I would never move in with you unless we could marry. But that can't happen now.

"Before the shooting, I was planning to ask you. I dreamed of the future we could have together. But now, that's become impossible. I would never burden you with the person I've become— the constant work, the dressing and bathing, all the ugly, intimate details involved in caring for someone like me. I don't know if I'd be able to provide for you. I don't know if I'd be able to satisfy you as a husband or give you children."

His gaze held hers across the table. A muscle twitched in his cheek. "You're a wonderful woman, Britta. You deserve so much better than anything I could offer you. That's why my answer— my final answer—is no."

Britta held back tears. "That's your pride talking," she said. "Pride won't give you a place to heal or provide a home for your little girl."

"It's not pride," he said. "It's love."

"You're wrong," she said. "But if you don't understand, I can't force you." She pushed out her chair and stood. "Finish your dinner. I need some air, but I'll be back to clean up the kitchen and check your wounds. I won't bring this up again."

Turning away, she walked out of the kitchen. Her heart was aching, but she wasn't about to let Jake see her cry. She had her own pride.

Picking up her thick merino shawl, which she'd tossed over a chair, she crossed the front room, opened the door, and stepped out onto the porch. The air was biting cold. She pulled the shawl tighter around her body.

Sunset stained the deepening sky with streaks of crimson, a sign that the early storm had moved on and the warm fall weather would return. But Britta's own storm still raged inside her. Jake needed help, and she was more than willing to give it, along with her love. Why couldn't he understand that?

She would gladly spend the rest of their lives serving as his helpmate and raising his little girl. As for the rest—at twenty-nine she was still a virgin. Even being kissed by Jake was a thrill. As long as there was love between them—and already a child—wouldn't that be enough?

But she knew better than to present that argument to Jake. He was in no frame of mind to listen.

The sun had gone down. Britta had begun to shiver beneath her shawl. It was time to go in and do whatever Jake would allow her to do.

In the kitchen, he had cleared the table and set the dishes on the counter next to the sink. There were two plates, water glasses, and a few utensils. Britta washed, dried, and stacked them for the next meal.

The light was on in the room where Jake slept. Coming down the hall, she could hear the sound of bumping and struggling. The door was partway closed. Hesitating, she called out to alert him that she was nearby. He was a private man, and she had to respect that. But he would have to accept being helped.

She heard another thump and a muffled curse. "All right, come in," he muttered.

She walked into the room and found him in his chair, trying to reach the empty enameled chamber pot where it lay upended on the floor. To get it, he would have to lean over far enough to risk falling out of the wheelchair.

"I've got it." Britta picked it up.

He sighed. "Give it to me and step out of the room."

Britta did as he'd asked. Moments later she returned, took the pot from him, and emptied it in the bathroom. Returning, she placed it on a side chair, within easy reach. Jake was fumbling to fasten his trousers. He paused to gaze up at her.

"See what you'd be in for if I accepted your offer? Can you imagine a lifetime of this, and worse?"

"You'll get stronger and more able to do things," Britta said. "It will just take time. Talk to the doctor. She worked in a veterans' hospital after the war. She'll be able to give you some suggestions and maybe order some devices to make things easier."

"You know I was in the war," Jake said. "I came home from France without a damned scratch. I used to look at those poor bastards in wheelchairs and think how lucky I was. And now this. Maybe I had it coming."

"Nobody has it coming, Jake. But at least, the man who shot you is dead."

"Yes. I know. Too bad he didn't have a better aim."

"I'm going to assume you didn't really mean that," Britta said. "Leave your trousers undone. I'll need to check your wounds and change the dressing."

"Don't bother. I'm fine."

"And we want you to stay that way. Those wounds could still become infected."

"You sound like my mother, God rest her soul." He watched her get the gauze, tape, and salve out of the wall cabinet and carry it to the nightstand.

"You've never told me about your family, Jake." She unbuttoned the top of his flannel shirt and slipped it off his shoulder. The blood-soaked clothes he'd worn the night of the shooting had been thrown away, but Britta had brought more clothing from his quarters above the jail.

"I've not much family left," he said. "My folks were Kansas farmers, fine stock. They died in the Spanish Flu epidemic while I was in the army. Two sisters married and moved away—I don't even know where. By the time I came home, the bank had taken what was left of the farm. I had an army buddy from Blue Moon. We got separated, but after the war I decided to look him up. He never made it home, but the town needed a sheriff, so I took the job and stayed."

"Tell me his name. Maybe I know him." She lifted the dressing off his shoulder wound. Healthy pink flesh was closing around the bullet hole.

He told her the name. It wasn't one she recognized. But talking like this seemed to make the delicate process of tending his wounds easier.

"I lost a brother in the war." She picked up the tin of salve and tried to twist off the lid, but it was screwed on tight. "Axel—but you already knew that." She twisted the lid harder. It was stuck.

"Here, let me do that." He took the tin from her and gave the lid a turn. The lid popped loose. He handed it back to her.

"At least I'm still good for something," he said.

As Britta dabbed the salve around the wound, her patience snapped. "You're still good for a lot of things, Jake Calhoun," she scolded. "You've got a brain, eyes, ears, and two good hands. That's more than some people. The sooner you stop feeling sorry for yourself, the sooner you can move on with your life."

He was silent for a long moment. "I was a sharpshooter in the army. That's what got me hired as sheriff. But who wants a sheriff who can't ride, drive a car, or even walk?"

"You could hire deputies for that. They could do the legwork and drive you when you needed to go somewhere." Britta applied a fresh dressing to the shoulder wound and pulled his shirt back into place.

"That won't be my call," he said. "I'll be up for reelection in November. I was planning to run, but nobody's going to vote for a sheriff who can't do his job. I should probably withdraw now and give others a chance to campaign."

"Why close that door so soon? I know people respect you. Let them decide on election day. You might be surprised."

"Or humiliated."

"Oh, hush! Hold still." Bending close, she pulled away the tops of his trousers and drawers, needing to reach the dressing on the crest of his hip. She had never touched him—or any man—in such an intimate place. Her senses tingled as she leaned close to loosen the dressing over his wound. His hair brushed against her cheek. His skin smelled of sweat and disinfectant—the mixture strangely erotic as it seeped through her senses. His uncovered skin was pale and satiny, his lower body sculpted with muscle. A line of crisp, dark hair traced a narrow path down his belly that vanished under the edge of his open trousers.

The house was chilly, but Britta felt strangely warm. As she uncovered the dressing, the words he'd spoken earlier came back to her.

I don't know if I'd be able to satisfy you as a husband or give you children.

Britta had spent her early years on a farm. She knew the facts of life. But knowing and experiencing were two different things. Now, looking down at his body, imagining what her eyes couldn't quite see, she understood the real reason why Jake had refused to marry her. And she had no answers.

CHAPTER SIXTEEN

*H*UDDLED IN THE FRIGID SECOND-CLASS CAR, RUBY RODE THE EAST-bound Northern Pacific train as far as Glendive. By the time the morning sky had begun to pale, she'd made up her mind that she was traveling in the wrong direction.

There might be safety in the East. But how could she leave Mason to risk his life avenging her father's murder? She knew that she couldn't go inside the prison. But at least she could stay close by in case he needed her.

After leaving the train, she checked the schedule posted next to the ticket window. The westbound train wouldn't be coming through until late this afternoon. Until then, she'd have a few hours to rest and make plans.

In a drab café across from the station, she treated herself to coffee, toast, and scrambled eggs. Mason had given her several hundred dollars, enough to give her a new start anywhere she wanted to go. But when she imagined him walking defenseless into that prison, dressed in the ugly black-and-white prison garb, and meeting his old enemies face-to-face, a shudder of dread passed through her body. Her father had been murdered in that place. Mason could easily meet the same fate.

She couldn't just disappear and leave him there.

But if she went back, her life would be in danger, too. Mason's prison boss had ordered her killed. Colucci could be looking for her, as well. And she couldn't count on any help from the two government agents. They'd be just as likely to put her behind bars.

The waitress stopped by the table and refilled her thick porcelain coffee cup. As Ruby sipped the hot, black liquid, a plan sprouted in her mind. By the time the cup was empty, she'd thought it through and made her decision.

That afternoon, as the westbound train pulled into the station, a changed figure waited on the platform. Only the duffel and sturdy work boots were the same as before. The shorn hair, the workman's clothes, purchased in a secondhand shop, the cap that shaded a beardless face, and the warm sheepskin coat, painted a convincing picture of a boy in his teens.

Ruby's transformation had been as complete as she could make it. She had abandoned her purse for a wallet. Even her underclothes and the extra things in her duffel were made for a male. Only her voice, and furtive visits to the women's restroom, threatened her disguise.

She had bought a ticket for Miles City. From there, she could transfer to the Milwaukee Road, which would take her directly to Deer Lodge.

Boarding the train, she found an empty seat at the back of the car, pulled her cap down to conceal her eyes from above, and pretended to sleep.

She lost track of the times the train stopped to deliver passengers and cargo and take on more. It was night once again when the train pulled into Miles City. This was the most dangerous part of her journey. There could be people looking for her here. No one would have expected her to be on this train, especially in disguise. But she couldn't be too careful.

After checking in both directions, she made her way to the smaller Milwaukee Road station house, which was closed. A lone bench stood against one outer wall. Turning up the collar of her coat, she huddled in the shadows to wait for the morning train to Deer Lodge.

The snow was gone, but the night was cold. A stray dog, its ribs outlined through its brindled hide, padded along the platform, looking for tidbits. It sniffed at Ruby's shoe, then moved on to gobble a discarded sandwich crust.

Ruby was tired, but she was too nervous to sleep. When a big man in a ragged Mackinaw meandered past her, slowing his step for a closer look, she shrank into her coat. Why hadn't she bought some kind of weapon—a knife or even the gun she'd been forced to leave in her hotel room? When the man moved on, she began to breathe normally again. But danger was every-where, and she was as defenseless as that poor, hungry dog.

By morning, other passengers had gathered to buy tickets and wait for the train. Ruby joined the line. Many of the passengers, she noticed, were sad-looking women, a few with older children. Maybe it was visiting day at the prison.

When the train came in, gliding under the power of overhead electric wires, she found a seat. A middle-aged woman in a shabby coat sat down beside her. Ruby gazed out of the side window, hop-ing to be ignored, but that wasn't to be.

"Who are you going to visit, young man? Your pa?"

Ruby nodded, not wanting to use her voice.

"Johnny, my boy, isn't much older than you," the woman said. "He got locked up for stealing a watch to sell. Three years just for that. And him in there with those awful men. What kind of devil-try will they be teaching him? It breaks my heart, I tell you." She dabbed at her eyes with a wadded handkerchief. "I tell him to say his prayers every night. I only hope God can hear him through those thick prison walls."

The woman chatted on. She didn't seem to care whether Ruby replied. But her description of prison life brought home the enormity of Mason's sacrifice. He could have left her to face the two agents on her own. If he had, he would be free.

He had done that for her.

The woman stopped talking as the train slowed for Deer Lodge and stopped at the station. The visitors filed out of the car, wear-ing their badges. Ruby followed, keeping to the rear of the pro-cession.

The prison wasn't far. Of course, there'd be no way she could get inside to see Mason. Even if she could, making her presence known could get them both killed. She could only stand across the street and gaze at the enormous structure, seething with cold hatred. Her father had died here. And as long as Mason was inside, he was in danger every minute.

Built by convict labor more than fifty years earlier, the thick red brick walls, fortified with stone and rising out of a deep trench, were bounded at all four corners by massive turreted towers where armed guards kept constant watch. Heavy iron bars covered every window. Looking from an angle, she glimpsed more structures built onto the back of the main building, all of them fortified and guarded.

Escape from such a place would be unthinkable. Privacy would be rare and hard to come by. Yet one clever, ruthless man had found a way to run an entire smuggling operation from inside the prison. And that same man had found a way to murder her father.

Staring up at the looming structure, Ruby was overcome by a sense of helplessness. What happened inside these walls was beyond her control. Mason would be on his own, and there was nothing she could do to help him.

All she could do was keep herself safe and be there for him when he got out of prison. Her most useful refuge would be a place where Mason had friends and family, a place where he could find her once he was finally free.

She turned away from the prison and walked down the main street, looking for someplace to buy a cheap car. She needed a way to Blue Moon.

Mason faced his old mentor in the prison exercise yard. He'd been gone for just a few months, but Julius Taviani appeared to have shriveled with the passing of time. The old man had to be seventy, at least, and it showed. Even so, he exuded power and an evil aura that Mason could feel like the touch of an icy hand.

Taviani's new bodyguard stood behind him, a hulk of a man with the physique of a gone-to-seed professional fighter. He was as tall as Mason, with shoulders like a barn door and huge hands that looked strong enough to bend iron bars . . . *or snap the neck of a slight man like Art Murchison.*

His eyes narrowed to a squint as he took Mason's measure. Clearly the big man saw him as a threat. Without a word spoken, Mason sensed that he'd already made a dangerous enemy. But it was Taviani who wielded the power here—Taviani whose word would be obeyed.

The old man scowled up at Mason. "Well, you didn't waste much time getting back here," he said. "What the hell happened?"

Mason shrugged. "I got busted by the feds. The woman already had them tailing me."

"So, did you do what I asked you to?"

"I didn't have time. The woman's gone. The feds told me she left the state for parts unknown. So you can call off your hounds if they're out there. She won't be back, and she can't do you any more damage."

Taviani swore, his breath hissing out through a gap in his yellowed front teeth. "What about Colucci?"

"I thought you were going to take care of him."

"I was. But thanks to your screw-up, I'll have to keep him around until I can figure out a replacement. Meanwhile, with his pilot gone, he'll be about as much use as tits on a boar. I can't send more product unless he's got the means to deliver it." He hawked and spat on the gravel. "This whole airplane delivery thing has been a bust. Maybe I should go back to using trucks. They had their problems, but at least they didn't crash."

Falling silent, the old man surveyed the prison yard. The area was surrounded by high stone walls, with guards at all stations. The guards on the wall had high-powered rifles. The ones on the ground were armed with clubs. The prisoners, dressed like Mason in humiliating black-and-white striped pajamas, jogged the inside perimeter, tossed a half-deflated ball, or stood around watching and chatting. Some smoked.

Now and again a prisoner would glance toward Taviani, then quickly look away. Everyone knew who the old man was. It was rumored that even the warden feared him.

Mason moved casually among the men, taking stock of who was gone, who was new, and which of them were hanging together.

He hadn't expected Taviani to be pleased with him, but the old man had been downright cold. It might take time to get back into his confidence. At least Ruby had made a safe escape. Now he had to stop thinking about her and do the job he'd come for.

"Dollarhide, I thought that was you." Mason wheeled at the sound of a cocky voice behind him. Wallace Timbo, a rat-faced little man doing time for forgery, wasn't exactly a friend. There were no real friends in this place where the rule was every man for himself; but Timbo could be counted on as a source of the latest prison gossip.

"Nobody expected you to be back, especially so soon," Timbo said. "What happened?"

"Maybe I missed your ugly face," Mason said.

Timbo chuckled, then nodded toward Taviani and the big man who stood behind him. "It looks like somebody stepped into your old job. And something tells me he won't be moving aside for you."

"That's what I figured," Mason said. "Tell me what you know about him."

"Everybody calls him Piston. Don't know what his real name is, but he's doing twenty to life for second-degree murder. Killed a guy with his bare hands in a fight over a woman."

"Murder? Why isn't he in solitary?"

Timbo shrugged. "Taviani wanted him. And what Taviani wants, Taviani gets. The big guy doesn't say much. I get the impression he's not the sharpest nail in the keg. But he's got Taviani to do his thinking for him. All he has to do is take orders."

Timbo glanced around, then leaned closer. "You can thank me for this later, Dollarhide. You made some enemies while you were working for the old man. They'll be out for payback, and this time, Taviani won't protect you. So be ready."

With another glance over his shoulder, Timbo scuttled away like the little rat he was. Looking across the compound, Mason could see a group of three husky men. He recognized all of them. Two he'd punished with his fists, just because Taviani had told him to do it. The other man had probably resented his being Taviani's right-hand man and welcomed the chance to take him down.

Mason watched as they moved toward him. He knew how the fight would go. The guards on the ground would look the other way during the worst of it. Only when the melee was slowing down, and after the target had taken a brutal beating would they wade in with their clubs, march the combatants back to their cells and, if need be, drag the loser to the infirmary.

Mason knew something else as he met Taviani's stony gaze. Timbo had been right. The old man would not step in to save him.

Mason prepared to fight. He could have taken on any one of them, maybe even two. But with three coming at him, he was about to be beaten senseless. The best he could hope for was to do some damage before he went down.

They were coming closer, like wolves circling their prey, hatred blazing in their eyes. The crowd of prisoners opened a path, then closed behind them, forming a ring of watchers. Mason stood his ground, facing his enemies. Taviani, flanked by Piston, stood a few yards behind him.

As the trio closed in, Mason dropped to a slight crouch, shifting on the balls of his feet as he waited for the attack.

It never came.

The leering hostility faded from the faces of the three men as they backed into the crowd. Mason turned to find Piston standing like a brick wall behind him.

For an instant he almost believed he'd been saved from a pounding. Only when he saw the reptilian smile on Taviani's face did he understand what was about to happen. Piston would be defending his job. Mason would be given a fighting chance to take it from him. The loser of the brawl would be stripped of all respect and become the target of any bully in the prison.

The ring of watchers widened as the two men faced each other. Even the guards had become spectators—all of them probably expecting to see Mason crushed. Piston outweighed him by a good thirty pounds. The brute had a roll of belly fat, but the extra weight was mostly muscle. And his fists were like wrecking balls.

This man had, in all likelihood, killed Ruby's father. And be-hind him was the evil mastermind of it all. Mason used that thought to fuel his anger as he aimed the first strike—a hard punch to Piston's gut.

The big man grunted, but his body was as solid as a sack of ce-ment. Mason felt the pain shoot up his arm all the way to his shoulder. He recovered in time to dodge the swinging hammer of Piston's left hand and step back. The big man was powerful but slow—that would give Mason a slight advantage. But if Piston landed the right punch, the match could be over except for the mauling that would likely continue until the guards had seen enough.

In prison fights, there were no rules. Biting, gouging, stomp-ing, and kicking brought cheers from the crowd. Sizing up the man who faced him, Mason knew he couldn't rule out anything. For all he knew, Piston had orders to destroy him.

As Piston lumbered toward him, Mason went for the most vul-nerable part of him—his face. He flung everything he had into a punch that delivered a crunching blow to the big man's nose. Blood spurted. Roaring in pain and rage, Piston waded into the fight, head down like a charging bull. Mason dodged the impact and countered with an uppercut to the brute's ironlike jaw. The blow landed hard, but the force of the collision threw Mason off balance. He reeled, struggling to stay upright.

Piston was quick to take advantage. A ham-sized fist slammed into the side of Mason's head. Reeling, he glimpsed Taviani's cold smile. As he went down, the last thing he saw was the twenty-pound concrete sole of Piston's boot, prison issue that unruly prisoners were forced to wear. The boot filled his vision. Then everything went black.

When Mason woke, it was night. He was lying on his back, a dim light shining through the bars of his cell. His left eye was swollen shut, with a tender bruise running from temple to chin. He worked his jaw, expecting it to be broken. But it was only damned sore. So, it seemed, was every joint and muscle in his body.

He struggled to sit up, then abandoned the effort because of the pain. Tomorrow would be worse—he'd traveled this road before. In a way, it was as if he'd never left this accursed place.

He forced himself to remember why he'd come here and what he had to do. He'd promised the feds he would give them Taviani. Ideally that meant getting enough evidence on the old man to end his power and have him moved to federal prison for life. It could also mean finding the secret source of his illegal whiskey. Even killing him might be a solution—but Mason would have to answer for that. It wasn't the best idea.

"So you're awake." The voice was familiar. Raising his head, he could see Taviani's diminutive silhouette standing outside the bars. "You can thank me for saving your life. Piston would have killed you before the guards got to him."

Mason took a breath, pain stabbing his ribs. "I've got one question for you. Why?"

"Why did I order Piston to attack you, or why did I order him to stop?"

"Both, starting with the first question. I knew you'd be unhappy because I didn't kill Colucci's pilot—and because I got caught. But I didn't expect to be beaten."

Taviani snorted. "You should know better than that. You were seen leaving the woman's hotel room with the feds and walking her to the train. You were even seen kissing her goodbye."

Mason was startled into silence. Ruby had suspected that Colucci employed a maid at the hotel as a spy. But Ruby had been mistaken. The maid had been working for Taviani, not Colucci; and she'd seen everything that went on outside the room.

"I've seen more men ruined by love than by money," Taviani said. "But if you think I'll forget about your little pilot, you're wrong. She needs to be silenced. And she can't run fast enough or far enough to get away. As for you, Dollarhide, you're a traitor. I wanted to make an example of you. That's why I told Piston to give you a beating."

"So why am I still alive?"

The silence lasted several seconds before the old man replied. "Because there's a chance you could still be of use to me. You've seen what Piston can do. But he has the mind of an eight-year-old child. He belongs in an institution, not here. But he'll do whatever I tell him—even if I order him to kill."

A chill crept through Mason's body. He lay frozen with horror, staring up at the frame of the empty bunk above his head. To the old man, Piston was no more than a trained dog who, without judgment, would do anything for its master.

"What about those cement soles?" Mason ventured to ask. "What did Piston do to earn those?"

"When he first came here, right after you left, he was terrified. He kept trying to run away. The staff replaced the soles of his boots with concrete to slow him down. I saw an opportunity in the boy. All it took was a bit of kindness to make him mine."

Mason suppressed a shudder. He, too, in his own way, had been taken in by this coldly evil old man.

"Timbo told me about the reason for Piston's arrest. I hear he killed a man. What happened?" Mason asked.

"Piston's sister was a whore, working the streets in Billings. Piston was hanging around, looking out for her. A customer got rough, started slapping her. Piston threw him against a brick wall. I can't imagine he meant to kill the bastard, but he did, and he wound up here."

"What happened to the sister?"

"She was gone when the police got there. Her testimony could've helped her brother. But she never showed up. Neither did any of the family, if he's even got one."

And what about Art Murchison, old man? Did Piston kill him, too, on your order?

Mason knew better than to ask that question. But if he could get proof that Taviani had ordered the killing of Ruby's father, that should be enough to get the old man retried and put away for murder.

Collecting evidence wouldn't be easy—especially here, where any of the prisoners or guards, or even the warden, could be in Taviani's pocket. Talk to the wrong person, and he'd be as good as dead.

"You mentioned that you could still use me," he said. "How?"

"The same as before—passing on messages, collecting debts, keeping me informed. I'd keep Piston as my bodyguard and enforcer. You'd pick up the slack. It would be a demotion, but you've lost the right to be choosy. All right?"

"I guess it's better than nothing."

"One more thing." His tone hardened. "Cross me again, and I'll turn Piston loose on you—and next time I won't call him off. I'll see you in the yard after breakfast."

The old man's footsteps faded down the hall. Mason heard the door of his cell open and close. He could probably get out anytime he wanted.

Mason closed his eyes. He was too sore to sleep but he had to try. In the darkness, he could hear the snores and muttered curses of men in their cells, the flushing of a toilet, and the faint jingle of keys as the guard patrolled the floor. The old smells of sweat and tobacco were familiar. It was almost as if he'd never been away.

He thought about Ruby, and how they'd made love. He was doing this for her, Mason reminded himself. But not just for her. He wanted to make a clean break with the past, and this was the only way.

Ruby was the future he wanted. It worried him that Taviani was still determined to find her. He could only hope that she'd found a safe refuge.

Ruby, still dressed as a boy, had bought a cheap two-seater from a used auto lot in Deer Lodge. It had a crumpled fender, and the front seat was worn through, but the engine started on the first try, a good sign.

After gassing it up, she took the back roads south, cutting around Miles City. She had seen the countryside from the air, so she knew her way. Approaching Blue Moon at sunset, she had a decision to make. Mason had given her the name of his sister, the doctor, whom she could find in town by asking. But it was getting late. The doctor wouldn't be in her office at this hour. And Ruby had no idea how to find the ranch where she lived with her husband and children. In any case, Ruby wouldn't want to expose an innocent family to the danger of armed mobsters who might still be looking for her.

She had made deliveries to Mason's ranch, which lay south of the town. She knew how to find the airstrip and the cave, but she'd never been inside the house or met the elderly mother he'd mentioned in passing.

She could hide in the cave. That struck her as a good idea until she remembered that she would have no water, no food, no heat, and no bathroom facilities. She wouldn't last more than a few miserable days. She would have to take her chances at the house.

She was still disguised as a boy. Maybe she could ask for work. She didn't know much about ranching. But she was a good mechanic. Asking to earn her keep would be better than begging for shelter.

Blue Moon was quiet except for the two-story building that appeared to be some kind of restaurant. Lights were on inside. Autos and buggies were pulled up outside. The aromas that drifted on the air made Ruby's mouth water. She had barely eaten all day. But even though she had money for a meal, stopping could be a dangerous idea. There was no telling who might be inside that place.

She kept driving, switching on the car's headlamps as the twilight deepened. The countryside had begun to look familiar. She remembered Mason driving her after the plane crash, the dim impression of a hedge surrounding a stately brick house. Ahead, to the left of the road, she could see lighted windows and a broad front porch. This had to be the place.

As she switched off the engine and climbed out of the Model T, a wave of fatigue swept over her. She hadn't had a decent meal since that breakfast in Glendive, and she couldn't even remember the last time she'd slept well. She was exhausted. Her vision blurred slightly as she stumbled up the front walk. She cleared her throat, hoping she could make herself sound like a boy.

As she knocked on the door, a hellacious barking came from

the other side. Ruby liked dogs, but this one sounded like a monster, waiting to attack and tear her to pieces as soon as the door was opened. But she was too far gone to give up and leave.

Hand shaking, she knocked again. Through the door, she heard a woman's sharp voice. The barking faded. The door opened.

A white-haired man in a threadbare tuxedo, tall but stoop-shouldered, stood before her. He looked as ancient as a gnarled oak tree. His blue eyes were all but lost in wrinkles, but Ruby recognized a spark of kindness in them.

The room behind him was dimly lit. Ruby glimpsed a woman in a high-backed chair, one hand on the collar of a huge mastiff. She looked too frail to control the dog, but the creature was making no effort to pull away and attack.

The old man spoke in a formal voice. "Kindly state your business, young man."

Ruby blinked the room into focus. "I'm a friend of Mason's," she said. "He told me that if I came here, I could find work. I'm—"

The words died in her throat. Her legs folded beneath her. The world went black as she collapsed across the threshold.

CHAPTER SEVENTEEN

RUBY OPENED HER EYES. SHE WAS LYING ON A LUMPY DIVAN WITH an afghan over her legs and a damp cloth laid across her forehead. The monster dog sat nearby, staring at her with cataract-veiled eyes. It growled as she stirred and tried to sit up.

"You gave us quite a scare, young lady." The elderly man stepped into sight, carrying a tray.

Young lady. Her disguise hadn't worked.

"Forgive me," the man said as if reading her thoughts. "I needed to pick you up and move you inside. It was hard not to notice certain . . ." He colored slightly. "I've got some tea and sandwiches here, if you're hungry."

"Thank you, I'm starved, but I don't dare move. The dog—"

"Oh. Brutus is just curious. Get over there, boy."

Still growling, the dog retreated to the side of the high-backed chair where the woman sat. Her striking green eyes glared at Ruby, their color the same as Mason's. She would be his mother, of course. But there was nothing welcoming in her sour expression.

Ruby pushed herself to a sitting position. The man placed the tray on her lap. It held a delicate china cup filled with amber tea and a sliced beef sandwich with mustard on white bread. "If you'll allow me to introduce myself, miss, I'm Sidney, Mrs. Dollarhide's butler, at your service."

A butler? Here? Ruby felt as if she'd stumbled down the rabbit hole. ""It's a pleasure to meet you, Sidney," she said. "I'm Mrs. Ruby Weaver. Thank you for your kindness."

The old man inclined his head. "It's Mrs. Dollarhide you should thank. This is her home. I have the honor of serving her."

"You may go, Sidney." The woman waved him away and turned her attention to Ruby. "Please go ahead and eat while we talk. Can I trust that you fainted from hunger, and not because my son has fathered yet another bastard?"

"You needn't worry on that account. I was just tired and hungry. It's been a long day." Ruby hid her shock at Mrs. Dollarhide's frankness. She knew that Mason had a past. He'd even spoken with some pride about his grown son. What surprised her was that his mother would speak of it in such a way. She took dainty bites of the sandwich, trying to eat like a well-mannered lady.

The dog had remained at his mistress's side. She stroked the massive head with one blue-veined hand. An emerald set in gold adorned her middle finger. "Since you claim to be a friend of Mason's, maybe you can tell me where he's gone off to," she said. "It's been days since I've seen him. He even took my automobile and left me with no way to get to town."

Lying would only complicate things later. "Mason's back in prison," Ruby said. "But it's not what you think. He's working with the Bureau of Investigation to catch an evil man who's running a crime ring from behind bars. Once that's done, he'll be released."

"A likely story!" Mason's mother snorted. "I'm not a fool. I know what's been going on—the late nights, with Mason coming home at all hours. The phone calls when he thought I wasn't listening. He tried to make me believe he was sneaking around, seeing women. But I knew better. It was that wretched bootleg whiskey business. He couldn't leave it alone, and now he's been caught again."

She leaned forward in her chair. "And what about you, missy? Galivanting around, pretending to be a boy. Were you in on that filthy business, too?"

"Yes, but I was working for the Bureau, as an informant. I was found out, and now some very bad people want to silence me. I had to go on the run, in disguise."

"And so now you've come here—to hide."

Fear and exhaustion broke through Ruby's pride. "Please," she begged. "I have no family and no place to go. I could sleep anywhere, even in the barn. And I'd work for my keep. I'm an excellent mechanic. I even have an old car outside. I could fix it up for you to use—"

"That's enough whining, girl," the woman snapped. "I may be short on kindness, but I would never force a woman to sleep in the barn. You can stay in my son's old room and work in the house. Sidney's getting feeble. He could use some help. Pity I don't have a maid's uniform, but I have some old work clothes that would fit you. I might even have a lace cap that would cover that awful hair of yours. Understand, you'll be working for room and board only. You'll be expected to earn your keep. No slacking. And if I find out you're pregnant, you and your bastard will be out the door."

"I understand. And I'm not pregnant." The memory of Mason's loving was still fresh. But after her tragic miscarriage, the doctor had told her that she wasn't likely to have more children.

Ruby had finished her sandwich. She glanced toward the dog. "And what about him?"

"Leave him alone until he's had time to get used to you. Sidney will show you to your room tonight. I'll have him find you some clothes and leave them outside your door. You'll start work at first light. The place could use a good scrubbing—floors, walls, everything. Don't make me sorry I let you stay."

"I'll do my best. And thank you for taking me in, Mrs. Dollarhide. I mean to repay you for your kindness."

"We'll see about that in the morning when I put you to work." Mason's mother glanced back toward the kitchen, where the butler had gone. "Sidney, I'll take my tea now," she said.

"Coming up, ma'am." The old man spoke from the next room.

Keeping a wary eye on the dog, Ruby stood and carried her tray to the kitchen. She'd hoped for a warmer welcome here. But at least she could be grateful for a safe refuge.

How long would that refuge last? With danger afoot, anything could go wrong. Her best and only hope was to be here when Mason came home.

Jake sat in his wheelchair, on the back porch of the house he still thought of as Britta's. The night breeze was chilly, the moon a silver crescent above the mountains. Across the back lot, he saw the light go out in the rooms above the jail. His heart lightened. Britta would soon be here to share supper with him and his daughter.

Two weeks had passed since the shooting at the dance. Jake's gunshot wounds had nearly healed, and he was gaining enough upper body strength to pull himself into and out of the chair. He'd even figured out how to bathe himself with a bucket and a sponge. But so far, there'd been no improvement in his legs. They were as useless as ever.

It was Marissa who'd solved the problem of his living quarters. After he'd explained to her why they couldn't live over the jail and why social custom dictated that he couldn't move in with Britta, the little girl had suggested, "Why don't we trade places? Britta could live upstairs in our old place, and we could live in her house by the school."

Britta had agreed, and it was done. It was a practical arrangement, although not a fair one. The prisoners in the jail, most of them drunk on illegal moonshine, tended to be unruly—snoring, arguing, and cussing—especially at night when Jake left them alone. The noise found its way upstairs, as did some of the odors. Although Britta never complained, Jake was eaten with guilt over the discomfort and inconvenience the new arrangement caused her. This was only temporary, he vowed. But his options were limited, including the one he refused to consider—marrying the woman who had done so much for him. The woman he still loved.

The city council had hired a young cowboy as a deputy to do the leg work and drive him where he needed to go. Jake spent most of his days in the office, babysitting the jail prisoners, reviewing case files, filling out paperwork, and dealing with visitors. He hated being tied to a desk, but at least he had a job—although that was likely to change with the November election.

Now, in the moonlight, he could see Britta's graceful silhouette coming down the path toward him. The yearning that rose in him was like silent torture. He wanted her—and he knew that she was willing to be his. But the miracle he'd hoped for had yet to happen.

"Come on in." He greeted her warmly, but the tension—the unspoken longing between them—was always there. Tonight, he'd ordered a dinner of roast beef, vegetables, and sourdough bread from the restaurant. It was warming in the oven. Marissa had set the table with the dishes Britta had left in the kitchen. The little girl already knew how to arrange the plates, glasses, napkins, and cutlery for each place setting. It was one of the lessons Britta had taught her.

Now Marissa came bounding outside, her golden curls flying as she ran to meet the visitor. Britta often shared meals with Jake and his daughter. The third-rate kitchen in the rooms above the jail was barely suitable for making coffee and toast. Sometimes Britta cooked for them at her former home. But it was easy enough for Jake to call in a delivery order to the restaurant.

The three of them were becoming a family. Jake could see how attached his motherless child was becoming to Britta. Britta sensed it, too. Jake could tell that she was concerned.

Clasping Britta's hand, Marissa pulled her into the kitchen. Jake followed through the door that she held open. "How nicely you've set the table, Marissa," Britta said. "Everything looks perfect."

"I wanted to have flowers on the table," Marissa said. "But the flowers are all gone."

"It's too cold for flowers now," Britta said. "There'll be more in the spring. Until then we can pretend. What kind of pretend flowers would you have on the table?"

"Roses! Red ones, like the ones at my grandma's house."

"And I would have wildflowers because they make the land so pretty in the spring," Britta said.

"What kind of pretend flowers would you have, Daddy?" Marissa asked.

Jake hesitated, thinking, then smiled. "I don't need to pretend," he said. "I have two beautiful flowers right here, and I'm about to have supper with them."

Britta raised an eyebrow as she transferred the food from the oven to the table. "What a charmer you are, Jake Calhoun. Sit down, Marissa. Let's eat."

Marissa slipped into her seat, made higher by two thick books. After the little girl took her turn at blessing the meal, she waited while Britta filled her plate.

"I can pretend about something better than flowers," she announced. "I can pretend that you two are married. And Britta can be my real mom. And we can all live together."

Jake saw the shock that passed across Britta's face, followed by a flush of color. How could he explain their situation to a child so young? Heaven help him, he didn't know where to begin.

Marissa looked from Jake to Britta, as if puzzled by their reactions. "Is that all right—to pretend?"

"It's . . . fine, honey," Britta said. "As long as you know that you're just pretending."

"But—" the little girl began.

"That's enough, Marissa," Jake said. "Eat your supper. We'll talk later."

The meal continued with some awkwardness. When it was finished, Britta began cleaning up while Jake helped his daughter get ready for bed and tucked her in.

"You said we'd talk." She gazed up at him from her pillow.

"Tomorrow," he said. "It's late. It's time you were asleep."

"I want to talk now," she said. "Why can't you and Britta get married? I can tell you love each other. Why don't you ask her?"

He sighed. "Because I want her to be happy. How can she be happy with a man who can't walk?"

"That's silly, Daddy. You're still you. I still love you. So does Britta."

He kissed her forehead and backed away from her bed. "That's enough talk for now. Go to sleep."

He left the room. She didn't understand, he told himself. Or maybe he didn't. He envied his daughter's innocent wisdom. If only things were that simple.

He found Britta in the kitchen, drying the last of the dishes. She gave him a questioning look.

"She's not giving up on the idea," he said. "I suppose she will, in time."

Britta hung the damp towel over the back of a chair and reached for her shawl. "I should go," she said.

"No, stay, please," he said, his chair blocking her path out the back door. "Come sit with me in the parlor. We can't leave things like this."

He ushered her into the parlor, a cozy room with a cushioned settee, an armchair, an overfilled bookshelf, and a miniature pot-bellied stove. He'd kindled a fire earlier. Flames glowed behind the mica panes in the door.

She took a place on the settee. He turned his wheelchair to face her.

"Do you have something to say to me, Jake?" He could read the apprehension in her lovely azure eyes. For as long as he'd known her, Britta had seemed unaware of her beauty. She was vulnerable, unable to believe that a man could love her—that *he* loved her.

"I just wanted to apologize." Fumbling his way word by word, he stumbled on. "This living arrangement is working for me, but not for you. Those quarters above the jail aren't fit for a lady. With winter coming on, the noise and the smell are going to get worse. You mustn't stay there."

She flashed him a startled look. Then swiftly composed herself. "I suppose I could find a room to rent somewhere. But it isn't such a hardship living over the jail. I've enjoyed doing for you and Marissa. This is the first I've felt useful since I lost my family. I never realized how much I've missed having someone to care for. Jake, I've needed this—"

She broke off, staring down at her hands. "I'm sorry. I do understand that Marissa is becoming too attached, and you want to—"

"Stop talking, Britta." He seized her hands. Suddenly he knew what had to be said—what he'd wanted to say all along. "Listen to me. I don't know what's going to happen in the future. I don't know how much of a recovery I'll make—but does anybody know what life is going to throw at them? I only know that I love you. I need you. And Marissa needs us both. If you'll have me, and if you think we can be a family, I'm asking you to marry me."

"Oh!" Tears welled in her eyes and flowed down her cheeks. "You big, proud fool, of course I'll marry you!"

Gripping her hands, he pulled her onto his lap. She came willingly, her soft curves melting into him, her mouth meeting his in a long, passionate kiss. He felt her close to him, her breasts full and warm, her hips fitting the curve of his body.

There was more than one way to love a woman and make her heart sing. He would learn them all, Jake vowed. But he would never stop hoping.

Mason surveyed the exercise yard. The morning was cold, the prisoners moving briskly to keep warm. They circulated, exhaling puffs of vapor that hung over them like a fog bank. Watching them was like scanning a herd of zebras in a shifting kaleidoscope of black and white.

Julius Taviani had ordered him to find a man named Harvey McGill, whose family owed money on the outside. Mason's job, for now, was to remind McGill what would happen if they didn't pay up.

He hated being Taviani's errand boy, and he hated Taviani. Worse, he was having a hard time finding any solid evidence against the old man—evidence that Taviani had ordered the murder of Art Murchison or any of the other prisoners who'd been found dead and quietly buried in a weedy plot behind the prison.

As Taviani's man, he had more freedom than most of the prisoners. But that didn't mean he could waltz into the records office and start going through the files. Even the library, where Art had worked and died, was a problem to access alone. So far, it had been either attended or locked.

Mason was getting impatient—and worried. If he didn't deliver on his promise to nail Taviani, the federal agents were capable of leaving him here to rot.

As he eyed the crowd, searching for McGill's thatch of white-blond hair, Piston appeared beside him. The husky man gave Mason a nod and a smile that was almost childlike. When Taviani wasn't around, Piston's gentle nature came through. But with the old man, he was like a fighting dog, trained to attack, even kill—one more reason for Mason to hate Julius Taviani.

Mason fished in his pocket and found the biscuit he'd saved from breakfast. Piston never got enough food to satisfy the needs of his body. He was always hungry. Mason passed him the biscuit.

"Thanks." The big man downed it in a couple of bites. Piston wasn't much of a talker, so it wasn't easy to know what was on his mind. Mason had formed a cautious friendship with him. He felt genuinely sorry for the childlike giant. Piston didn't belong here. He belonged in an institution where there were no people like Taviani to take advantage of his trust. But what could be done with a man who'd killed, likely more than once?

Piston nudged Mason and pointed. There was McGill, having a smoke at the fringe of the crowd. With Piston following him like a shadow, Mason approached the man. McGill dropped his cigarette and backed away. "Give me two more days," he pleaded. "My brother will have the money by then!"

"I'll pass that along," Mason said. "But you know the deal you made, and you know what will happen if your family doesn't pay."

McGill's pale eyes shifted toward Piston, who stood at Mason's shoulder. No more words were needed. The man slunk away to lose himself in the crowd. Message delivered.

Mason and Piston moved to a sheltered spot next to the wall. A guard with a club glanced at them, then turned away. "Where's Taviani this morning?" Mason asked.

"He's talking on the telephone with his friend, Mr. Colucci. I heard before he sent me out here," Piston said.

A chill crawled over Mason's skin. He couldn't help wondering about the danger to Ruby. But he'd seen her safely on the train. Right now, he had a little time with Piston alone. He needed to make the most of it.

"You do a lot of things for Mr. Taviani, don't you, Piston?" he asked.

"Yes. He treats me nice when I help him."

"Do you hurt people?"

"Just when he tells me to," Piston said.

"Do you do everything Mr. Taviani tells you to?"

Piston nodded. "He gives me good things. Sometimes I even get ice cream."

"Do you ever kill people?" Mason held his breath as he waited for an answer.

"I don't like to. It makes me feel bad."

"Does Mr. Taviani tell you to kill people?"

Piston pressed his lips together and shook his head. "We don't talk about that."

Mason cast his gaze around the yard. There was no sign of Taviani. Playing it safe was getting him nowhere. It was time to take a dangerous risk.

"Do you like books, Piston?" he asked.

"I like pictures. Mostly pictures of animals. But I can't read the writing."

"There are some good picture books in the library. Have you seen them?"

"No." He sounded nervous.

"Let's go and have a look. Come on."

Piston followed him inside the main building. The library would be open at this hour. There would be people inside, but having Piston along would give Mason an excuse to paw through the shelves. Finding any solid evidence linked to Art Murchison's murder would be a long shot. But if that evidence existed, that would be the most likely place to find it.

The library was in a room off the open second-floor walkway. The rows of shelves were all visible from the front counter. An elderly man Mason recognized as one of the lifers was watching the room and checking out books. There were two other prisoners in the library, one reading a newspaper at a long table, the other perusing the shelves. Both of them were past middle age, peaceful men, known and trusted.

It might have been helpful to question the men about the murder, but when Mason walked through the door with Piston, all three of them made a hasty exit. If there was going to be trouble, they wanted no part of it.

"Come on in, Piston. Let's find you something to look at." Mason guided the big man to a low shelf that held easy picture books, along with some larger photographic volumes. The books had been donated and were well-worn, some missing pages and covers. At one end of the shelf was a stack of tattered magazines, mostly old issues of *The Saturday Evening Post.*

Mason began thrusting books toward his companion. "Do you like dinosaurs? Or maybe trains? Here's a good book about Africa." It had been Mason's intent to get Piston interested in the books, while he searched as much of the room as he could, but the big man seemed distracted. Maybe he hadn't had much exposure to books.

Mason tried again. "Look, Piston. Here's a big book about ships, or maybe you'd like this one about—" He stopped, his pulse lurching. He had just picked up a book about airplanes.

On the cover was a picture of a Jenny, like the one Art had flown. Surely Art would have held this book in his hands. He would probably have read every page. That he'd left any kind of message was probably wishful thinking. But it was worth looking inside.

Piston had chosen a book about horses and taken a seat to look at the pictures. Mason held the airplane book spine-up and gave it a careful shake. A sheet of torn-off notepad paper fluttered from between the pages and settled to the floor. Pulse racing, Mason picked it up and began to read the neatly penciled script.

> *To whomever finds this note:*
>
> *I have just made a terrible mistake. In my foolish vanity, I shared a secret with a man I trusted, a man I believed to be my friend—Julius Taviani. I have since learned more about the man from people who fear him. I have come to understand that in confiding my secret, I have compromised my daughter's safety and my own life. Mr. Taviani has arranged the deaths of others, and I fear that I will be next.*
>
> *Mr. Taviani relies on others to do his killing for him. But if I am dead by the time you read this, know that it was on Taviani's orders. He is as guilty of murder as if he'd committed the act with his own hands.*
>
> *To my daughter, Ruby, I send my love and a plea for forgiveness. I can only pray that she escapes this net of evil and finds her way to a happy life.*
>
> *Arthur Murchison*

Heart pounding, Mason read the letter again. It was evidence, but it wasn't proof. He needed more.

He was folding the letter, planning to replace it in the book, when Piston looked up at him. "What's that paper?" he asked.

It was now or never. "It's a letter from a man who died in here. A man with graying hair and a little moustache. Did you know him?"

"Uh-huh." Mason nodded. "He was nice."

"Did you have to hurt him, Piston?"

The big man nodded again, gazing down at the table. "Mr. Taviani made me do it. With my hands. He wouldn't let me stop."

"So Mr. Taviani was there with you when the man died?"

A tear rolled down Piston's cheek. "I didn't mean to kill him. He was nice. Mr. Taviani gave me ice cream after, but I still felt bad."

And there it was. Mason had the letter and he had Piston's confession. But would the authorities believe a man with diminished capacity, a man who couldn't read or write?

Mason tucked the book, with the hidden letter, inside his undershirt. "What if I told you that you'd never have to hurt anybody again?" he asked. But Piston wasn't paying attention. His gaze was riveted on the library door, which had just opened.

Mason turned. Taviani stood in the doorway with the open walkway behind him, a brutally cold expression on his face. Clearly, he'd heard everything, or at least enough.

Piston was on his feet now, looking confused. His gaze darted from Mason to the old man.

Taviani pointed to Mason. "Kill him, Piston," he ordered. "Do it now."

Piston hesitated, then raised his head and squared his massive shoulders. "No," he said.

The old man's face went livid. He drew a small revolver from his pocket. It was hard to believe that a prisoner could have a pistol, but Taviani had ways of getting what he wanted. "I mean it," he said, pointing the gun at Piston. "Do what I say. Now."

"You're not going to fire that gun, Taviani," Mason said. "If it's loaded, which I doubt, the sound would bring every guard in the place, and even you would be in big trouble." He turned to the big man. "You don't have to do what he says, Piston. You can be free of him. No more killing. You've already taken the first step. You've said no."

"Don't listen to him, Piston," Taviani snarled, pointing the gun. "I'm giving you to the count of three. If you haven't made a move, I'll pull this trigger." He took a deep breath. Beads of nervous sweat stood out on the old man's forehead as he began the count. "One . . . two . . . three!"

On the count of three, Piston charged him. Lunging through the open door, he pushed Taviani out onto the walkway. The momentum carried both men to the railing and over it. Piston had his hands around the old man's throat as they plummeted to the concrete floor below and lay still.

Mason raced out of the library and down the nearby steps. He reached the two men ahead of the guards. Piston was moaning, badly injured but alive. Taviani lay on his back, blood pooling around his head. His grin was like a death's head as Mason leaned over him.

"I'm done for, Dollarhide," he said in a gurgling voice. "But there's one thing I meant to tell you. Colucci told me he's tracked down your little pilot. As it turns out, she's at your ranch." His laugh was hideous, spraying drops of blood. "I told him to go ahead and kill her, along with any witnesses."

CHAPTER EIGHTEEN

RUBY HAD HER WORK CUT OUT FOR HER. THE HOUSE ON THE Hollister Ranch hadn't had a thorough cleaning in years. The two people who lived here were neat in their habits. But Sidney, the butler, had a bad back and hadn't been able to give the place more than a passing swipe with a feather duster or a kitchen towel. Mrs. Dollarhide—whose given name, Amelia, Ruby wasn't allowed to use—was much too fine to soil her hands with house-cleaning, and she didn't trust anyone from town to come in and do the work—they would either steal valuables or carry tales back to their friends.

The walls and ceilings were dingy with coal dust. The worn and matted carpets were gray with dirt and dog hair.

The outside of the windows was layered with road dust and rain spatters. And that was only the beginning.

Ruby suspected that the house's aging residents were too near-sighted to see all that needed to be done, or maybe they'd been here too long to notice.

Taking advantage of the mild fall weather, she'd washed the windows. She'd also had one of the hired men haul the rugs out-side to the clothesline. Ruby had spent an afternoon beating them until her arms ached. Then they were carried back inside to be laid on the floors she'd mopped.

The work kept Ruby occupied. She liked being busy. But her thoughts dwelt constantly on Mason, especially when she lay in his bed, in the darkness of his boyhood room. Was he still in prison? Was he safe? Could she trust the federal agents to get him out when the time came, or would they break their word and turn on him the way they'd turned on her?

One incident worried her, although not in the way she worried about Mason. She'd been outside, beating the rugs, when an airplane—a Jenny—had flown over the house, coming in so low that its wheels almost skimmed the trees. The roar of the engine had rattled the windows.

These days, airplanes were becoming a common sight. Ruby hadn't been unduly alarmed—until she saw the identification number stenciled on the fuselage. The plane was the one she had flown for Colucci.

Panic had shot through her body. Ruby had willed the fear away as the plane flew south over the airstrip and the cave, then rose, banked, and headed back toward Miles City and the farm.

Colucci must have hired a new pilot, she reasoned. It made sense that they would be checking out the delivery routes. Maybe they wanted to see if the site was still active or if any cargo had been left behind. Now that Mason had been re-arrested, they would have no reason to come back.

Putting her worries aside, she'd done her best to focus on the tasks at hand. She'd cleaned and polished the big coal stove in the kitchen and scrubbed the floor and fixtures in the bathroom. Then, after consulting with Amelia, she'd turned her efforts to the parlor.

The floors had been mopped and the rugs laid back into place, but the rest of the room hadn't been touched. The shabby furniture, although it needed replacing, would probably have to stay, especially Amelia's high-backed armchair with its worn brocade upholstery. But the walls and ceiling were in want of a thorough cleaning.

Ruby started early with a stepladder from the tool shed and a pile of cotton rags she'd gathered the day before. The plastered ceiling needed wiping to remove the coal dust and cobwebs. While the ladder was in place, she cleaned and polished the electric chandelier. The room was looking brighter already. But the papered walls would probably take hours.

Amelia, dressed and coiffed for the day, came into the parlor, followed by the loyal Brutus. Ruby had covered the chair with a sheet while she cleaned the ceiling, then uncovered it again. Like a queen ascending her throne, Amelia took her seat and waited for Sidney to bring her breakfast of tea and toast.

"So you're working in here today, are you?" she asked Ruby.

"That's what we decided." Ruby was perched partway up the ladder. "I was about to start on the walls."

"You'll want to be very careful," Amelia said. "That wallpaper is old, but it was made in Italy before the war and cost a great deal of money. Damage it, and you'll be out the door."

"Thank you for the warning," Ruby said. "First, I'll need to take down those pictures on the walls. I'll clean the glass and polish the frames before I hang them up again."

"That will be fine." Amelia sipped the tea her butler had brought. "Leave the nails in place. We don't want to hammer new holes in the walls, do we?"

"I'll be very careful."

Framed photographs of different sizes and ages decorated the parlor walls. Ruby counted sixteen of them. She found it odd that whoever had hung them over the years hadn't hesitated to hammer nails into the costly Italian wallpaper. But that wasn't her problem.

Taking care, she began lifting each picture off its nail and laying it on a sheet she'd spread on the floor. The wallpaper she uncovered behind each one was almost pristine, a lovely white and gold damask. The framed pictures, like the wall between them, were grimy with dust. But the photographs, she realized, showed the history of the ranch and the people who'd lived here—including Mason. Ruby wanted to know more. Maybe Amelia would tell her.

"Who's this?" She held up one of the smaller photographs as she wiped away the dust with a clean cloth. It showed a slender, handsome man in an old-fashioned suit.

Amelia leaned forward, her green eyes squinting slightly.

"That's my father, Loren Hollister. He bought this land and built this house. It was one of the few choice parcels Benteen Calder didn't get his greedy hands on first. My father was a gentleman, not a roughneck like Benteen. He raised fine cattle and blooded horses."

"And your mother? Is her picture here, too?"

"No. My parents separated when I was a little girl. My mother never came here. I stayed in the city with her until I grew into my teens. Oh, I was a handful—there, that picture with the silver frame. That's me at sixteen."

Ruby picked up the photograph and wiped off the dust. The young woman in the picture, wearing ecru lace and holding a fan, was gazing at the camera with a roguish smile on her face. She was stunning. "What a beauty you were!" Ruby exclaimed.

Amelia chuckled. "That was a long time ago. I had plenty of beaux, but I was a wild and willful little thing. When my mother couldn't control me, she sent me to my father with orders to find me a husband who could keep me in line. He found me Joe Dollarhide." She pointed to a larger picture. "Over there."

Ruby cleaned off the wedding photo—the bride wearing a veil and a radiant smile, the groom tall, dark and rugged, with a restless look about him, as if he were anxious to be done with the wedding and get back to building his kingdom.

These were Mason's parents. She could see parts of him in each of them. His mother's green eyes and chestnut hair. His father's athletic build and chiseled features. And what about Mason's reckless, passionate nature—had that come from the young Amelia?

"I'd have burned that picture a long time ago, but I wanted Mason to see where he came from. I loved Joe, but it wasn't meant to be. He didn't want to work for my father, even if it meant inheriting this ranch as my husband. He wanted his own land, his own kingdom on the bluff. And when his first love, Sarah, showed up with their son, that finished it for us. Our divorce gave me sole ownership of this ranch. I never married again."

"So you ran the ranch yourself, all these years." Ruby dusted off the picture of a woman seated on a tall bay horse. She was strong, confident, and beautiful. A rifle in a scabbard was slung from the saddle. One gloved hand held a coiled whip. It was a younger Amelia.

"I did, with hired help, of course," she said. "But why should that matter to you? Why should you even care about our family and how it fell apart? Is it because of Mason?" Her eyes drilled into Ruby. "Do you love him?"

Ruby's silence answered the question.

Amelia shook her head. "You poor, foolish girl! My son's got no more sense of responsibility than a tomcat. I raised him to take over this ranch. But he wasn't interested. First, he got some poor girl pregnant and had to leave town. He stayed away for years. When he came back all he wanted was to make money boot-legging. Now look where he is! Run away, girl, or he'll break your heart, just like his father broke mine!"

"You're wrong," Ruby said. "Mason went back into prison to save me. He's changed."

"Nonsense!" Amelia snorted. "Men don't change—least of all men like my son. He's disappointed me every day of his adult life."

"And yet, you love him," Ruby said. "You've never stopped be-lieving in him. I can tell. And I can tell that you worry about him, just as I do. I see the way you wait for the mail and how you jump every time the telephone rings."

"That's enough talk for now!" Amelia snapped. "Get back to work. I want those walls clean by tonight."

Ruby picked up another rag and moved the ladder closer to the front door. "What about that?" She nodded toward the gun rack that was bolted to the wall next to the door. It had brackets for several guns but held only one, a Winchester rifle that looked like the one in Amelia's photograph.

"Just clean around it," Amelia said. "And don't touch the gun. It's loaded. I've kept it there for varmints—coyotes and such, in-cluding the human kind. I used to be a deadly shot, though I haven't fired a gun in years. There was a time when problems could be taken care of with a bullet or two. But these days, the world has grown too civilized."

She set her tray on the side table, picked up a thick-looking book, and began to read. After a time, her head began to droop. Her eyes closed. The book slipped from her hands, onto her lap. Strange that Amelia would fall asleep when she'd been so alert earlier, Ruby thought. Maybe she should ask Sidney about that tea he was making for her.

The cotton rag she was using was getting the surface dust off the wallpaper. But the pattern, where it hadn't been covered, was still dingy. It needed more cleaning. Soap could damage the fragile paper. But Ruby remembered, growing up, how a neighbor woman had rubbed her walls with hunks of bread. As she recalled, the bread had done a good job. She would have to ask Sidney for some leftover bread to try.

The dog got up and lumbered over to the foot of the ladder. Ruby had never tried to pet the beast. But at least it seemed to tolerate her now. It looked up at her with clouded eyes. Its white muzzle twitched as it investigated her scent.

"Hello, Brutus," Ruby said in a friendly voice. "Are you looking for company? Would you let me pet you?" She reached down and put out a hand. Brutus sniffed it, drooling onto her knuckles. When she stroked the huge head, the dog's tail thumped against the floor.

Suddenly Brutus stiffened and growled. A line of hairs bristled along its back. Ruby stepped off the ladder, moved to the window, and peered out through the glass, remembering the plane, expecting anything.

But it was only the mailman, stopping his Model T to place several envelopes in the roadside mailbox. Maybe one of them was a letter from Mason.

Amelia was still asleep. Not wanting to wake her, Ruby slipped out onto the porch. Keeping the dog inside, she closed the door behind her and hurried down the sidewalk to the opening in the hedge. Fallen leaves crunched under her feet.

By the time Ruby reached the box, the mailman had driven

away. From inside the house, she could hear the dog barking. What was wrong with the beast?

She opened the box and took out the mail. None of the pieces looked promising—just bills and advertisements. Shuffling them in her hands, she turned around to walk back to the house. Only then did she see the two men in suits and fedoras, standing on either side of her.

The shorter man was a stranger with a fat, babyish face. He carried a Thompson submachine gun with a 100-round drum magazine. The other, taller man was Leo Colucci.

Pieces of mail fluttered to the ground.

Colucci grinned, showing his yellowed teeth. "We meet again, Ruby. Too bad. We could've made a good team, you and me. But now it's too late. I know you were working with the feds. Nobody gets a free ride after that."

"So what are you going to do? Kill me?" Ruby knew better than to grovel. That would only goad him.

"Kill you?" Colucci laughed. "That's a good guess. But first we're going through that front door to kill everybody in the house, including that damned dog that won't shut up. And you're going to watch them die. After that we'll figure out what to do with you."

Brutus was barking frantically, lunging at the door from the inside. Ruby remembered the gun on the rack. There'd be no way to get to it before Colucci's friend sprayed the place with bullets from the deadly submachine gun. The two ranch hands would be out with the cattle at this hour. If the men had any sense, they'd stay away.

"Please," she begged. "There are just two people in the house. They're elderly—and they're harmless. They don't deserve to die."

The man with the gun spat in the dirt. Colucci grinned. "Sorry, baby. Leave no witnesses, that's the rule. Larry, here, will get it over fast. They won't feel much—at least not for long. But I can't promise the same for you."

She could see their late-model auto parked down the road, out of sight from the house. "Just take me with you," she pleaded. "I'll go willingly. They won't have to see you at all."

"That's not the way it works, sweetheart," Colucci said. "I want you to see your friends die before we take care of you. Larry, here, can make it fast or slow. With you, I'm thinking it'll be slow. Come on, let's get it over with."

As they moved up the walk toward the porch, Ruby began to struggle, squirming and kicking. But Colucci's huge hands manacled her arms behind her back, holding her with an iron grip. He was too big for her, too tall and too strong.

Brutus was still barking and pawing at the door. Colucci swore. "Kill that damned dog, Larry. Just shoot him through the door."

Larry raised the submachine gun. That was when the scene exploded.

The door flew open. A single shot rang out. Larry dropped the gun and pitched backward with a red hole between his eyes. Brutus leaped at Colucci. As the big man struggled to fend off the dog, Ruby was shoved aside. A second shot, just as deadly as the first, struck Colucci. He spun and collapsed on top of his companion.

In the silence that followed, Ruby scrambled to her feet.

The two thugs lay dead on the front steps. As the dog sniffed at the bodies, Amelia strode out onto the porch, the rifle in her hands.

"Haven't lost my touch," she said.

Ruby, Amelia, and Sidney, who'd been in the kitchen, were waiting for the deputies to arrive when the telephone rang. Amelia took the call. Her face was transformed as she conversed for a few moments, then held the receiver out to Ruby.

"It's Mason," she said. "He's in Miles City. He's found the car and he's coming home. He wants to talk to you."

EPILOGUE

Three weeks later

LATE THAT NIGHT, A SNOWSTORM HAD BLOWN IN, FILLING THE DARKness with airy flakes that blanketed the ground like eiderdown. In the parlor of the ranch house, the flames in the fireplace had burned down to glowing coals. On the sofa, Ruby and Mason snuggled beneath a warm quilt, watching the storm through the windows.

Amelia, trailed by Brutus, had gone to bed earlier—without her special tea. Mason had discovered that the so-called "health tea" she'd been buying for years at the Chinese store in Miles City contained a torpor-inducing drug. With the drug's effects filtering out of her system, her sharpness was returning.

"She's still going to be a handful," Ruby teased, resting her head against his shoulder. "I like your mother."

"Amazingly, I think she likes you, too," Mason said. "She always wanted me to marry a rich girl. But she's realized that what this family needs more than money is a woman who can help me run the ranch." He gave her a playful kiss. "Don't worry, I'm not putting you to work until after the wedding. Then it'll be too late for you to quit. But I promise you, we're going to make something of this place. Even the Calders will envy us."

She laughed. "That'll be the day. This is Calder country, and they make sure everybody knows it."

His arm tightened around her. "I heard from the prison doctor today," he said. "Piston passed away in the hospital. The fall he took broke his ribs and affected his lungs. He saved my life. But there's no place for someone like him—a killer as innocent as a child. Most hospitals for the criminally insane are worse than prison these days. I don't know what waits for us on the other side, but I like to imagine Piston walking through the pearly gates as pure as an angel."

"At least he's at peace. So is my father." Ruby wiped away a tear. She would be a long time mourning the man who'd only wanted to see her happy. "What about Taviani's secret bootleg whiskey source? Did the feds ever find it?"

"The old man took that secret to his grave," Mason said. "It doesn't concern me anymore. I'm giving that cave back to the bats."

"And what about the airstrip?" she asked.

He looked down at her, frowning. "We haven't talked about that, have we? I'd never stand in the way of what you want, but if you were to crash and die, my life would be over."

She smiled. "You can give the airstrip, and your worries, a rest. I can't promise I'll never want to fly again. But for now, other things are more important."

More important than you know. Ruby's body was sending subtle messages of change—the tenderness in her breasts, the absence of her usual monthly period, the slight nausea. It was too soon to tell Mason. She would wait a few more weeks to be sure the miracle had really happened. Then, if all went well, she would give him a happy surprise.

Webb Calder was waiting at a table when Blake walked into the restaurant. The lunch hour was busy. Webb had managed to find a quiet corner where they could talk, but his invitation, by telephone, had given Blake no hint of what he had in mind.

Webb rose as Blake approached the table. "Thanks for coming, Blake. Have a seat. Lunch is on me today."

"I'll buy my own lunch, thanks." If Webb wanted a favor, Blake didn't want to feel obligated. He sat down. Chili was on the menu today. That sounded all right. But damn, he missed having it with a cold beer. From the look of things, Prohibition could last forever.

"I guess you heard about the election," Webb said as the waitress brought their coffee.

"Yup. Jake's been a good sheriff, even on wheels. I'm glad the people voted to keep him. But now that he's married to Britta, he's got a family to think of. My brother-in-law, Logan, has offered Jake a job managing his horse and cattle operation. Britta and Kristin are friends. Raising their children together would be ideal for both of them."

"We'd have to find a new schoolmarm."

"True, but not right away. If Jake takes the ranch job, they'll be having a home built out there, so they'll both be in town over the winter, at least. Plenty of time to make up their minds." Blake seasoned his chili with extra sauce. "But that's not why you asked me here today. What's on your mind, Webb?"

"Just something for you to think about." Webb leaned back in his chair, the rival ranchers sizing each other up like two dominant herd bulls.

"You probably know I'm building an airstrip," Webb said. "I've got a new engineer on the project, and it should be finished next spring."

"So what's that got to do with me?" Blake asked.

"Your son, Joseph, came to dinner with Chase a while back. He appeared interested in flying—not just interested, but passionate. He said he hoped to be a pilot."

Blake's stomach clenched like a fist.

"Of course, I want to clear this with you before I speak to him. I can tell he's a bright lad and a fast learner. I'm going to need pilots on the ranch. If you're willing, I would pay for his training and hire him if he does well. What do you say? Do I have your permission to bring this up to him?"

"Hell, no!" Blake's fist slammed the tabletop, so hard that it spattered the chili in his bowl.

"Why not?" Webb looked surprised. "I'm offering him a great

opportunity. I could tell how much he wants this. It's his dream. Are you upset because Joseph would be working for a Calder?"

Blake was on his feet. He took a deep breath. "Not so much that," he said. "But Joseph is the future of my family. If anything were to happen to him, the family wouldn't continue. I love him, Webb. I can't give him up. Especially not to you."

"You're sure that's your final decision?" Webb remained seated.

"It is. Thank you for asking me first, but I won't change my mind. And don't you dare go behind my back."

Blake opened his wallet and slapped enough money on the table to pay for both lunches. Then he turned and stalked out the door.

Joseph stood on the covered porch of the log house on the bluff. The storm had moved on. The land was frosted with silver, and the sky was a glory of stars.

But the beauty of the night was lost on Joseph. Earlier, Blake had laid down the law in no uncertain terms. As long as he lived under the family roof, Joseph would not be allowed to pilot an airplane.

Once he might have thought of leaving. But over the past weeks, he had learned a hard lesson in responsibility. His reckless behavior had robbed a man of his ability to use his legs. Maybe this was a consequence, Joseph thought, a penance for what he had done. True or not, his father was right. The family needed him. Running off to fly planes would be an act of pure selfishness.

So he would plan a life of servitude, like his father's—a life of sawdust, cow manure, and backbreaking work. And if he had sons one day, he would raise them to do the same.

There had to be something more—something to give him a touch of the joy he'd felt in the air. But maybe he was asking too much. Maybe it was time to give up.

With a sigh, Joseph walked back into the silent parlor, the family asleep, the coals smoldering on the hearth. The portrait of his grandfather, Joe Dollarhide, tall, rugged, and resolute, hung next to the fireplace—except for the eyes, Joseph was growing up in his image. But he was growing up in a different time. Joe Dollarhide had come to Montana with nothing. He had made his start breaking wild horses, married an heiress, and carved his own kingdom on the bluff.

But the wild mustangs were gone from this part of Montana. Joe's kingdom existed as a financial empire of cattle and lumber. The only challenge was to keep everything running smoothly.

Joseph looked up at the stern face, remembering the man and the vitality that had lingered into his old age. The hunger and ambition that had driven Joe Dollarhide had not been passed on to his son. They could have no place in the heart of his only grandson.

Joseph turned away, went up to his room, and got ready for bed. The day had been emotional. No sooner had his head settled on the pillow than he fell into an exhausted sleep.

The dream came from somewhere deep inside, perhaps from some inherited part of him. Horses—a wild band, thundering across the prairie—bays and blacks, paints, duns, and buckskins, snorting, calling, and tossing their manes.

In the lead, fearless and powerful, was a stallion . . . a magnificent blue roan.